THE 86th VILLAGE

THE 86th VILLAGE

SENA DESAI GOPAL

Copyright © 2022 by Sena Desai Gopal
Cover and jacket design by Mimi Bark
Interior formatted by emtippettsbookdesigns.com

ISBN 978-1-951709-74-7
eISBN: 978-1-951709-95-2
Library of Congress Control Number:
available upon request

First Trade Paperback edition April 2022 by Agora Books
An imprint of Polis Books, LLC
44 Brookview Lane
Aberdeen, NJ 07747
www.PolisBooks.com

For my two families, the one I was born into and the one I married into.

And, of course, for Harsha, Surya, and Anya

PROLOGUE

In 1964, the Indian government sanctioned the Arjuna dam across the Krishna river. The backwater reservoir would submerge 86 villages and irrigate an arid region three times the size. Everyone supported the dam—the thinkers, the progressives, the idealists, the people. The only opposition, which was quickly silenced, came from the residents of the 86 villages who knew the government would not compensate them fairly for their houses and lands that would submerge.

The diligent architects of the country took five years to draw up the plans by which time most of the project funds had disappeared in the fancy houses and expensive cars of politicians. To save face, and to avert public criticism, the government began construction but money ran out when the dam was a few dozen feet high.

Meanwhile, the area fell victim to National Mining, a corrupt iron-ore mining company in which politicians and prominent citizens had shares. Forests disappeared. Whole hills were blasted out and rainwater gushed unhindered down barren slopes, emptying soil debris into the Krishna, causing it to swell its banks. A verdant, bucolic countryside turned into a stark, desolate landscape. A suffocating cloud of dust enveloped everything, instigating a mass exodus of people. The farmers left first, after being bullied into selling their land to National Mining for a pittance. The tailors, blacksmiths, temple priests, carpenters and grocers followed.

Only the rich survived. They moved to the cities but maintained homes in their villages, returning once a year to confirm their status in a rural society that no longer existed.

The village streets which used to be filled with running, shrieking children became deserted. Stray dogs and cats wandered listlessly, hoping for scraps. Even the monkeys left, looking for banana groves and orchards that had disappeared, little knowing they would not find them for many, many miles. The monkeys that remained behind became aggressive, snatching food from passersby and invading meager pantries in homes.

Abandoned houses were bought by National Mining for its workers who never stayed more than a few months. After a decade of mining and making a hefty profit, the company quietly moved on, selling the land it had bought from farmers back to them at rock-bottom prices. The newspapers wrote about the generosity of the company, first creating jobs for locals and then allowing them to buy land for next to nothing. The politicians and citizens with shares in the company were congratulated for their forward thinking, their vision for a better, capitalist society.

Many moved back to their villages hoping to rebuild their lives but it was hard especially for farmers whose fertile lands had been destroyed. Still, people trudged on, waiting for the topsoil to form again, for the trees and grass to come back. It would take a long time but they did not mind. They knew how beautiful their villages could be.

The mines had stripped the groundcover, making it vulnerable to floods. Every monsoon, people watched the rains praying there would be enough for their crops but no more or their villages would flood.

Then the threat of submergence returned as a local politician decided to resume dam construction, thirty years after it had been stopped. It was an attempt to make money but was presented to the people as something they would benefit from. However, the people of the 86 villages were now aware of their rights and protested, refusing to leave until they were fairly compensated. To appease the people, the government said it would build the dam to a lower height so no village would submerge. In a few years, after the displacees were resettled, the government would complete the dam and drown the 86 villages.

With this irrefutable argument, a lower dam was built but even that caused flooding in the monsoon in villages laid bare by the mines. The government refused to take responsibility, claiming that the floods were because of aggressive farming practices. Reluctantly, it started a Displacement and Rehabilitation program, dispatching officers to the 86 villages to help people resettle when the dam was completed.

Then rumors began about the government's plan to raise the dam without resettling the victims as it had promised. People sought the help of the landlord of Nilgi, the only village spared by mines and floods.

CHAPTER ONE

October 2004

Reshma's coming to Nilgi was neither accident nor coincidence. Nilgi was a village easily avoided, set at the end of a road, on the banks of the Krishna river. It was not a village people casually passed through. If you came to Nilgi, it was because you wanted to.

Only one real road led to Nilgi or away from it, whichever way you chose to look at it, and it was the potholed tar road connecting it to the nearest town and district capital, Shantur.

Perched on the Deccan plateau's southwestern edge, Nilgi was far enough from the ocean's moderating influence that its seasons were distinct. Summers here were hot and dry, winters cold and dry, and it rained incessantly for four months from June to September. The last monsoon rains had passed when Reshma came, painting the countryside in brushstrokes dipped in shades of green. Hills cast their viridescent shadow over deep-green banana groves, patches of uncleared forest and fruit orchards bursting with guava, pomegranate, and sweet lime. Stretching from the base of the hills

4

were gently undulating fields of maize, jowar and groundnuts through which early winter sunflowers poked their impish heads.

It was a particularly beautiful evening when Reshma came to the Hanuman temple, a kilometer northeast of Nilgi. The Krishna river, full and clear, glistened through emerald fields like a snake shedding its skin. The setting sun—bathed the earth in a clean, soft light making the whitewashed temple walls whiter, the shadows in the trees darker, deeper.

The village was gathered outside the temple, men and women in separate groups. The elite sat on the stone platforms beneath the trees, the less elite squatted on the ground. The world's problems were being sorted that evening, just like any other evening— religion, politics, illnesses, local scandal, soured milk—and no one noticed the beggar girl.

Samar Chandar, the thirty-three-year-old government liaison officer stationed in Nilgi to help people move and resettle when the village drowned in the backwaters of the Arjuna dam, first noticed a movement in the shadows behind the trees, too large to be a stray dog or cat. He stood up to look and at that very moment Reshma came out of her hiding place. There was a lull in the conversation, seconds of hesitation, before Samar stepped forward.

"Are you lost?" he asked.

Silence.

"Looking for someone?" he pressed.

And there she stood, a four-foot-high figure, no more than nine, skinny and slight, clothed in a dress of indistinguishable color falling off thin shoulders. Two arms and two legs protruded from the oversized dress, twig-like and all angles. Long, black, waist-length matted locks of hair framed a small, oval face. The features were covered in grime, barely distinguishable except for the eyes, large and almond-shaped, the pupils black. And it was the eyes that captivated and disturbed the watching crowd. They were not the eyes of a child, sheltered and loved, fed on sweets, and rocked at night. These eyes had known much pain. Not the pain a child feels when it falls or is scolded, but the pain fate should inflict, if it must, on an adult.

The gathered crowd held a hasty consultation, and everyone agreed it was not the right time for questions. Who knew how long the girl had walked and when she had last eaten? A beggar, they decided, with no real past and no future. But even they could not get away from the stench of the present—the smell of sweat and tears, of urine and dirt, of acid in an empty stomach and rotten food.

"Where can she stay the night?" Samar asked, looking around at the crowd, hoping for a volunteer and seeing only puzzlement. "We cannot leave her here."

"You have lived here four years and still don't know the ways of Nilgi," said a grey-haired man bent so low he spoke to the ground. "Anyone with no place to go, goes to the vada. Take her there."

An acquiescing murmur from the crowd and the decision was made. The girl would go to the vada, the home of the Nayaks, the village landlords. It was the biggest house in Nilgi, a mansion with enough space so a beggar's presence would not be disruptive and could be ignored if necessary.

It was not clear how Samar ended up being the one to accompany Reshma to the vada, but as darkness descended and the air turned chilly, he found himself leading her to the only house in the village that would—could—have her.

Samar shone his flashlight on the dark footpath and the girl walked by his side, deftly stepping around loose stones and kikar thorns, silvery under the rising crescent moon. At some point, worried Reshma would trip, Samar took her small, grimy hand in his and she did not resist. A passerby would have never guessed the two had just met. Samar's tall, lanky frame was bent slightly towards Reshma's small figure. A strand of his thick, oiled hair had escaped, marring his broad, intelligent forehead as he concentrated on the path. He was careful with his feelings, giving the impression that he lacked warmth, and felt confused at the unexpected protectiveness he felt towards the little barefooted girl. Was it because he was an orphan and the village in such a short time had already assumed, she was one, too?

The screeches of the monkeys swinging in the trees by the temple grew increasingly faint and when they reached the northeastern corner of the village, Samar turned east along a narrow-paved road towards the vada.

The vada was removed from the rest of the village, a half-kilometer on the eastern side, easily accessible while keeping a respectable distance from the common folk. Entering the twenty-foot-high main gate, Samar noticed Guru, the servant boy, hanging oil lanterns on iron poles entrenched in the soil of the front yard. It was the second day of a power outage and no one could say when it would be back. It could be in the next few minutes. Or it could be another day or two. Or longer.

"I am short-staffed," the power station supervisor explained to disgruntled callers. "I don't have an engineer here and am waiting for one to be sent from the city." He, of course, did not mention that the quota of electricity meant for Nilgi was being diverted to Santosh, the local politician who had been repeatedly elected to the state's legislative assembly despite proven allegations of demanding and taking millions of rupees in bribes. MLA (Member of the Legislative Assembly) Santosh was hosting his friend's daughter's wedding and the gardens around his thirty-eight-room opulent mansion were being lit with the stolen electricity. The supervisor did not feel the slightest twinge of guilt about accepting a lakh of rupees from Santosh for this favor. Power for the powerful was his motto and it had served him well. He had saved enough money from bribes so he could send his engineer son to the United States for a master's program.

When Guru saw Samar stepping through the gates, a bedraggled little girl in tow, he stopped the lantern-lighting and ran to alert the cook and head servant.

"Basu, Basu, Samar is here with a girl. She looks like a beggar."

Basu, in the kitchen, sighed resignedly, annoyed at the interruptions in his dinner preparations. Really, did people have no manners showing up at odd hours with strangers, vagabonds, and drunks? He was only slightly mollified when Samar greeted him respectfully, bending his head and folding his hands in a namaskar.

"What's the matter?" Basu barked, wiping his hands on the towel always slung over his shoulder, even when he was not cooking. "Who is this?"

He pointed a stubby finger at Reshma, cocking his head to one side. She disappeared behind Samar's legs, tucking her head between his knees.

In that moment, Samar felt a sudden, unexpected tightening in his chest.

"She showed up at the temple earlier," Samar said tilting his head back to where Reshma stood, her head still tucked in his knees. Then, more belligerently than he intended, "Everyone thought she should stay here but if it is an inconvenience, I can take her back and leave her at the temple."

Basu felt a twinge of guilt and shot Samar an admiring look. Almost every government official he knew turned the tables skillfully, making you feel responsible for an unfortunate situation that was none of your doing. In the dim flickering light of the oil lanterns, Basu looked at Reshma closely, hesitating only a moment before sending a hovering Guru to fetch the landlord, Raj Nayak, and his wife, Daya.

Guru hurried upstairs. Life had been dull these last few months and Samar and the girl were welcome distractions. If he was lucky, the situation would distract the household enough so he could sneak out and smoke his stash of hand-rolled bidis. He was sure he was suffering tobacco withdrawal symptoms, not to mention how it was beginning to grate on his nerves the way everyone watched his every move. The constant questions: *Where were you last night after dinner, Guru? Have you been smoking again, you monkey? Guru, you should know better than anyone not to drink, your father is a drunk.*

"Samar is here with a beggar girl, dhani," Guru informed Raj, addressing him formally as everyone did. "He says she needs a place to stay."

"So let her stay," Raj responded, glancing up from the book he was reading in the light of the oil lamp, Charles Dickens' *Tale of Two Cities.*

"We should go downstairs, Raj," Daya said, standing up from her chair. Raj's reluctance to get involved in household matters still irked Daya after more than two decades of marriage, and she stared at him as he continued reading. She looked, distractedly, at his still-youthful face with his mother's black eyes and his father's hooked nose, topped by thick brown, hair that fell back from his forehead in perfect waves. Even today, decades after they first met, Daya's heart missed a beat when her gaze fell upon her husband. Her eyes traveled down to his thickening waistline and she made a mental note to talk to Basu about not indulging Raj's sweet tooth.

Raj, aware that Daya was staring at him in frustration, put down his book reluctantly. He understood the goings-on in his house were more important than Dickens, but Dickens was surely more gripping. He had no idea, then, just how much Reshma's arrival would grip him and the rest of the village. How it would turn carefully constructed lives inside out like shirts discarded in haste, every seam and knot visible.

A few minutes later, Raj strode into the front room. Daya and Guru followed.

"What is the commotion about Basu?" he asked.

Another round of explanations.

"We don't know her name," Guru offered.

Daya walked up to the girl and knelt before her, resisting the urge to turn her head away from the stench.

"What is your name?" she asked tender-voiced.

Reshma stared at the slim woman kneeling before her. She had seen women like Daya, getting in and out of cars, always impeccably dressed, not a hair out of place. Their clothes were dull-colored, and they wore very little jewelry, but it was their demeanor which established, beyond doubt, that they were wealthy. Reshma remained silent.

"Don't be scared, you are safe here," Daya pressed.

"Reshma," a small voice answered. Reshma, meaning silk. Soft as silk.

"Are you lost? Do you have any family? Parents we can help you find?"

"No," Reshma shook her head, her lips quivering. "Nobody."

Samar felt a stinging behind his eyes. He remembered a little boy, no more than eight, standing as Reshma now stood, in a roomful of strangers. Being assessed, watched. Noted. Strangers who took the boy in not because they wanted to but because they had to. The boy's parents, both dead, were relatives and what would people say if they did not do the right thing and take in an orphaned relative?

The bile rose in Samar's throat.

"I think she needs to be fed first," Samar said to Daya. "Don't you agree?"

"Yes, yes," Daya agreed standing up, smoothing the pleats of her cotton sari. "Poor child."

Daya summoned Bharati, the youngest maid, who led Reshma to the servants' quarters by the kitchen. The kitchen women took over then, fussing over the bewildered child and Reshma submitted to their ministrations without protest while they undressed her, bathed her, burned her filthy clothes and dressed her in an outfit Bharati had outgrown.

"Give her some ghee," Sharada, the toothless roti-maker suggested, clicking her tongue at Reshma's thin body, every rib a complete arc. "She needs fattening."

Bharati added a dollop of ghee to the dal on Reshma's plate before placing it on the floor in front of the jute dinner mat. The kitchen women hovered, watching Reshma shove the rotis in her mouth first, then the dal.

"Poor child doesn't even know how to eat," one of the women whispered, wiping a tear with the end of her sari.

"Shh, let her eat," Sharada said.

A silence settled in the kitchen as rotis burned over open hearths, eggplants charred, and the women watched the tiny, waiflike child eat as if it was her last meal. Or her first. Basu came in to tell the women to hurry with dinner preparations for Raj and Daya, stood at the door for a few moments, then turned on his heels and left. Dinner would be late.

Sharada watched Reshma intently. She had stood straight and tall once but was hunched over now, like an inverted V-shaped twig that has snapped in the center but is still, miraculously, in one piece. She did not know her exact age and had come to the vada when she had a mouthful of teeth and her smooth, brown skin glowed like polished amber. Now, Sharada's skin was shriveled as if she had been in the water too long and she had lost all her teeth. She had been hired as Raj's nanny and when he was old enough that he did not need her, she had taught herself to make rotis and remained in the vada. Sharada's rotis were famous; she could make several dozen within an hour and each one fluffed up like a balloon and melted in your mouth.

Guru, taking advantage of the chaos and commotion, snuck out to smoke bidis. He needed to make up for weeks of deprivation. He knew everyone at the vada had his best interests at heart, but he was well over twenty and wanted to be treated like an adult. No one believed he was as old as he said he was—years of malnourishment as a child had stunted his growth and he was no taller than the average fifteen-year-old.

Sharada noticed Guru sneaking away but did not stop him. She was preoccupied with something else—the white birthmark she had seen on Reshma's back, the size of a thumbprint, its edges uneven. She remembered seeing a mark like this years ago, when she was young, on the back of a boy she knew well.

From the vada, Samar walked back to the temple, his steps leading him there without conscious intention or purpose. The place was deserted, cold and dark, and he knew his wife was waiting at home with their dinner, but Samar wanted to be alone.

The simple act of Reshma hiding behind his knees had roused unfamiliar emotions in Samar, unsettling him. He wondered if Reshma had unwittingly declared her trust in him with that gesture. Or was it that Basu's presence had sent her scurrying to hide behind the only pair of knees she could find?

The image of Basu caused Samar to smile ruefully. His bald head, his huge paunch, his short, stubby fingers made Basu seem childlike, innocent even. But his loud laugh, his booming voice, abrupt no-nonsense attitude could intimidate easily. Samar understood a little girl's apprehension on meeting Basu for the first time, but he could not understand his own emotions towards a beggar he had met a few hours ago.

Sitting under the trees outside the temple, Samar let the tranquility of the place soothe him. He was an atheist and did not believe that Lord Hanuman, the Hindu monkey deity residing inside the temple, was responsible for calming shot nerves. But even he could not deny there was something mystical, powerful, even peaceful, about the place.

During the day there was a stillness about the temple despite the small sounds. The aerial roots of the banyan trees turned and twisted like the gnarled hands of an old woman, creeping towards the soil, forming a thick trellis around the main trunks. Birds flitted in and out of the thick green canopy, squirrels scampered up and down the giant tree trunks, and monkeys swung on the branches munching on sweet, red fruit. Sometimes, a cobra or a rat snake slithered through the afternoon shadows, disappearing in the surrounding fields. In the morning, the sound of the pujari's chants drowned all sound. In the evening, the chatter of the gathered crowd and the call of roosting birds made the world outside disappear, as if the temple was the center of the universe, grabbing all its energy and taking it for its own.

Behind the temple, the land sloped sharply into the Krishna river, its waters calm in the summer and winter, turbulent and muddy in the monsoon. The villagers believed the temple stood like a gatekeeper, keeping the outside world outside. They knew that Lord Hanuman protected them from the monsoon floods that ravaged the surrounding countryside year after year, made worse by the incomplete Arjuna dam downstream. No one had the nerve to point out that Nilgi escaped flooding because it was on higher ground.

Nilgi was one of 86 villages that would submerge when the dam was completed and Samar had come to Nilgi four years ago with his wife, Usha, as a Displacement and Rehabilitation Officer to help people move and resettle.

Their own village, Samar and Usha's, had been idyllic until the mines came and destroyed it and the surrounding fields and forests. Usha's wealthy father had relocated his family to the city and Samar had been devastated to see Usha, his closest friend and confidante, go. His father, a grocer, had planned on moving to Shantur but Samar's mother had fallen ill and died from throat cancer, almost certainly caused by the noxious fumes from the mines. Samar's father died a few months later from malaria, which had become a huge threat as potholes in the road, caused by barreling mine trucks, filled with water every monsoon, the perfect breeding ground for mosquitoes.

Samar had been raised by reluctant relatives forced to take him in. He'd put himself through college and returned to his village to reopen his father's grocery store with the meager savings his parents had left him. But business was poor as most of the village had been abandoned because of the mines. He had been ready to give up when he met Usha again, visiting the village. The two rekindled their friendship but now there was something else neither could deny: an attraction. They got married, against the wishes of Usha's family, and Samar tried even harder to make the grocery store work but made barely enough to get by. Things became worse when there was yet another exodus from the village because of the threat of floods from the dam whose construction had resumed under Santosh.

A tension crept in between Samar and Usha as she struggled to live in poverty after spending all her life in luxury. A child would have helped, but after three years marriage, Usha had not conceived. Frustrated, Samar began looking for a job and his eyes fell on an advertisement in the newspaper—the government was training young graduates as Displacement and Rehabilitation Officers. He shut down the grocery store, underwent his training and moved to Nilgi.

To Nilgi, he brought the only thing dear to him. Usha.

Together, they rebuilt their life in a place where they knew no one and no one knew them. Samar, initially, had a two-year contract in Nilgi but at the end of it he asked to stay longer, and his boss agreed wondering, idly, why anyone would want to stay in a tiny, doomed village. But, for Samar and Usha, Nilgi had become an escape from their own troubles. Coming here had smoothed the wrinkles in their marriage, lessened the pain of childlessness, and soothed Samar's childhood demons.

Until now.

Reshma's coming had unsettled Samar, somehow. In the distance, across dark fields, he could make out the tall walls of the vada's tower, the outline of the squat, sprawling main house. Reshma was probably asleep by now.

Or not asleep, Samar thought to himself angrily. *If her demons are anything like mine, the ones that afflict helpless orphans, she is probably wide awake.*

Samar watched as Nilgi's lights went out one by one. Only a few households were still up, and he knew one of them was his. Usha was probably beginning to worry. Samar stood up determinedly and began walking home.

As QUICKLY as the village woke every morning, it died down every evening. Oil and kerosene lamps stopped burning by 10 p.m. and the only sounds were the village dogs barking and the grunt of wild boars as they dug for roots in nearby fields. Far in the darkness, a jackal howled, a sound mothers used to scare their restless babies to sleep.

CHAPTER TWO

Reshma's pitifully vulnerable demeanor brought out the maternal instincts in the kitchen women and they fussed over her like hens in a chicken coop; sewing her clothes, braiding her hair with jasmine flowers, and feeding her ghee so she would put on some weight. She had been in Nilgi a few months, but no one had come to claim her. At night, she slept on a thin mattress in the kitchen corner next to Sharada who, without being asked, took it upon herself to be Reshma's surrogate grandmother. It was an implicit arrangement that everyone seemed happy with.

"Do you think she should go to school?" Daya asked Sharada a few weeks after Reshma arrived. "I can talk to the school headmaster and maybe he will let her start mid-year."

"Going to school, being with other children might help," Sharada replied, sitting cross-legged on the floor by Daya's chair, sorting through a pile of rice grains on a plate, picking out pieces of husk, sand particles and small stones. "If the headmaster doesn't agree you can ask Raj dhani to put some pressure. He *is* the chair of the district's education committee."

"I hope I don't have to use Raj's influence. He does not like it. If the headmaster refuses, we can ask if Reshma can sit in on some classes without being formally enrolled."

Sharada nodded and went back to cleaning the rice. *Poor child*, she thought to herself once again.

The headmaster agreed and Reshma began attending school in the mornings. In the afternoons she did chores in the vada. Evenings were hers as long as she returned before dark. On the surface, Reshma took to her new life well. Below the surface, she was still the same lost, wandering beggar who first came to the temple. Even when she talked, laughed, or smiled, there was a part of her that did not. A part of her, deep inside, that no one could reach.

Days became weeks, winter peaked, guavas ripened, and tuberoses bloomed under the soft sun. Reshma, by now, was accepted as part of the vada though she still never spoke of her past and even Sharada, widely respected for her ability to extract information from the most reticent and secretive people, could uncover nothing. Any personal questions, no matter how gentle and innocent, merely drove the child further into her silent cocoon where she often lived smothered by the dark, silken threads that her private demons wove around her slight body. Often, a servant found her crouching in a dark corner of an unused room and would coax her back to the kitchen. In the kitchen, Reshma seemed happiest, surrounded by the constant chatter of women cooking and serving food to the stream of hungry help trickling in from the Nayak's fields.

The kitchen was a happy place, filled with chatter that ceased briefly when Basu came in to chide the women for the cacophony they were causing. The women, then, almost always turned on Basu, tormenting him with sarcastic comments about men interfering in kitchen matters, followed immediately by sly, flirtatious remarks that drove the man away with a smile on his face.

It was in the kitchen, where smells of freshly-ground spices congealed with laughter and tears and sank into the thick stone walls, that a friendship sparked among the three youngest servants: Bharati, a few years older than Reshma, Guru of indeterminate age and a silent Reshma. The friendship grew by the burning fires in the six hearths, encouraged by the kitchen staff, endorsed by Daya, nurtured by three children who had been forced to leave their childhoods behind because of unfortunate circumstances.

"Why don't you attend school like Bharati and Reshma?" Sharada chided Guru every morning when she saw him loitering in the kitchen while the girls were in school.

"I am meant for bigger things than school," Guru, proudly illiterate, always responded.

"Like what, you useless monkey? A little education won't do you any harm."

"It won't do me any good either! Look at you. No education and see how well you have done Sharada mami. Bright as a sun, you are."

And so, the conversation proceeded every morning with Sharada cajoling and Guru teasing until the girls came home and the three did their chores before racing to the temple to play under the banyan trees.

It was under the trees that another curious friendship developed, this one between Reshma and Samar. The basis of a friendship between a thirty-plus man and a little beggar girl was unclear but it was obvious to any onlooker that the two were close. Perhaps because Samar had been the one to walk Reshma to the vada that first night or perhaps because they were both orphans.

Samar, as the Displacement and Rehabilitation Officer, had not wanted to be the harbinger of bad news but quickly discovered that no one in Nilgi believed him. When he tried explaining to people that they must make plans to move, start a new life elsewhere because their village would submerge in the dam backwaters, they looked at him sympathetically.

"Lord Hanuman will protect us from drowning," they assured Samar, as if he were a child.

Samar finally realized that submergence had been hanging over Nilgi for so long that people did not believe it would happen. They listened to Samar politely, then pushed the sad myth to the back of their minds and continued adding to their houses and improving their fields despite being advised not to invest any more time or money into their doomed properties.

While the sad gloom of impending destruction permeated the neighboring countryside making mud walls chip and crumble, roofs leak, and abandoned fields turn white with accumulated salt, Nilgi only flourished. Mud houses were replaced with brick structures painted blue, green, and even a shade of pink that astonished the eye. Farmers installed new irrigation systems and PVC pipes in their fields and harvests improved year after year.

At some point even Samar began believing it was all a lie. The blueprints he had seen in his office in the city, delineating the area of submergence, became lost in his mind as an illusion from another life. He, too, allowed himself to be soothed by Nilgi's timeless charm, its optimism and unwavering faith.

SHORTLY AFTER MOVING to Nilgi and confiding her longing for a child, Usha had been advised to pray at the temple every evening. "Pray to Lord Hanuman and you will have a child within a year or two," one of the women had promised.

Almost four years later, Usha was still childless but continued praying at the temple. Samar, despite his dismissal of religion and god, took Usha to the temple every evening on his motorcycle and waited outside until she was done.

Usually, Samar enjoyed chatting with the people under the banyan trees while he waited but there was a restlessness in him that evening. Waiting at home was a letter from his boss telling him about the recent government order to raise the dam's height and complete the project, but there was no mention of the compensation due to the 86 villages.

There was already a sizeable population displaced by the mines and that would only increase if the dam was completed without a sound resettlement plan. It would turn the district into a place with no moorings, where desperate poverty and crime reigned.

Nilgi was one of the few villages untouched by mining and flooding, but not for long.

"So, why don't you ever enter the temple?" a voice at Samar's elbow asked, breaking his reverie. A question he had heard a hundred times.

"Because I don't believe in god," Samar answered for the hundredth time, looking down at Reshma. "You startled me. Where did you come from?"

"There," Reshma replied, pointing seriously in the general direction of the vada. "You just didn't notice."

"How was school today?" he asked, gazing down at her small, upturned face, the almond-shaped eyes filled with deep secrets.

"We had a geography test, and I don't think I did well," she replied, her mouth turning down.

"Why do you think that? You studied for it, didn't you?"

"I did but I haven't taken a test before."

Samar could have asked why she had not taken a test before. He could have asked her where she attended school before this, if she had attended school at all. But he did not ask despite the questions buzzing in his head.

"Would you like to go on a motorcycle ride?" he said instead.

"Yes, yes," she squealed, hurling herself at his legs, almost knocking him down.

"Wow, you really don't want to go, do you?" he teased. "Well, let's ask Usha if she wants to come, too."

He let Reshma place her feet over his, her back against his knees, and holding her steady under the armpits walked them both to the temple entrance.

"Would you like to go as well?" Samar said seeing Bharati and Guru hovering by the entrance, waiting for the priest to bring out the laddus, balls of sugar, roasted gram flour, cashews and raisins, offered to Lord Hanuman that he would distribute to the gathered children. "I promise I will ride very slow."

"I am not scared," Bharati replied, squaring her shoulders. "I don't trust your riding."

Samar laughed. For all her bravado and non-stop chatter, Bharati was a fearful girl who believed djinns haunted banyan trees and made apocalyptic predictions about the world every time she saw bad news on television. She was banned from watching the news at the vada but managed to sneak into the living room where the television was before someone scolded and took her away.

"Guru, can you ask my wife to be done for today? Tell her enough prayers. We want to go on a motorcycle ride."

Guru went in and returned to report that Usha said Samar could either go home and leave her alone or come in and pray with her.

"Why does she pray every day?" Guru, fellow-atheist, belief-challenger, pot-stirrer wanted to know.

"Because someone has told her it will bring great happiness," Samar replied, an edge to his voice.

At that moment, Usha stepped out of the temple and shook her head at Samar. In her hands was a brass plate with marigold flowers and pieces of coconut and jaggery that she offered Samar, knowing he would refuse. Which he always did, even though he loved coconut and jaggery, but this came from the temple and had no place in his life.

"I promised Reshma I would take her on a ride," Samar said. "Would you like to come along?"

"No, I will wait here," Usha said, sitting down cross-legged by the temple wall, adjusting her burnt orange sari over her knees, making sure it covered her properly. "You two go too fast for me. It makes me dizzy."

She watched Samar and Reshma walking to the motorcycle, holding hands. Reshma was chattering up to him and, at one point, he bent his head down towards her and laughed. They were too far for Usha to see their faces, but she knew that expression on her husband's face—part adoration, part indulgence, part unadulterated joy. Only around Reshma did Usha see the carefree man her husband could be—his thick, dark, curly hair tousled, his handsome face free of worry, his tall, gangly frame relaxed.

Lately, Samar was visiting the general store in Shantur at least twice a week on the pretext of shopping for the household. He returned with supplies they did not need and a doll, bead necklace or ribbon for Reshma. Usha teased him saying he was getting soft in his old age to which he replied, seriously, that only one orphan could understand the life of another. Usha never teased him after that.

Samar assured Usha, repeatedly, that he did not care they were childless, but she had known this man for most of her life and did not believe him. He wanted children, she was certain, to reaffirm his own identity, his own life, his own worth.

And just like that, as Usha sat leaning her back to the temple wall, a thought tiptoed unbidden into her mind.

Maybe Reshma is the child we want. Maybe Lord Hanuman has blessed us with a child, and we are just not seeing it.

CHAPTER THREE

"**D**inner is ready," Basu announced. Daya, cradling a cup of Darjeeling tea in her hands, continued rocking in the wicker chair beneath the jasmine canopy of the vada's kitchen courtyard.

"I'm not hungry, but could you bring me more tea?" she asked, handing Basu her empty cup.

"What about Inspector Veera? He is coming to dinner."

"He's here to see Raj on some business and won't even notice my absence. In fact, he might prefer it. He has little respect for women, and I don't want to be ignored while he discusses this important matter with Raj."

Basu sensed something was wrong. Daya spent every sundown in this wicker chair, nursing the same cup of tea for an hour or so before pouring it, untouched, into the jasmine roots before coming in to dinner.

Today she had refused dinner, finished her first cup of tea and asked for a second. It made Basu nervous. He sensed her anger in the soft light of the single bulb in the courtyard. He guessed it was directed at the inseparable three—Reshma, Guru, and Bharati—but did not know the exact reason. This past week, Daya had commented several times on the laziness of the children, both at school and in the vada.

Daya was angry, angry enough that she knew it would be best to absent herself from the dinner table where she would have to make polite conversation with Raj and Inspector Veera from the Shantur Police Station. There was no love lost between the inspector, who was in the pockets of Santosh, and the Nayaks. Santosh never missed a chance to undermine them. He had political power, but Raj and his family were more respected because they were the local landlords. It made Santosh furious, and it never occurred to him that people did not dislike him because his roots were humble but for his corruption and how he carried on with impunity and arrogance. He had been re-elected several times only because the opposition's candidate was weak, incapable and lacked the resources for a successful campaign.

Daya was in no mood to hide her feelings. By now, she knew the entire household was aware of her anger and she was surprised no one had been dispatched to calm her. She was glad because she was in no mood to be calmed. She wanted to hold onto her anger until she had finished saying what she needed to, to Reshma, Guru, and Bharati.

Daya had never punished the three children and their minor misdemeanors were always attributed to their age and excused after a quick scolding. But, today, they were more than an hour late returning home from the Hanuman temple and Daya was livid. Not because they were late, but because the three were becoming increasingly insolent and followed none of her instructions.

The friendship and affection blossoming between Reshma, Guru, and Bharati gladdened Daya's heart; none of the three had families they could count on for love and support and having each other was a good thing. But their negligence towards work—school and household chores—irked her. She felt she still had some control over the girls, but Guru was a problem. His intractability, impossible dreams, and a genetic disposition towards addiction, alcohol, and smoking, worried Daya. Just yesterday, a bangle-seller from Shantur who went from door to door selling her goods, had asked after Guru and slyly remarked that she often saw him buying bidis from a street hawker.

Daya noticed a brief lull in the kitchen's buzz and knew the children had arrived. She could hear Basu telling them, quietly, to see the mistress in the courtyard and smiled despite herself. She knew Basu spoke quietly only when he was very annoyed or very worried; his calmness was more dreadful than his abundant curses and obscenities. And, this evening, Basu was annoyed that Daya had refused dinner.

"You have made her so angry she refused dinner," Basu was saying.

Then a shuffling of six feet as the offenders filed into the courtyard, the girls trying to hide behind Guru. Showing repentance had worked before but it did not today. Daya watched them in silence, holding back her usual scolding and cajoling. It made the children uncomfortable, and they stood, shifting from foot to foot, heads bowed, sneaking looks at Daya from beneath downcast eyes.

"I've promised your mothers," Daya began, causing Reshma jerk her head up in alarm. "Yes, yours, too Reshma, though we never met. Wherever she is, I know she would want a better life for you than this."

Reshma, Guru, and Bharati were watching her closely, wondering if anger had made their mistress lose her mind.

"I promised your mothers, in my heart, that I would raise

25

you to be good, hardworking, independent adults. That is a big responsibility for me, but it is a bigger one for you. I am trying my best to provide you with as many opportunities as I can but how you use them to make something of yourselves is up to you. From how you have been behaving recently, I am wondering if I have been a fool in taking you all in. If your present enthusiasm for work continues, I am confident you will end up loafers."

Reshma, Guru, and Bharati stared at her. It was unlike Daya to be sarcastic, and they were not sure how to react, so they said nothing.

"From now on I'd like to see more enthusiasm for work, both in school and at home," Daya continued. "Guru, I know you think yourself above school, so I won't force a much-needed education on you. But you are the oldest and I expect you to pull your weight more, be more responsible. Your whole family depends on you."

Then, turning to the girls, "And do you want to end up uneducated, helpless, dependent on your husbands? From now on there will be no play until you have finished all your work. Am I making myself clear?"

Her voice rose and shook on the "clear," and since her expression was hard to fathom in the light of the courtyard's bulb, the three perpetrators stood still, unsure what to say.

"We didn't want to make you mad," Guru finally murmured into the silence. "We weren't thinking."

"The sun will rise in the west the day you begin thinking, Guru," Daya said, smiling in the dark. "But even that day might come. Now, go and have your dinner."

Daya watched the three leave the courtyard, an air of such dejection about them, that the anger she had so stubbornly been holding onto dissipated. It was wrong burdening children with the responsibility of success as the world perceived it—getting a job, marrying, having children—but Reshma, Guru, and Bharati had to be reminded they were on their own, unprotected by parental love and support.

Guru's family, from a nearby village, depended on him to provide what his alcoholic, useless father could not. There had been sixteen in his family including his always-passed-out father, two mothers, one legal and one not-so-legal, with thirteen children between them. One of Guru's sisters had run away, one sister had married and moved out, two brothers married and continued living in the house with their wives and children, so there were now eighteen in a two-room house. Guru lived in the vada. He often wondered if god assigned people numbers and if he was the inauspicious thirteenth sibling, though he was neither the oldest nor the youngest. Numbering or no numbering, Guru knew he was the unluckiest. His oldest brother had escaped the burden of supporting the family as he was the firstborn and had to be preserved. His other brothers were let off the hook because they were either married with children or were mediocre students trying to finish school or simply incapable of working. His sisters escaped because they were girls, so Guru, the fourth offspring of the younger, less-legal wife, was now the breadwinner.

Guru, however, knew he was better off than most in a district where villages had been ruined first by mines and then by floods because of the dam. Nilgi, miraculously, had escaped disaster and life there was still good. Guru was a servant, but the Nayaks treated him well and the vada staff had become his family. He had a roof over his head and enough food to eat so he could send all his salary to his family. He should have been content, but he was not. He wanted to be rich, so rich he never needed to work again. And when he was rich, he could start looking for his older sister who had run away.

Bharati's mother, a young woman abandoned by her errant husband, worked for a building contractor, moving from place to place, wherever there was work. Because she had rejected the overtures of the overseer, she was paid less than she deserved for carrying bricks and bags of concrete. She barely made enough to support herself and had come to the vada one listless summer night a year ago to barter Bharati's services as a house servant in return for room and board. She was terrified the overseer would start propositioning her pubescent daughter and knew Bharati would be safe with the Nayaks.

Daya took in the thirteen-year-old and went a step further, enrolling her in the village school. For that, Daya earned the mother's gratitude and the burden of eventually finding Bharati a good fellow to marry—a difficult task as the girl was not particularly attractive.

As for Reshma, Daya did not know who she was but there was little doubt she would grow up to be a beauty. Her exquisite looks, her gentleness, would drive men mad when she came of age. There would be problems when families of prospective grooms began inquiring about Reshma's background. Daya knew nothing except that the village believed she was an orphan and if Reshma continued her silence, her origins would remain shrouded in conjecture and gossip.

RAJ LOOKED QUIZZICALLY at his stout, pot-bellied guest in a crisp, khaki policeman's uniform. When Raj had taken his usual seat at the head of the dining table, the man, Veera, had rushed, almost run, to take the chair at the opposite end. Raj understood the inspector did not want to be seated anywhere except at the head or foot of the Nayak table, and was making sure Daya did not get the seat at the other end. Raj smiled to himself because Daya was not joining them for dinner and even if she had, she preferred sitting on Raj's left side so Basu could serve them both quickly and not have to walk up and down the twelve-seat dining table.

Basu, a sour look on his face, served Veera the stuffed eggplant, potato curry, dal and roti.

"Is that enough?" he asked when Veera remained silent after Basu had served him the third spoonful of dal.

"Just a little bit more," Veera said, reaching for the ghee in front of him.

"Only rice for me, Basu," Raj said. "I still haven't digested my lunch."

"I hope your health is alright?" Veera said, fingering the baton he had carelessly and conspicuously placed on the table.

"It is fine, thank you," Raj responded. "So, what brings you here? It sounded urgent when you called this morning."

"Nothing urgent," Veera laughed. "I was craving Basu's food, that's all."

"I hear the cook is outstanding at Santosh's house. Surely, this is a step down for you?"

Veera laughed, uncertainly, his clean left hand going up to his badge, his fingers running over the three stars.

"How would I know?" he asked.

"Come, come, Inspector," Raj said, smiling. "It isn't Basu's food that brought you here."

"You are right," Veera replied, licking his thick fingers, and sitting up from his slouch. "I am here about Samar. Samar Chandar. You know him?"

"Yes, we are acquainted. Everyone knows everyone else in Nilgi."

Samar and Usha had spent the previous day—a Sunday—at the vada, playing with Reshma, leaving after dinner, but Veera did not need to know that the Chandars were good friends with him and Daya.

"Samar is a government official and there are rumors he is

29

inciting people against the government because dam compensation has not yet been paid to those who will be displaced."

"Well, it hasn't been paid and it seems it is not likely to be paid and someone needs to stick up for the people. Even at its present height, the dam is causing villages to flood. If the height is raised, as it seems the government plans on doing, it will obliterate the whole region."

"That is not the point. Samar is a government servant, and he is breaking the law by triggering anti-government sentiment."

"You just said it was a rumor," Raj said looking at his guest, his gaze unwavering. "Moreover, I would know by now if Samar was organizing protests against the government. Nothing escapes my notice in Nilgi."

"It isn't a rumor," Veera said, flustered. "We can throw him in jail."

"You will have to prove he is, indeed, doing what you say he is doing."

"The government is aware that you, too, are organizing people to protest," Veera tried, changing tracks.

"Everyone knows that I am against the dam. I was against it ten years ago when the government decided to build it at a lower-than-planned height, reassuring people their villages wouldn't flood. But I knew floods were unavoidable and wrote several letters of protest to the authorities and politicians. No one heeded the letters, especially your Santosh, who openly ridiculed me. He didn't realize that by doing so, he was bringing the issue to the attention of people who had been silent until then. He, unwittingly, gave me and the activists, people to organize into a protest. There hasn't been a protest *yet*, but if the dam height is raised more without compensating the people, be sure there will be riots."

"The government may try stopping you," Veera said, realizing he was losing the argument.

"It is not a crime to oppose the government," Raj said. "And if the government did succeed in stopping me, a few hundred thousand people will take to the streets."

It was true, Veera reluctantly accepted. The zamindari system, a feudal system, had long been abolished, but the Nayak family was still influential and loved in these parts. Openly antagonizing the family was not in the government's best interests.

"I am only telling you what I have heard," Veera said in a conciliatory tone. "Just keep an eye on that Samar Chandar for us. I don't want him to get in trouble. As you must know, my loyalties lie with the people. I am here to serve them."

"I am sure they do," Raj said, softly. "You don't seem like a person who acts with only his own self-interests in mind."

"Of course...of course, I don't," Veera said, standing up, not sure how to read Raj's comment. "I must leave now."

Raj stood up, shook his guest's hand and went up to his room.

Veera, baffled and unsure of what had just transpired, ambled to his Vespa scooter parked in the front yard and rode to his modest, lonely, bachelor's home in Shantur.

APPROACHING FOOTSTEPS BROKE into Daya's thoughts. Sharada entered the courtyard and sat cross-legged on the floor even though there was an empty chair. It was audacious to sit in a chair in her employer's presence.

"Are you not feeling well?" Sharada asked.

"I am fine, just not hungry," Daya replied. "Did the inspector leave?"

"Yes, he has left."

"I wonder why he was here. He doesn't usually seek us out."

Sharada shrugged.

"Something is bothering you," she said. "What is it? Basu said you had a talk with the children."

"I am worried about Reshma, Bharati and Guru," Daya confided. "I have taken on the responsibility of raising them in this house, seeing they are settled in life, but I am not succeeding. They are becoming defiant."

"They will be alright, don't worry. They are good children."

Daya nodded.

"Guru and Bharati will be, but I worry about Reshma," Daya said. "She is so quiet, and we know nothing of her past. And until we know, we can't really help her."

"She is close with Samar. Maybe we can ask him if he knows anything."

"No, never, Sharada. If Reshma finds out she may withdraw further and stop trusting us completely."

RAJ WAS ON the terrace of his room. The night sky was clear and in the soft moonlight he could make out the outline of the banyan trees on the horizon, like dark clouds trembling in the slight breeze. The Hanuman temple was behind the trees and in his mind's eye Raj could see the whitewashed walls, the open veranda, the deceptive calm.

He had played there with his friends when he was a child. He smiled, remembering how they had raced down the slope behind the temple, hurling themselves, laughing, into the Krishna river. Sharada used to stand at the top of the slope shouting, threatening, pleading, telling them they would drown.

Frustrated, Sharada would go into the temple and pray. "Give the boys some sense so they don't kill themselves." And Lord Hanuman had listened, the smile never leaving his face, despite being constantly pestered by prayers, homilies, resolutions, and promises. And when Raj and his friends returned, exhausted from their play, Sharada smeared holy ash on their foreheads to calm them. The boys sniggered knowing the prayers were meant to calm Sharada's nerves more than anything else.

And then, one day Raj had stopped racing down the slope. Adulthood had crept upon him, unnoticed. Life stopped being simple. Suddenly, things were no longer black and white. There was a huge gray area trolled by doubts, suspicions, and misgivings. The gray area had grown as Raj had put more and more years behind him, as he navigated through marriage, fatherhood, manhood, and landlord-hood. He had done things he was not proud of but could not regret. Questions with no answers bubbled in his mind, spilling over. At some point, he had stopped wondering what was real and what was not. He began focusing his energy on just one thing—helping the people who would be displaced by the dam.

"Won't you come to bed?" Daya asked, making Raj start. "I thought you would be asleep by now."

"You didn't come to dinner," Raj responded. "Isn't the night sky beautiful?"

"It is," Daya agreed. "What did Veera have to say?"

"This and that," Raj shrugged. "Mostly warned me and Samar not to participate in anti-dam activism."

"It isn't any of his business, really. Besides, people are already furious. You are just enabling them to express their resentment."

"Have Jai and Rohan called today?"

"No, Jai said yesterday that he was busy studying for his boards and Rohan is out playing in the school cricket tournament."

"We are lucky," Raj said. "They are good kids. Jai is only sixteen and much more responsible than I ever was at that age. I think we were right in sending them to boarding school."

Daya nodded and put an arm around Raj's waist, resting her head on his shoulder.

"What's the matter?" he asked, lifting Daya's chin, searching her eyes. "You only lean on me like this when you are upset."

"I am worried about Reshma, Guru, and Bharati. I am responsible for them, but losing control. They are doing as they please, neglecting work and studies. I am most concerned about Reshma. We know nothing about her."

"Do you know what?" Raj asked suddenly. "Every time I see Reshma, I have this feeling that I know her. Like we have met before."

"Now, *that* is absurd," Daya laughed. "You are getting old and your mind is in overdrive from all those books you are reading."

Raj did not respond. He was certain his imagination was not running riot. He had not really paid Reshma much attention when she first came to the vada with Samar. She was covered in grime and so filthy it was difficult to see what she looked like. A few days later, Raj ran into Reshma and Bharati in the hallway outside his bedroom and really seen her for the first time. He had stared, not because it was an exquisite face, but because he felt he knew it. He had dismissed his thoughts as fantastical, but the feeling kept growing stronger and stronger each time he saw her.

"Look, the Raat ki Rani creeper is blooming," Daya said, pointing to a plant in the corner, drooping under the weight of dozens of white blossoms. "The Queen of Darkness. Do you believe the flowers attract snakes at night?"

Daya held a flower under Raj's nose.

"Sharada says there was a cobra with white hood markings under the creeper the night you were born," Daya said. "She says it portends good luck."

"I don't believe in such superstition but, yes, I am a lucky man. No one could ask for a better life companion and you have given me two wonderful boys."

"Yes, you are lucky," Daya teased. "Won't you come to bed?"

"In a little bit. Samar has 'discreetly' told me the government plans to complete the dam—there is no displacement and rehabilitation plan for people. I need to meet with the leaders of the 86 villages to plan a protest. We have no friends in the government anymore, no politicians left who are truly interested in helping the people. Santosh is the worst. He is the state's agriculture minister and has instigated plans to complete the project. There is a lot of money to be made."

"I love you even more for taking this on," Daya said. "You are getting involved even though Nilgi may never flood."

RAJ WALKED TO the Hanuman temple through the cobbled streets of the village, Sharada by his side. He slowed his steps to match hers.

"You go on. I'll catch up."

Raj did not answer or pick up his pace. The previous night, after Veera had left, he had gone down to the kitchen and asked Sharada to make payasam, a sweet cream of wheat and milk pudding, as an offering to Lord Hanuman. The temple always cleared his head and he needed to think logically, come up with a sound strategy for the anti-dam movement. Veera's visit worried him; if the government was trying to silence dissension, there was little hope.

It was a cold morning and a fog had descended, hiding the houses and fields in a white cottony blanket. Over the Krishna, fog and water joined, becoming one. The sun was just rising as the cowherds trudged out of their houses wrapped in coarse, black sheep wool blankets, bright-eyed and ready for the day. They gathered the village cattle, coaxing them out of slumber, driving them towards the hills, clicking their tongues to keep the animals in line. Their bare feet trod noiselessly, their path lit by oil lanterns swinging from their arms. They bowed to Raj as he passed them, and he returned the greeting.

Smoke was rising from houses as women made rotis for their husbands and children. They packed the rotis with red chili chutney and a dollop of sunflower oil, wrapping them in a piece of cloth so they stayed moist until lunch.

On reaching the temple, Raj and Sharada ascended the few steps, entered the inner sanctum, and rang the bells hanging from the ceiling. Raj bowed down, touched his head to the floor and prayed silently. Then, he stood up, lit the two oil lamps by Lord Hanuman and placed the bowl of payasam Sharada handed him on the floor, in front of the deity.

"Let's sit outside for a little while," he said to Sharada. "No one is here and it is so quiet."

"Something is bothering you," Sharada said.

"Yes. I am worried the people won't get the compensation they deserve. That they *need*. Our government is too corrupt but it isn't just that. There is a bigger power at play, something larger than us that is causing us to self-destruct. This cloud of hopelessness and despair hanging over our heads."

"There is nothing you can do about that, my son, but you can make sure you keep the protest alive, prevent people from becoming hopeless. You have always been a worrier. It is not good for you."

Raj smiled. He was glad Sharada had insisted on going with him. She had known him since the moment he was born and her loyalty to him and the Nayaks was absolute.

Raj's mother had hired Sharada fifty years ago, a few weeks before he was born, against the advice and homilies of the household staff, well-wishers and not-so-well-wishers. Sharada was a sixteen-year-old widow and certain to bring bad luck, they assured Raj's mother who dismissed the prophecies as ignorance and superstition.

Sharada's husband had died from a cobra bite while foraging

for wild berries in the forest where he was grazing his cattle. He lay on the ground by a kikar shrub, frothing at the mouth, until a passing cowherd saw him and ran to the village for help. By the time a group of villagers arrived the boy was dead and with his life, Sharada's life, too, had ended.

As a widow, Sharada was destined to live on society's fringes as an outcast, her head shaven, all the color in her life purged by the white saris she had to wear. She would live the rest of her life in a widow's ashram with unfortunate women like herself. She could eat only what she got from begging for alms on the streets. Life stretched before her filled with blame, shame and pain. She would be blamed for her husband's untimely death because who could have brought that on except a vicious, inauspicious wife? Her widowhood was her shame and society's unrelenting chastisement of her would be her pain.

Sharada's in-laws, predictably, held her responsible for their third son's death. They accused her of dark magic—she had killed her husband for the man in black with ash on his forehead living on the village's outskirts luring weak, young women with his vile art. It did not matter that Sharada had never met him. *Look*, they said to anyone who would listen. *She refuses to shave her head or wear white because she wants to look attractive and trap another man, destroy another home.* Sharada endured the abuses of her in-laws, but when they began insisting, she move to an ashram, she fled to her widowed father's house.

Sharada's father, an old man with hopeless eyes and camphor-white hair, brought his daughter to the vada hoping she could live out her life there. The Nayaks did not always conform to custom and traditional ways and in the past widows had sought refuge at the vada living and working there until they died. Of course, they were used as servants and not a single widow had remarried but it was still a better life than the ashram.

Raj's mother had liked Sharada immediately.

"No widow in the vada has worn white," she said to the protesting servants. "Sharada will keep her hair and her colorful saris. She will dress as she did when her husband was alive, and I expect you all to treat her as you would any sixteen-year-old. If I hear otherwise, there will be repercussions. Times are changing and so will we."

So, just like that, Raj's mother laid down the law. That a widow was permitted, even encouraged, to look attractive, eat with the rest of the household and mix with people freely was inconceivable and such a deviation from custom that it did not even warrant comment. The traditional whispered about the decline of values. The jealous predicted that Sharada would end the lives of many more men. Most women, especially the widows who begged for a handful of rice on the streets and slept on stone floors, rejoiced secretly.

Initially, Sharada was terrified of living like a widow and even more terrified of not. When a married woman made herself attractive, it was for her husband. When a widow made herself look attractive, she was a loose woman out to seduce men.

Hesitantly, and initially fearful, Sharada left behind the life she was supposed to live. She wore colorful saris, flowers in her hair, glass bangles on her wrists. To be truthful, she had been married less than three months and hardly known her husband. His death saddened her but it was not the kind of grief that tears you apart, making life seem futile. It was the kind of sadness that time heals with few scars, except for the occasional sigh or missed heartbeat for a life that could have been.

It is wonderful what people can get used to and Nilgi's residents reluctantly accepted a widow in their midst who behaved as a young, unmarried girl would. They looked the other way as long as Sharada stayed away from their husbands and sons.

Raj was born a few weeks after Sharada came to the vada, on an unusually warm spring night, just before the clock struck twelve. As he left the warmth of his mother's womb, his gusty cries penetrated the vada's deep stone walls and spilled into the moonless darkness outside. The midwife wiped Raj's mother's sweaty brow with a muslin cloth soaked in rose water before taking the baby to the bathroom to clean up. Sharada helped the midwife; she had considerable experience taking care of babies, being the oldest of her siblings.

The instant the midwife placed the screaming infant in Sharada's arms, she fell in love. The crying ceased for a brief moment and two large, unfocused eyes stared at Sharada before the tiny face scrunched up again and the wailing resumed with renewed vigor.

Raj came into the world like anybody else—naked, shriveled, vulnerable, his future filled with question marks and no guarantees—but was considered special because he was the landlord's son. On the night Raj was born, Sharada saw a cobra under the fragrant blossoms of the Raat ki Rani creeper in the kitchen courtyard. She saw the same cobra, unmistakable with its white hood markings, the next night and the night after for a week after Raj's birth. She was convinced the cobra sightings confirmed beyond doubt that Raj was truly special.

Decades later, as an old woman, Sharada would describe that night in detail. When she narrated the story of the night of Raj's birth, her eyes sparkled and the loose skin hanging from her arms trembled in delight. She described the beat of the dholak, a hand drum worn with a rope around the neck, from the vada, announcing the birth of a boy. If the mother or baby or, worse, both had not made it through childbirth the dholak would have remained silent and, instead, the haunting notes of the flute would have rent the night air. If her listeners were still listening,

Sharada would tell them about the loud, happy hullabaloo from the vada that could be heard by nomadic shepherds camping a few kilometers away, The next day, it was, her, Sharada who distributed boxes of saffron pedas to the entire village to celebrate Raj's birth.

CHAPTER FOUR

Address at once, Raj wrote in his notebook.

1. *Contact Rao and Sons, Builders and Contractors, for estimate to repair roof leak.*
2. *Order desks and chairs for Lower KG and Upper KG in all district schools.*
3. *Start discussions with Department of State Transport to organize subsidized bus passes for students.*
4. *Find replacement for retiring Rampur school headmistress.*

At five, Raj put down his fountain pen, leaned back in his chair and took a deep breath. His bones were stiff and his muscles numb from hours of sitting at his desk. The clock on the wall showed just after six. The night, chilly and moonless, infiltrated the school grounds through dark, still trees. In a nearby house, an infant wailed. The newborn in the Bisnal family, Raj guessed and wondered idly if the seventeen-year-old mother knew how to care

41

for her baby. He wondered, more seriously, if he should abandon his work for now and go home; he had been in his office since seven in the morning.

The school was single-storied, built with stone and capped by a leaking red-tiled roof. A deep veranda, with red-oxide floors ran around it successfully keeping the sun out so the summer heat was tolerable, the winter cold intolerable. From the outside, the building seemed small but it was surprisingly spacious on the inside. There were ten classrooms, from grades one to ten, a common faculty and staff room, an office for the headmaster and, in the eastern corner, a reasonable-sized office for Raj. On the door was a black iron plaque with faded gold lettering, Raj Nayak, Chair, Shantur District Education Committee.

Raj had become chair after his father passed away. The position had been held by his father and before him, his grandfather. Raj's great grandfather had built the school which had initially run only up to grade five. Over time, more and more classes were added and now it provided instruction right up to matriculation in grade ten, after which students could go to college if they wished.

Raj had been a visionary when it came to education. He had helped pass laws that made it mandatory for families to send their children to school until grade ten. Though this law was not always enforced, fewer families were sending their minor children to work and school attendance had increased. Lately, however, Raj's ambition and enthusiasm for education was flagging. He wondered if it was because of the impending doom of the dam. *Perhaps old age,* Raj thought, even though he was barely fifty, pushing back his vinyl-covered wooden chair from the desk and standing up. He walked to the window and opened it. The cold air rushed in making him shiver in his thin sweater but he did not move away from the window or close it.

Or maybe I have nothing left to give, he philosophized, gazing into the darkness.

Raj had grown old in this school. He had first walked through the front door as a five-year-old and left for college after graduating at sixteen. It had taken him six years to finish his bachelor's and get his law degree after which he returned to Nilgi to take over the running of the family estate and later, after his father died, became the chair of the district's education committee.

He had dreamed his biggest dreams not for himself or his family but for others and education had been just one of the things he had been involved with. Initially, there had been plenty of like-minded people to work with but in the last decade that pool had shrunk. The outside world had crept in, annihilating a simple life with tantalizing glimpses of luxury—palatial homes, fancy cars, and exotic vacations. People's dreams had grown unhindered, fed and enabled by a corrupt system that made it possible for the unscrupulous to amass wealth.

The term nouveau riche tiptoed in, sinking into society and was given a permanent place. It was becoming harder and harder to launch improvement projects when politicians like Santosh reigned. That was why Raj appreciated government officials like Samar who still had the best interests of the people they served at heart.

Raj was not sure how long people like Samar would last. The visit from Veera had rattled him more than he let on. There was little hope when the government began threatening to shut the voices raised against it. It was only a matter of time before India descended into anarchy.

Fifty-eight years after independence from British rule and India had become what it had vowed to never become: a nation where materialism was obliterating idealism and where dishonesty and corruption were acceptable. So, of course, Raj's views often clashed with others and he was advised to accept corruption and work within its paradigm. He wondered if he was a fool for not letting go of his ideals.

Everyone knows the difference between right and wrong, Raj's mother used to say. *But it is discipline that keeps you on the right path. Discipline makes you a moral person.*

That had been the core of his education and Raj had worked hard to stay on the right path. Morality had been his goal and achieving it had made him strong, winning him the respect of not just Nilgi but the entire district.

Then he had strayed and begun to doubt the solidness of his own education and the soundness of his morality. No one knew of his transgression but it kept him awake night after night. It wrapped its sticky tentacles around his mind and squeezed so tightly that he writhed in pain.

Perhaps that is why I can no longer fight for what I believe in, he thought. *How can I preach to others when my own convictions are uncertain?*

Raj went to his desk, unlocked the middle drawer and took out a brown envelope. He pulled out a black and white photo from the envelope, faded and frayed at the edges. There was a young woman in the picture standing by a window, her dark, straight hair cascading down to her waist. She was wearing an oversize white kurta that concealed her knees but exposed her slim legs and bare feet. Raj closed his eyes remembering how vulnerable and beautiful she had looked. He had taken the photograph just before they parted, not knowing just how final that goodbye would be. At the time, Raj had hoped to see her again. He had hoped to convince her to see him again.

Raj ran his fingers gently over the photograph wondering, for the millionth time, where she had disappeared. If he did not have the picture, she could have easily become a figment of his imagination, a dream to be chased, a wave touching briefly upon the sand. But Raj did not have that luxury. He had the picture and the memories it evoked. Memories that were at once joyful and painful, right and wrong.

The sound of approaching footsteps made Raj start and he hastily shoved the photograph into its envelope and put it back in the drawer.

"Dhani?" he heard Guru's voice.

"I am here," Raj called, realizing he had not turned on the lights.

"In the dark?" Guru said walking in and turning on the lights. "What are you doing in the dark, dhani?" Then without pausing for an answer, "Daya awwa wants to know if you will be home for dinner."

"Basu packed me enough food that I don't need to eat for a while," Raj replied, leaning his head back and rubbing the back of his neck.

"Are you all right, dhani?"

"Yes, yes, just very tired. I haven't seen you in a while. Any new ideas? Daya tells me you are full of ideas."

"Oh, I have lots of ideas but no time or money to implement them," Guru said carelessly. "I cannot reveal them because they might be stolen."

"Really? That good, eh?" Raj said.

"Yes, that good."

Raj sighed.

"Guru, son, why don't you start attending school? Education is very important."

"What for, dhani? You don't need an education to get rich. Look at all the politicians. How many have even finished high school?'

Damn right you are, you monkey, Raj thought.

"Education is true wealth," Raj persisted. "Don't you want to pass knowledge on to your children and grandchildren?"

"No offense, dhani, but education is a luxury only for those sure of three meals a day. I have gone without food for days so my younger brothers and sisters could eat. My only goal is to become rich, have feasts every day. My children will be fat and spoilt and I will not drink and beat them."

The blood vessels around Raj's heart constricted.

"Did you father beat you?" he asked gently.

Guru hesitated a moment, then squared his shoulders and replied.

"Yes, he beat all of us. My mother, my stepmother, and all the children. But I got the most beatings because I fought back. One time, he was beating my older sister and I grabbed his hand and spat in his face. That drove him crazy."

"What did he do?" Raj asked, reluctant to pry but wanting to know.

Guru hesitated again, then turned around and pulled up his shirt.

There were three scars running across a skinny, brown back. Perfectly parallel, straight lines.

What perfect marksmanship, Raj thought, the blood boiling in his veins.

"That was my father. He had promised my sixteen-year-old sister's hand in marriage to a rich, old man for ten thousand rupees. When she refused, my father beat her. That is when I intervened. He turned and looked at me with such hate in his eyes, took off his belt and struck me with so much fury that I collapsed. The pain was excruciating, and I went numb after he struck me the third time. The wounds were deep, and I lost so much blood I remained unconscious in the hospital for three days. I was ten at the time."

"What happened to your sister?" Raj asked and then wished he had not, seeing a fleeting, pain-filled expression cross Guru's face.

"We don't know," Guru answered. "Three days after the beating, after she made sure I was recovering, she ran away. She was so kind and smart and beautiful. People said her eyes were like an apsara's. Any one would have married her but my father was selling her to a lecherous old man. My mother and stepmother still cry for her."

Raj, suddenly, felt weary. Years of mining and the dam had ruined the district. Farmers could barely harvest one crop because of the depleted soil and monsoon floods. Poverty led people to desperate measures, and in Guru's case, his family's condition was exacerbated by an alcoholic, abusive father.

"Did you try to find your sister?" Raj asked.

"My older brother and I looked for her for years, then we stopped."

"Why?"

Guru thought a moment, then answered. "Someone in the village told us that my sister was working as a prostitute in a city brothel and my brother decided to stop the search. If we did find her and it was true she was a prostitute, it would bring shame upon the family. No one would marry my other sisters."

Night's chill wrapped its ice-cold arms around Raj. Darkness deepened and jumped in glee at having chased all the light away.

A beautiful girl in a city brothel, Raj thought. *With apsara's eyes that looked into your very soul, teasing its secrets out.*

"When I have some money, I will start looking for her again," Guru was saying. "I don't care what my brother thinks. She and I were so close, and I need to find her."

"What was…is her name?" Raj wanted to know.

An irrelevant question, perhaps, that should have remained unasked.

"Priya," Guru answered. "My Priya akka."

Raj's world tilted; everything went black as he fell from his chair. The last thing he remembered was the terrified look on Guru's face.

WHEN RAJ BECAME conscious, he was lying on his office floor, a cushion beneath his head, something cool on his forehead. The village doctor was on his knees, holding his wrist, a worried look on his face.

"Ah, there he is," the doctor said, relieved, when Raj opened his eyes. "Nothing to worry about. Pulse is back to normal."

"I don't know what he has eaten today," Raj heard Daya saying. "He has not been eating well these past few weeks."

"Yes, that is true," Sharada, in the background, said. "He was not a good eater, even as a child, but it has become worse."

Raj drifted off again to a place between consciousness and unconsciousness. A happy, numb place. When lucidity returned fully, he was on a sofa in the vada's living room surrounded by familiar faces: Daya, the vada staff, Samar and Usha. And Guru.

Guru.

Guru was Priya's brother.

Priya was Guru's sister.

There are so many Priyas, Raj told himself. *Guru's Priya may be different from mine.*

His eyes sought Daya's kneeling by the sofa, gently rubbing his chest.

"The doctor thinks you are overworked and not taking care of yourself," Daya said. "But he wants to run some tests just in case."

Raj nodded, held Daya's hand, closed his eyes and silently apologized to her. How had all this happened? They, he and Daya, had been happy together since the first time they met.

RAJ HAD SEEN Daya's picture and she, his. They knew each other's birthdates, height, weight, skin color (fair, medium-fair, brown), birthmarks, all the information that goes into a passport or ration card. In addition, the bio-datas their families exchanged stated their education, family backgrounds, current salary (for him), future aspirations (for him), and hobbies (for her). Their horoscopes matched, their stars aligned perfectly, and both agreed to get married because there was not a good enough reason to refuse. The first time they saw each other was in a roomful of people, at their engagement ceremony.

Daya had been in the far corner of the vada's main hall surrounded by a group of giggling girls who ogled Raj and his friends with unabashed interest. The girls whispered in Daya's ear, burst into laughter, then turned once again to stare at the young men. This curious interaction went on all evening while the elders continued with the formalities of the engagement, throwing distracted, indulgent smiles at the young people. Daya never looked up even once the entire evening. All Raj saw was a broad forehead adorned with a mango-shaped bindi and downcast lashes. His friends stared back at Daya's friends insolently, nonchalant smirks on their faces while they checked out the girls, sizing them up, gauging each one's potential as a bride and bedmate.

To be truthful, Raj had no expectations or requirements for the girl he would marry, but realized the photograph of Daya did not do her justice. He saw a hint of a heart-shaped face and full lips. Her black hair with a straight center-part was pulled back into a braid. He saw slender arms weighed down with glass bangles—green to match her sari. When she stood up to accept the clothes and jewelry Raj's mother gave her to seal the engagement, he noticed she was slim, but curvy. Not stunning but very, very attractive. Raj allowed himself a smile.

Daya would have preferred to ogle Raj as her friends were doing, but if she did, they would tease her without mercy. His friends would laugh, outrageous remarks would be passed about the eagerness of the bride and bridegroom. How unfair, Daya thought, that she could not even look at the man she was marrying, and her friends could. She did sneak a look and saw a tall, straight man with light skin and dark brown hair. She had been told he was handsome, absolutely brilliant, friendly—but appropriately reserved as a landlord should be. He exuded confidence, but beneath it, Daya sensed a vulnerability she wanted to wrap her arms around. She blushed and looked down.

The wedding date was set, the number of guests decided, and the engagement party broke up without the bride and bridegroom-to-be exchanging a single word or coming within four feet of each other. As Daya walked to the hired bus for the ride home with her family, her best friend pulled her aside whispering that an elderly woman, probably Raj's aunt, wanted to see her. Old women had a reputation for examining brides closely, as if they were horses or dogs on display, and Daya felt a wave of anger. She had little choice and followed her friend to the back of a row of nerium trees. Strange that an older woman, probably with bad eyesight, wanted to see her in the dark, Daya thought, before noticing the two people waiting for her: an old woman and Raj. Daya panicked when the woman and her friend left her with Raj. Alone. She had heard stories of impatient bridegrooms orchestrating secret rendezvous before the wedding. Several thoughts rushed through Daya's mind. She had not had her haldi ceremony, her skin was not soft enough, she was sweaty, her hair a mess. And lastly, was it even right to touch her betrothed before the wedding?

Later, she would feel foolish for thinking those thoughts because Raj simply walked to her, stood three feet away and said, "Sorry for this but I have a question to ask if it is all right with you?"

"Yes?" she choked.

"Are you marrying me of your own free will or have you been forced into it?"

She looked at him, shocked. She wanted to tell him any girl

would marry the handsome son of the landlord. Instead, she shook her head no.

"That is fine, then. I wanted to make sure this was what you wanted."

That was the moment Daya felt the first pang of what she would later realize was love. Having never interacted with any men except the ones she was related to, she had no way of knowing Raj's worth. But she instinctively knew he was decent, sensitive, with not a shred of arrogance. He did not consider himself a catch even though he was probably the most eligible bachelor in the district. He did not take his bride-to-be's assent for granted. If there had been doubts in Daya's mind, they simply melted away. He suddenly smiled at her. She smiled back at him and in that moment, Raj saw just how lovely Daya was.

"Are you done with your questioning?" the old woman said, reappearing. "Daya, go now and don't worry too much about your future husband's strangeness."

"Meet my nanny, Sharada," Raj said. "You will be seeing her a lot. She appears at your elbow out of nowhere."

After the engagement, Raj had gone to bed every night with Daya's photo under his pillow. In his mind she became the perfect woman and her imperfections, when he did see them, only made her more desirable.

Raj had gone into his room on their wedding night, to find Daya sitting at the edge of the bed strewn with red rose petals. She had changed from her heavy silk and gold wedding sari to a simple cotton Chanderi sari in cream. Her feet, decorated with dainty henna patterns, peeped from beneath her sari, the silver anklets tinkling every time she moved, which was often.

She sensed Raj's uncertainty and looked up, saw him standing at the door, asking for permission to be let into their marital bed. She must have given her assent because he came and sat by her, his hand reaching out to close over both of hers, resting in her lap.

"I will never hurt you, at least not knowingly, I promise you that. We don't know each other but I love and respect you already."

She turned to him; her doe-like eyes wide with surprise.

"You love me? Really?" the words were out, and she blushed.

"Yes, it is easy to love someone so dainty," he murmured, turning her face to his, lifted her chin and brushed his lips over hers.

"And you? How do you feel, Daya?"

"The same. I have thought of you every single moment since our meeting after the engagement. If you had not orchestrated that, I would have taken my time falling for you."

He chuckled.

"I believe we were destined to meet, and I was meant to love you, marriage or no marriage," Raj said, his fingers tracing the glass bangle marks on her wrist. "So, let me relieve you of all the trappings of marriage so you are free to love me."

He removed the gold and glass bangles on her wrists, piling them on the bedside table. Then, he reached behind her neck, releasing the clasp of the gold necklace, letting it fall. The skin on the back of her neck tingled, goose bumps rose where his fingers had been. She watched with her eyes, he listened with his. She gasped as he dropped to his knees by the bed and removed her silver anklets, her silver wedding toe rings. Her toes curled.

Daya felt as light as a piece of cotton escaped from a ripe, bursting pod and knew it was not just because of the jewelry Raj had removed. She felt his hands lifting her weightless body off the bed. He removed her sari, deliberately and slowly, reaching behind her in a loose embrace several times until the fabric fell to the floor and she stood in a cream cloud wearing just a petticoat and blouse, her midriff bare. He stepped back to look at her and she opened her eyes, swaying as desire shot through her and seeing the same in his eyes.

Then, his lips were on hers, his arms pulling her close, pressing the whole length of her against him, his tongue inside her mouth. How did the body know what to do when it had never done it before, Raj marveled? They undressed each other, their heads bumping, buttons tearing, giggling as they began their journey of discovering each other.

"Are you ready?" Raj asked as they lay naked on the bed, existing only where their bodies touched.

She nodded her head, closing her eyes at the sudden pain as he entered her.

Pleasure took the edge off the pain. It did not matter that he was inexperienced, and they had never touched before this night. They were meant to be, and her body shook with Raj's as he covered her mouth with his.

Raj and Daya. Daya and Raj. Raj's Daya. Daya's Raj.

RAJ'S PARENTS HAD passed away less than a year after he married and Daya and he had stepped into their shoes easily, taking over the family business and running of the vada. Their relationship was a simple one, as marital relationships should be. He loved her and she loved him, and they were a team. It had been like that, all-accepting from the start.

Then, Raj had broken all his promises to Daya. It was worse that she did not know, that she did not even suspect something was wrong.

CHAPTER FIVE

Ten Years Ago

"The meeting is over for today," the secretary to the Minister of Education announced in his pompous, government-official voice. "We will meet again tomorrow in this room at 8 a.m."

"What is the point of meeting again when the minister himself is not here?" a woman's voice challenged. "We have been here for days discussing the same things, but no final decisions can be made without the minister."

"Madam, this is not in my hands or yours but in god's," the secretary answered, peering at the woman from the top of his reading glasses. "These are difficult times for the minister, and we must support him."

"Support him when we don't even know the nature of this so-called 'crisis' for which he had to leave the city the night before the convention began?" the woman said, her starched sari stiffening. "How can we, mere principals, teachers, and members of education committees, make decisions about the future of our schools when the Minister of Education is absent?"

"Well said, madam, well said," another man said. Her starched sari stiffened further, and she patted her neat, sparse bun. "It was the minister's idea to have this meeting so we could decide on much-needed curriculum reform and he has disappeared. Where is he?"

Sniggers, suppressed coughs, and snorts in the room as sweat ran down the personal secretary's face. His smug smile disappeared, and he wilted in his chair. He shuffled the papers on his desk, gathering them.

"The minister is occupied with urgent family matters beyond his control," the secretary said after a few seconds, his government official voice back. "He will be back tomorrow, and I will cancel all his meetings and reschedule his appointments for the next few days so he can give this convention his undivided attention. Remember, he is a family man first, a minister second."

Sniggers and snorts again but the secretary was back in charge. He knew what he had to do but why, oh why, had the minister been brash enough to leave the country the night before the convention began? The arrangements had been made over months. Principals, teachers, and educators from all over the state had been handpicked to attend the meeting. Hotel rooms were booked, and train reservations made for more than two hundred attendees. It was the minister's idea to begin with—curriculum reform to take the schools into the 21st century. But, at the last minute, the day before the convention began, the minister had taken off to Mauritius with his mistress who was complaining that he was not paying her enough attention. If people found out, the minister and his staff would be forced to resign and the secretary had no intention of losing his job. He came up with a plan to silence the dissension of the meeting attendees, keep them happy. Anyone could be bought, he knew; it was only the price that varied.

LATER THAT EVENING, the secretary called the men he considered influential and invited them to dinner. He went home to bathe and yell at his lazy wife so he could leave the house in an apparent huff. Then dinner at Hotel Savera where food and whiskey would flow freely and a visit to Rati Mandir and the men would be happy as parrots.

There were only fifteen female attendees and they did not matter.

RAJ LAY DOWN on his hotel room bed and closed his weary eyes. The fan whirred, cars honked on the street outside and exhaust fumes drifted in through the open windows. He had been here less than three days and already missed the quiet of Nilgi. The pure air, the shouts of children, the green fields, the cobbled streets with their humble homes. Nilgi, haughty and untouchable on higher ground, an oasis among villages laid bare by mines, neglected by the government because the area would one day submerge in the dam. Raj wanted to return home and continue doing what he could as chair of his district's education committee, watch the worst students graduate high school and the best ones excel, prosper, and leave Nilgi for bigger dreams. He cherished letters from students informing him of their whereabouts, where they lived, what they did, their families. Many, who had moved to faraway places, invited him to visit and he always wrote back saying he would and never did. He did not need much more than Nilgi.

Raj had not wanted to attend this meeting, but the Minister of Education had written and invited him. The best educators in the state were invited, the letter said, to discuss serious curriculum reform. Raj wrote back, refusing politely, but the minister's secretary had called him and pleaded he come. "Your ideas and experiences will be invaluable," the secretary had said over the phone and Raj had come only to discover the minister was absent. Raj knew he could leave tomorrow, and his absence would go unnoticed, but he was too responsible and kept his word no matter how much it inconvenienced him.

THE SECRETARY LED a group of men through wrought-iron gates, to a three-storied house sprawled over manicured lawns. Creeping pink and orange bougainvillea defined the edges of impeccable, white-washed walls and a sign on the front door said, "Rati Mandir." What is this place? Raj wondered. And how had he been convinced to accompany a group of drunken men on this evening jaunt? At dinner, he had been shocked to see several men, who he thought were respectable, drink like fish, going through dozens of whiskey and rum bottles in less than two hours and misbehaving, making lewd remarks at the young waitress who was serving them. The only sober men were the secretary and himself. The secretary chose to stay sober because he was on a mission and Raj was sober because he did not drink.

The door swung open even before the secretary rang the bell and Raj realized where he was the instant he stepped in: a tastefully decorated, high-class brothel. The marble floor of the large front room, where he now stood with his drunken colleagues, was covered in Kashmiri rugs. Silk cushions and bolsters lined the room and oil lamps flickered on the walls. Elegantly dressed women darted through the room serving drinks and paan to men lounging against the cushions in different states of inebriation.

Raj had heard of this place. The temple of pleasure, where there were no whores or prostitutes but courtesans, dancing girls and long-term mistresses. You came only if you were invited or well-connected. No truck drivers, rickshaw wallahs or vendors could cross the front threshold. It was not a place where sex could be easily bought or sold; it was bestowed on you as a favor the first time. If the man survived the price and the pleasure, he could come back again and pick the girl he wanted. Some semblance of respectability had to be maintained because the girls who worked here were not vulgar street girls. They were trained in classical music, dance, love and literature.

The bile rose in Raj's throat and he turned to leave but the secretary's hand whipped out, grasping his elbow.

"Where are you going, sir? This is the best part."

"A brothel?" Raj shot back, angrily. "Is this your way of bribing us so we don't force you to reveal the minister's whereabouts?"

"This is not that kind of place," the secretary almost whined. "We are only going to watch a dance."

"You expect me to believe that? This is a group of decent men you are trying to corrupt."

"Really?" the secretary's eyebrows shot up. "I don't see any of your colleagues complaining."

What happened next was so quick that Raj did not have the time to react. A matronly woman in a red silk sari steered him gently and firmly onto the rug. She sat down next to him, plumped the cushions and offered him tea.

"You are about to see the best dancer in the city," she said in a soothing voice, her fingers touching his arm so fleetingly, he thought he had imagined it.

Speechless, indignant, and reluctant to make a scene, Raj stared down, not looking up even when the talk and laughter ceased and the soft strains of the sitar filled the room. But the notes were so gentle, so seductive, that he had to look up. His unwilling gaze fell on the veiled woman dancing into the room and, just like every man, he could not look away. The dancer was petite, dressed in a peacock blue lehenga and a bronze silk top, her bare midriff flat. She entered slowly, her hips swaying, as if she were walking on air.

When she was in the center of the room, the tempo picked up with the beat of the tabla and the notes of the harmonium. Her steps quickened, bare feet darting in and out from beneath the full-length skirt. She twirled and swayed so gracefully, so effortlessly, it seemed she was born to dance.

In the moment she threw back her veil, and her gaze locked with Raj, he knew the inevitability of what was going to happen. Maybe not that night or the next night but some night soon. It was written in stone and Raj closed his eyes, drew in a sharp, staggering breath and leaned into the cushions. He tried to conjure Daya's face and failed. He opened his eyes and found himself looking directly into her kohl-lined ones.

Everything stopped.

He saw the world in her eyes.

He stared at her oval face, the delicate features, the high cheekbones, the flawless skin. The smooth, untainted skin of an upper-class woman who has rarely stepped in the sun. But the skin of this woman was tainted. It had been touched, perhaps too many times, by men she may have cringed from. Callused fingers, smooth fingers, slick fingers on her skin. Groping boys' hands, frustrated men's hands on her body. They had all known her and Raj's blood pounded in his ears. He closed his eyes at his foolishness.

What did it matter? She was just a prostitute.

She was a beautiful woman whose eyes looked into his very soul; in whose eyes he could see the world.

Raj had never looked so boldly at any woman before, and certainly not in a roomful of strangers. Now, the dignified, respectable, happily married landlord with two children could not tear his gaze from the slenderness of a dancing girl's legs outlined beneath a chiffon skirt, the small breasts hidden beneath her bronze, silk blouse. Tiny diamonds glinted in her ears, the only jewelry she wore besides the anklets on her feet. She was looking at him, promise in her parted lips. With her eyes, she beseeched him to choose her tonight.

He refused her with his eyes. He stood up and left, to punish a woman he did not know, not knowing that he was punishing himself most as he stayed awake all of that night, imagining her in bed with one of his drunken colleagues. He hated himself for leaving, the other men for staying, her for existing.

This was madness, nothing good would come of it, he knew. Yet, he threw all caution to the wind and decided to see her again.

RAJ WAS UP before dawn, bathed and dressed in a fresh, white Raymond shirt and navy slacks. He combed back his hair and, with shaking hands, dabbed cologne behind his ears and on the inside of his wrists. He slipped his feet into black leather shoes and as the sun rose walked out of the hotel into the deserted street. The street looked different without traffic and crowds of people, the shop shutters still down. He did not know the way to Rati Mandir, but he knew it was behind Hotel Savera. He realized he did not know the way to Hotel Savera and wondered who to ask at this hour, then noticed the street sweeper.

"Namaste," he said walking up to the man. "Do you know where Hotel Savera is?"

The man stopped sweeping and looked at Raj.

"You want breakfast, Sir? Hotel Savera is not open for breakfast."

"No, no, I am looking for a place near the hotel. Can you give me directions?"

The man hesitated for a moment and Raj thought the sweeper was going to ask the name of the place he was looking for. There was no way Raj was going to reveal his destination.

"Go straight to the next corner, then turn left," the sweeper answered much to Raj's relief. "Keep going on that street until you reach Alka Talkies. Hotel Savera is right across."

Raj found the hotel, but Rati Mandir was not where he had thought it was. He looked frantically for a big, white house; its walls smothered with flowering bougainvillea. Had it all been a dream? Was she just an illusion? He hoped it was and, yet, felt relief when he spotted Rati Mandir behind a row of low houses. He ran down the street like a madman, through open gates, to the front door. Only after he had rung the bell did he stop to think. He did not know what he was doing. He had no plan, no idea what he wanted except that he must see her again.

The woman who opened the door was the same one who had coaxed him to sit the previous night. Wrapped in a simple, cotton sari, she looked different, like an aunt or a friendly neighbor, not someone who worked in a brothel persuading reluctant clients to stay.

"What can I do for you?" she asked, her eyes half-closed with sleep and Raj realized how early it was, barely six o'clock.

He hesitated, then said, "I would like to see the girl who danced yesterday. Last night."

Recognition dawned in the woman's eyes and her lips lifted in a sly smile.

"We are not open, sir," she said, rolling the "sir" off her tongue sarcastically. "You are welcome to come back tonight. The girls are resting now."

Irrational pain twisted in Raj. His mind raced. She was resting. Resting after a night of being with some strange man.

"I need to see her now, please."

"I told you we are not open," the woman said, sharply. "Weren't you the one who was about to leave last night? We were not good enough for you, eh?"

She started closing the door, but he stuck his foot so she could not close it.

"Please, madam. I just want to talk to her. Perhaps…. read her some poetry."

"Read to her?" the woman asked incredulously. "No man comes here to read poetry."

The mirth in her eyes died quickly when she saw the look in his. Serious. Sincere. Decent. They did not get much of decent at Rati Mandir. And, who knew, maybe this one got his kicks from reading to young women. To give him credit he seemed solid, clean, wholesome, very sophisticated.

"Alright, come back in an hour," she relented, then stressed. "You can read to Priya in the living room."

"Is that her name? Priya?"

"Yes, Priya. Meaning love. She is the most talented and beautiful one we have and quite unlike the others."

"What do you mean?" Raj asked.

"Well, you will see," the woman smiled. "She might actually enjoy being read to. See you in an hour, but you can't stay for more than thirty minutes."

It was only when Raj walked out the front gates that the flagrancy of what he had done dawned upon him. He sat down on a street bench, clutched his head between his shaking hands and whispered, "Shiva, hey Shiva," evoking the god of destruction. The next minute he was up again, walking back to the hotel. He needed to lie down and think.

RAJ WAS BACK outside the gates of Rati Mandir ten minutes before the hour was up with a plan, rehearsed lines, clutching a book of Mirza Ghalib's poems in his sweaty hands. He did not know if she liked to read or if she had even heard of Mirza Ghalib—one of the greatest Mughal poets of the 19th century—but words were all Raj had and, even those were someone else's. He could not understand this all-consuming need to be with a woman he had seen for less than twenty minutes in a crowded room. He understood even less why he was not fighting these feelings that unnerved and excited him at the same time.

He knocked on the door exactly an hour after he had left, and the same woman opened it. This time, she seemed slightly more amenable, affable even, and her expression softened when she saw the book in his hands.

"Come in, sir," she said, waving him in. "I am Sarla. And you are?"

"Raj. Raj Nayak," he said. "I am Chair of the Shantur District Education Committee and live in Nilgi. Do you know where Nilgi is?"

He wondered if he should have divulged so much information about himself and if brothel-goers hid their identities. But it was too late.

Sarla smiled again.

"No, sir, I don't know where Nilgi is."

"Call me Raj," he said, speculating hopelessly if he should encourage this degree of informality in such a depraved place.

"Call me Sarla. And remember we don't do this sort of thing. I am doing you a favor because you seem like a good, decent sort. Priya doesn't get much of that and I noticed how she was looking at you last night. She deserves some happiness. Just don't touch her. You have to pay for that privilege."

Raj's head told him to leave, his heart told him to stay and so he stayed hastening his own downfall.

Sarla led Raj to a smaller room off the main front room where Priya had danced last night. The room had four sofas with different patterns arranged around a square teak coffee table.

"Wait here," Sarla said. "I will bring Priya. Would you like some tea or cold drink?"

Raj shook his head. The absurdity of the situation, a respectable landlord being offered a drink in broad daylight in a brothel, was not lost upon him and he smiled ironically at himself. He sat down at the end of the bright orange sofa with a brown camel pattern, his back straight, his hands resting on his knees, Mirza Ghalib by his side.

The clock on the wall ticked, a tap ran somewhere upstairs, and a pressure cooker whistled in the kitchen. Like a normal household, Raj thought. Except this household had a young woman who could drive a happily married, self-contained man to distraction with a single look. He waited for the world to end. Or maybe it was about to begin.

He sensed her before he heard or saw her and stood up hastily, and the Mirza Ghalib slid to the floor. He stooped down to pick the book up and when he straightened, she was standing before him, her hands clasped in a formal namaste. He returned the greeting and they both sat down at opposite ends of the sofa. She looked down at her hands clasped in her lap. He clutched Mirza Ghalib to his chest.

Today, she wore a simple, cream, cotton salwar-kameez so all he could see was her face, her thin wrists and her bare feet. Her hair hung in a thick braid down her back. She wore no earrings, no anklets, and no makeup. He had hoped she was not as beautiful as he remembered and realized, with a sinking feeling, that she was even more breathtaking. She looked down and he looked at her because there was nothing else worth looking at. He gazed at her impossibly long lashes, the straight nose, the pointed chin, an escaped tendril of her hair. He wanted them all.

"Can we read together?" he asked, finding his voice.

She looked up startled and confused.

"Are you my tutor? Sarla aunty said she was arranging for a

tutor to teach me things so I can have intelligent conversations and get a better price."

The words were out, and her hands flew to her face, mortified.

Raj looked away. What was he to say?

"No, I am not a tutor," he said turning to look at her again. "I am one of the men who watched you dance last night."

"I recognize you," she said. *But you left yesterday when I was begging you to stay*, was what she did not say.

"Yes, I left, but I am back now. Priya."

She looked straight at him with those eyes he could drown in.

He saw the whole world in her eyes.

He saw his doom in her eyes.

"Do you know Mirza Ghalib?"

She shook her head.

"He was a great poet. I want to read one of his poems to you. It is called, 'Heart it Is, Not a Brick or Stone.'"

He cleared his throat. A car honked outside, and a group of sparrows twittered on the windowsill.

"Heart it is, not a brick or stone
Why shouldn't I feel the pain?
Or I shall cry and cry again."

He glanced up, she stared down. He turned a page. She shifted, rearranging her tunic. He continued.

"The amorous gaze is the deadly dagger
And the arrows of emotion are fatal
Your image may be equally powerful
Why should it appear before you?"

He looked at her again, carefully. She still looked down at her dainty hands, but a frown marred her brow.

"Love is laden with noble thoughts
Yet what remains is the carnal shame
Trust conscience the still little voice

Why do you want to test the rival?
There the pride of modesty resides
Here dwells the social morality
How shall we meet, on which road?"
She was staring at him now and he stopped.

"Why?" she whispered. "Why are you reading this to me?"

"Because you have bewitched me," he said, his heart suddenly light. "And I want all of you—your mind, your body, your heart. I am falling for you."

"I am not worthy of any love, any noble thoughts. I am a fallen woman with no future."

"Let me decide your worth," he said, gruffly. "You can't tell me you are indifferent to me, the way you were looking at me last night."

"Who are you?" she asked looking straight at him.

"I am Raj Nayak from Nilgi. You have probably never heard of Nilgi."

She looked at him, startled. She knew Nilgi and she knew of him. He was the man who might have helped her go to college, get her degree, get out of the drudgery of poverty. Back then, when she was a schoolgirl, she would have given anything to have him in her life. What a cruel twist of fate that when Raj Nayak did come into her life, he came as a stealthy lover. But she, Priya, would welcome him whichever way he chose. She would love him as best as she could because he was the face of her hopes and dreams. Her eyes filled with tears and she looked away.

Raj looked at the tears glistening on Priya's eyelashes and in that moment knew there was no escape from loving this woman. He wanted to reach over and wipe the tears but did not dare.

The clock continued ticking, the tap stopped running and Sarla walked in.

"Your half an hour is up," she said. "Priya has things to do. Her dance teacher will be here soon."

She noticed the silence in the room for the first time. She looked from Priya to Raj and then back at Priya. She understood some of what was happening, and it frightened her.

"Priya, can you go now, please?"

She turned on Raj as soon as Priya left the room.

"Next time you want to see Priya, please visit when she starts work in the evenings," she said. "I have allowed you to see her this time when we are closed but it won't happen again."

Raj looked at Sarla, shrugged and said, "I will be back."

Hard to say if fate conspired against Raj or with him because Sarla relented the next day and allowed Priya to leave the house with him. Sarla had interfered once before between a smitten man and one of the girls and paid a price. The young man had been offering the girl marriage and a chance at life outside Rati Mandir. Sarla had believed it was impossible for a brothel girl, no matter how well-educated, to lead a normal life and kept the lovers apart. The young man committed suicide first, the girl the day after. Two young people dead because of Sarla, the girl her own daughter. For what it was worth, Sarla loved Priya. She had seen the way Raj looked at Priya, the way Priya looked at him and Sarla knew she could not keep them apart.

Love itself is deceptive as it makes us believe, if only fleetingly, in life's permanence. Yet, the deceitful things we do for love, to experience it fully even if it is for only one moment, are considered immoral and inexcusable.

Raj's first deceit was to check out of his hotel after informing the education minister's secretary that he had to return home for an urgent matter.

His second deceit was spending the rest of the days when he should have been at the convention with Priya. Other deceits would follow, but his first two were the hardest as he searched inside himself for every reason to not be deceitful and found none.

Raj had never felt as alive as he did the four days he spent with Priya. He rented a room in a beachside hotel overlooking the Arabian Ocean in a town an hour away. During the day he and Priya walked along the beach eating bhel-poori and pav-bhaji sold by vendors from gaudily decorated open carts. He watched in delight as she ate plate after plate of the street food, accepted his public displays of affection. Daya, no matter how much she loved him, would have been embarrassed and would have never eaten street food, worrying about its hygiene. They must have looked strange together, but the town was filled with people like them—musicians, artists and puerile lovers living for today, grabbing every moment—and no one gave them a second glance.

Sadness, love, and fear hung in the air the night before Raj was to leave. The ocean breeze blew in through the windows as they lay side by side in bed knowing tomorrow was only a sunrise away. He turned and touched her face with his fingertips, ran the tip of his thumb across her lower lip. She closed her eyes and kissed the tip of his thumb. He lifted her chin with his forefinger and kissed one closed eyelid, moving his lips down slowly to the corner of her parted lips. He repeated the same on the other eyelid, the other cheek, the other corner of her mouth. A feather-light trail of kisses across the flawless skin of a tainted woman. Then an honorable man's lips on hers. She opened her mouth, sighing, and he stopped thinking she was not ready. He drew back, looked into her eyes and saw the pleasure, understood a woman's sigh of submission, one he had not heard in a long time.

He saw a panicked look and hesitated. She saw it and drew him as close as she could, so their bodies were pressing against each other their entire lengths. He could not stop himself then. He pleaded with her to be his alone. He begged at her throat, whispered in her ear, tasted the tears running down her cheeks.

She shook her head, "no."

"I can't," she whispered.

He made love to her gently, then desperately, savoring every sigh. He claimed her as his own, tried to fill her with his smell, his taste, his need.

The moon moved across the sky, an owl hooted, and street dogs howled into the darkness. At some point dawn shattered the sky and Raj had to leave for Nilgi, back to where it all started.

"I can't let you go," he said. "Come with me, please."

"And do what? Live where?"

"I can buy a house for you somewhere close to Nilgi," he said, knowing how absurd the idea was even before he finished the sentence.

"No, Raj. How is that possible? There will be a scandal if people find out you have a mistress stashed away in a house. You will start to hate me."

"I could never hate you."

"What about your wife and children? Have you thought about them?"

"I haven't thought of anything," he said gruffly. "I stopped thinking the minute I saw you. I love you. I never thought I could love two women, but I can."

"And you don't feel any guilt about having a mistress?" she asked quietly. "I will be your downfall."

"Can I come back and see you?"

"Where? In the brothel? No, this is enough. I am grateful I had this time with you. Now, go. I want to stand by the window and say goodbye."

He knew he could not convince her and was, in a way, relieved she had refused. He also knew he would never forget her and vowed to see her again, somehow. He dressed quickly and left her standing by the window wearing his kurta. He had taken that photograph, now in the middle drawer of his office desk, as he left the hotel room.

Raj did not know he would never see Priya again.

Priya stood at the window for a long time after Raj had gone. It seemed as if years, not days, had passed since she danced into the room at Rati Mandir and seen him for the first time. He had been sitting cross-legged but it was obvious he was tall and slender. His fingers formed a steeple on his stomach as he stared down. She had not seen his face at first, just a head of combed back, thick brown hair. There was discomfort in his posture, and she knew he had never been to a place like this. When he lifted his head, she was struck by the tenderness of it. She danced closer to get a better look and threw back her veil moments before she was supposed to, confusing the musicians. Their eyes locked. The world remained suspended for a moment as her heart flew out and landed somewhere by the quiet stranger. The inevitability of what would happen was clear to her; she would break the rules and love a lover.

CHAPTER SIX

Dreams and secrets filled Priya's eyes, and some people had to look away from her penetrating, unwavering gaze. The first thing Priya's mother, the older, legal, wife of her father, noticed about her newborn infant were the almond-shaped eyes, so large they took up half her tiny face. When her mother held Priya for the first time, she stared at her with pupils so black, they shone like polished onyx. Priya's mother forgot all the travails of her long labor as she gazed at her reflection in her tiny daughter's pupils. She sighed with pleasure and with sadness. Pleasure, because she knew her daughter would grow up to be a great beauty, and sadness because that beauty would most definitely be sacrificed at the altar of the family's wretched poverty. In the end, Priya's mother got very little happiness from giving birth to a much-wanted girl after producing five boys.

Life in Priya's village was hard. A few years before her birth, National Mining had started looking for iron-ore in the nearby farmlands and hills. Farmers were forced to sell at throwaway prices and people slowly began leaving the village. The ones who stayed behind were people like Priya's family who were so poor they could not leave. The family's poverty was made worse by an alcoholic father who drank away most of his meagre earnings.

The dreams began when she was not yet three. She knew this because she remembered her first dream clearly, as the circumstances in which she had dreamt it had been unusual and, for once, happy. She remembered going to the cinema with Awwa, her birth mother, and San Awwa, the young woman her father married secretly in a temple and brought home a few years before Priya came along. Her abusive father, in a very rare moment of affection for his family, bought tickets to a Bollywood movie showing in a nearby town, Shantur, which was also the district's capital. His two wives were initially shocked at this sudden display of generosity. They looked at each other in silence and the younger wife grabbed the tickets from her husband before he changed his mind.

The tickets were for a showing two days later and everyone walked on eggshells during that time, careful not to annoy the irrational head of the house. You could never tell with Appa, Priya remembered Awwa telling her. His mood could easily swing from amiable to foul and he might take away the movie tickets. Priya remembered how San Awwa had gathered her in her arms and promised a sweet if she could be on her best behavior until they had seen the movie.

"You can behave as you like after that," she had said and Awwa laughed as both women knew that Priya was incapable of even benign mischief, let alone causing disruption.

So, they all went to the movies, Priya, her two mothers, five older brothers and three older stepsisters. Priya remembered all this, even as an adult, and it always brought a smile to her lips.

The day of the movie had been filled with excitement. Everyone was dressed in their best, as if they were going to a wedding rather than a movie in town. Faces were scrubbed, hair combed, fluffed, braided. They thanked the head of the house, bade him a solemn goodbye and walked to the bus stop.

Priya did not remember the details of that morning or the bus ride but she remembered bits of the movie clearly. She remembered, for example, that it had been a movie about a family of four: a mother, a father, and two children. The girl, a few years older than her brother, was a loving sister to her sometimes—bratty sibling. The mother was the perfect housewife, always immaculately dressed, busy taking care of her home and family. There was almost nothing she could not do; she was a fine cook and seamstress, and the walls of her house were covered with her paintings. What impressed Priya the most as she sat in the dark, dank movie theater, was the father. He was a serious man who went to work every day with a black briefcase. It was not clear what he did, but he earned enough to keep his family in comfort. What astounded Priya was how loving and caring he was with his children. He played with them, made them laugh and indulged their cranky moods. He never raised his voice at his children even when they misbehaved.

What was even more surprising was the town the family lived in. There were tree-lined roads, parks and ponds. There were birds and flowers and butterflies. It was not the desolate, ravaged landscape of Priya's village where everything was laid bare, and fields were abandoned.

Before watching the movie, Priya had had no idea that what she was seeing on the screen was a reality for many people. The movie became her first dream, where she was the girl in the family. In her darkest moments, when her father was especially abusive, she would close her eyes and dream.

By the time she was six, so many dreams had settled in Priya's eyes that she always had a faraway look even when she was supposed to be engaging with people. Most people dismissed her as being slow and only her mothers were aware of the depth of her intelligence and curiosity. They tried cajoling her back to the land of the living, failed repeatedly, and, sighing, left her alone.

San Awwa, whose hopes were pinned on Priya rather than her own dimwitted daughters, vowed to show the world just how intelligent her stepdaughter was. In a way, Priya became San Awwa's dream; she was determined to see Priya grow up into a strong and successful woman, someone who would lift the family out of drudgery. Of all the children, only Priya had what it took.

On the side, San Awwa took on tailoring jobs to supplement the income her husband brought home working as a gardener in the house of the village leader who, taking pity on the family, kept him on despite the fact that he was too drunk most of the time to even show up for work. San Awwa had taken tailoring classes when she was younger and invested in a secondhand sewing machine with which she made everything from little girls' dresses to men's pants. She charged less than the other tailors and delivered on time, so the villagers sought her even though the fit and finish of her garments was never perfect. Her only challenge was keeping it a secret from her husband, which was easy to do as he was never home and when he was, he was too drunk to notice. Awwa did most of the housework so San Awwa could work undistracted.

When Priya was six and ready to start school, San Awwa bought her all the textbooks and school supplies with the money she had saved from tailoring. Because she was young and attractive, she held more sway with her husband than the older wife and used all her charms to convince her husband to let Priya go to school. At first, the husband resisted. What was the need? Most of his children had dropped out of school and the ones who had not, showed very little interest in learning. So why should Priya be sent to school, particularly because she seemed to be the dullest of his offspring?

San Awwa bit her tongue and argued that Priya was actually very bright, and they should give her the chance. If she did not do well on her first-grade examinations, they could remove her from school right away. What was the harm, she argued, when school was free and Priya was quite useless at house chores anyway?

The sixth year of Priya's life was one of her happiest. San Awwa gave birth to a baby boy that summer and Priya started school that monsoon. They named the baby Guru, and Priya was smitten. When she was studying, she put Guru next to her on a floor mattress. If her homework was especially hard, she would turn and gaze at her brother cooing and playing on the mattress and her anxieties melted away.

Priya thrived in school. Unlike most of her classmates she had been taught nothing at home, but still had caught up within months. She mastered all the alphabet and numbers and began reading simple story books. The faraway look left her eyes, but only when she was in school or doing homework. At the end of the year, she was first in class and there was no holding her back.

When Priya started third grade San Awwa taught her to tailor simple garments on the sewing machine. She told Priya she needed to start earning her own money so she could pay for college when the time came. Her own eyesight was weakening, and she would not be able to tailor for long.

"You are filling the child's head with impossible dreams," Awwa complained. "College is not for people like us. She needs to learn how to do housework."

"What's one more dream?" the younger woman challenged. "Priya is full of dreams and one more cannot hurt. Besides, she is terrible at housework."

So Priya continued dreaming. She did not dream hoping they

would turn into reality. She dreamed, instead, to get away from the reality of her life and college, too, seemed like a dream that would remain a dream. She lived in constant fear that her father, in one of his drunken rages, would force her to stop going to school. Still, she indulged San Awwa, learned to sew and took on small jobs. She stashed away her small earnings in an earthen pot she buried in the backyard, by a lantana bush that had not flowered in years.

School was Priya's refuge. Her father, who was once just an alcoholic and emotionally abusive, became violent. He administered beatings with such viciousness for the smallest of transgressions—his tea was too hot, the food lacking in salt, his shoes were unpolished. Initially, he just slapped his wives and older children around. Then, he began using whatever he could find—canes, belts, whips. Priya returned from school every day dreading the evenings when her father began his nightly ritual of abuse.

For some reason, he spared Priya. She never looked him in the eye and never raised her voice no matter what invectives he threw her way. She had an uncanny ability of knowing what he wanted at all times and was ready with it before he even asked. Perhaps, he mistook her fear for deference and left her alone. At night, Priya stuffed cotton in her ears so she would not hear the cries of her father's victim. She longed for the nights when he was so drunk, he just came home and passed out.

Priya began noticing how men looked at her when she was not yet eleven. Until then, she had no awareness of her beauty, at once smoldering and innocent. She did not know how mesmerizing her eyes were or how enticing her pointed chin was. She did not know that when she walked, there was a natural sway to her thin hips that drove men mad. She became uncomfortable at the glances of boys and men and, instinctively, began making efforts so as to not draw attention to herself. She walked in the shadows sneaking from home to school and school to home like a thief in the night. But there was a baffling fragrance to her beauty that heralded her approach, and she was unsuccessful in deterring attention. So, she did what she did best. She began pretending in earnest that she was someone else living somewhere else, in a safe place where no one could see her. The shutters came down further over her eyes, keeping the world out, but that only made her even more desirable.

By the time Priya was in tenth grade there was little doubt she would go to college. She was a stellar student and her teachers offered to help her get a scholarship. When the subject was broached at home, her father threatened to break her neck if she dared to think about going to another town alone to attend college.

"Are you a whore?" he asked. "No daughter of mine will bring shame on this family by going off alone. You will marry and go where your husband goes."

Priya wept that night and Guru tried consoling her. Perhaps their father would come around after he had a chance to think about it, he suggested. Or, better still, could she ask her headmaster to talk to their father and convince him?

Deep down, Priya knew there was no convincing her father. She told her teachers, anyway, and they were disappointed but not enough to try and change her father's mind. When she approached the headmaster, a good-hearted and timid man, he simply shook his head and told Priya he did not think he could convince her father.

"Your luck might have been different, my child, if you lived in Nilgi," he said patting Priya on her head. "The landlord there, Raj Nayak, manages to get most of the students in the village to go to college despite the protests from parents who want their sons to work and their daughters to marry rather than continue their education after tenth grade. Raj has enough clout that your father would not refuse him."

Priya had never wished for anything as much as she did to have lived in Nilgi where every student, it seemed, had the choice of going on to college. But, she accepted defeat reconciling herself to the same drudgery as her mothers.

"You will still be better off than your mother or me," San Awwa assured Priya, concealing her anger at being forced to let a misogynist man decide their fates. "You have finished school and one day you might marry a man who will let you go to college. Young, married women in the city do this all the time. They are allowed to have their dreams and not expected to stay home and become housewives if they don't want to. We will just have to find you a bridegroom from the city."

That hope, too, shattered two weeks after Priya finished tenth grade. Her father came home one evening and announced he had found the perfect match for Priya in their village. The man was wealthy, influential and the alliance would help the family.

"Who is the man?" San Awwa asked, as the village had no wealthy men of marriageable age.

Priya's father hesitated just for a fraction of a second before revealing the bridegroom's name. The family gathered in the front room went silent. They thought they had heard wrong.

"She will be very happy," he said, raising his chin in defiance.

That is when Awwa began screaming.

"You are marrying your beautiful, kind daughter to that lecherous old man just because he is the village leader?" she asked. "He already has a wife. What is he going to do with her?"

"He is a Muslim, and he can legally have four wives. He can have any woman he likes, and we are lucky his gaze has fallen on Priya."

"Of course he wants to marry her," Awwa cried, rubbing the tears on her cheeks. "The only respectable way he can have her is through marriage. What has he promised you? Money for alcohol?"

"Watch your mouth!" Priya's father shouted. "Or I will beat you until you beg for mercy."

"Beat me, then," Awwa said, sticking her chest out. "I would rather die than see my child sacrificed for your greed and the roaming eyes of your lewd boss. He will throw her out once he is done with her and she will never be able to show her face in the village again."

Priya never knew where the screams came from. Perhaps, they had always been in her, latent and desperate to be heard. So, she screamed and screamed into the shocked silence.

"I will not marry this man," she said, hysterical. "You haven't given any of us anything, Appa. At least have the heart to not take away the small pleasures we have found for ourselves. If you force me to marry this man, I will kill myself and you will go to hell for it. In fact, you will go to hell anyway for everything you have done."

Priya did not have a clear recollection of what happened after. She remembered seeing murder in her father's eyes as he lunged towards her and struck her across the face, then grabbed her by the braid and began hitting her wherever he could. In the background, she could hear her mother's screaming, her siblings crying.

Except, Guru. He had not screamed or cried but dove at his father, catching his arm in a vice-like grip.

"Don't you dare touch her," he shouted and spat in his father's face.

But Guru was a scrawny little boy of ten and his father a grown man with the strength of his fury. He had removed his belt and whipped Guru until the boy collapsed unconscious on the floor in a pool of blood. Finally, his anger spent, Appa had walked out of the house and the older brothers had carried Guru to the hospital.

Guru remained unconscious for three days and when he finally opened his eyes, he found his entire family, except his father, by his bedside. Priya grabbed his hand and kissed his fingers, weeping into them.

"I will make sure you will never marry him," he had mouthed, and she had shaken her head. He did not know what that meant until the next day when his mothers told him Priya had run away. What struck Guru was their calm—neither seemed sad nor upset.

"Perhaps, it is for the best," San Awwa said. "She was saving money for college and I hope she has taken it with her. She is a smart girl and might succeed on her own and return to us, rich and successful."

It did not, however, stop the family from looking for Priya. They searched for years, fearing the worst, hoping for the best. Their search ended when they heard rumors that she was working in the city brothel. The family even began hoping she would not return because, true or not, the rumors had tarnished her reputation forever. Only Guru never gave up—merely postponed—the idea of looking for Priya.

PRIYA'S SIBLINGS WERE asleep, her mothers were at the hospital, sleeping on the floor of the common ward beside Guru's bed where he moaned with pain despite the medicines pumped into him. In the stealth of darkness, Priya emptied the books out of her school bag. She put them in a neat pile on the floor, her fingers caressing them gently before she snatched her hand away as if burned. She filled the bag with other things, her entire life, in fact. Her clothes, a small soap bar, her toothbrush, her shattered dreams. She crept out into the backyard and walked to the place where her earthen pot was buried. She dug it out, emptied the money, exactly three thousand, four hundred and thirteen rupees, which she wrapped in a newspaper and carefully placed in the bag.

Then, she walked off into the night towards the bus stop where she spent the few remaining hours until dawn when the first bus rattled to a stop. She got in, the third passenger, and rode to Shantur. She had been to the Shantur bus stop only twice and it was smaller than she remembered. She asked the man at the dingy office for a ticket to the state capital, counted out the exact change and bought a ticket to what she hoped was a better life.

It was only when she got on the bus heading to the city that she began doubting her plans. When the bus entered the city eight hours later, terror overtook her usually calm mind. The place was bigger, busier, more intimidating than she had imagined. It was getting dark, and she began looking frantically for a lodge to spend the night in. The street outside the bus stop was lined with vendors selling food, shops and crowds of people walked along the asphalt pavement. She stopped a middle-aged woman walking by and asked where she could find a cheap lodge. The woman looked at her and pointed to a side street. "There are a few there," she said and walked on.

That night Priya stayed at Mayur Lodge for two hundred rupees after a dinner of vada-pav that cost her twenty rupees. It was the cheapest lodge on the street but still more expensive than she had expected. As her tired eyes closed on the sagging mattress of the first bed she had slept on, Priya decided to start looking for work first thing the next morning. Ideally, she wanted to work with a tailor, but was willing to do any job. Hope filled her heart and she smiled as she drifted off to sleep.

For the next three days, Priya scoured the streets for work, going farther and farther from the bus stop as she got her bearings and became confident she would find her way back to the lodge. Initially, she looked only at tailors' shops but when no one wanted her, she looked in other places—the grocers, the clothes' stores, small offices. She even offered to clean the filthy common bathrooms at Mayur Lodge in exchange of free room and board.

The lodge's manager, a kind-looking man, simply looked at her slight frame and shook his head.

At the end of the fourth day, she ventured even farther, ending up in one of the shabbiest areas she had seen. The buildings lining the filthy street seemed like they would collapse any minute. Peeling paint, broken windows, and dim lights within gave them an air of hopelessness, as if people came here when their lives hit rock-bottom. It was getting dark but the street was quiet and lacked the usual end-of-the-day, returning-home bustle. Priya shivered in the hot, humid air thick with the smells of deteriorating garbage and stench of open sewers. She continued walking down the street despairing at the idea of spending another night at Mayur Lodge for two hundred rupees. The doors of all the silent, still buildings were open but there was not a person in sight. What was this strange place? Priya wondered. Was it a ghost town? She stopped outside the most well-kept building, looking at the pile of bricks serving as the front steps, and wondered if she should go inside. Maybe she could find some work here.

A woman walked out as Priya hesitated. She was buxom, dressed in a bright pink sari and had so much makeup on, it was hard to make out what she really looked like.

"What do you want?" she asked in a voice that made Priya think she was choking.

"Nothing, nothing," Priya said, trying to ignore her rising fear. "I am looking for work and wandered onto this street. I better go now. I don't want to bother you."

The woman's eyes narrowed and disappeared beneath heavy-set eyebrows. Priya wondered, irrelevantly, if she was a woman or a man dressed as a woman. She had seen them—hijras or eunuchs— and was terrified because her mothers had told her they were cruel and brought bad luck.

"How old are you? Where do you live?" she asked. "Do you

have a home?"

Looking back, Priya wondered if things would have been different if she had lied and said she lived with her parents. But she did not and shook her head.

"Sixteen. I am good at sewing but willing to do anything for a roof over my head."

"Anything, huh" the woman said, almost to herself. "Come here into the light and let me look at you."

Priya's instincts told her to run but she did not want to annoy the woman and stepped into the light of the lamp over the front door.

The woman scrutinized Priya from head to toe. If the fear had not been rising in Priya, she would have noticed the appreciation and stealth creeping into the woman's eyes.

"There is work for you here," the woman said, suddenly gentle. "Why don't you come and look around?"

Something warned Priya not to trust the woman, but her desperation to find work made her walk into the house, right into a trap and towards her own downfall. As soon as they were inside, the woman closed the front door, locked it and yelled, "Come down you lazy fool! I have found something for us."

A sullen man in a white muslin dhoti came down the stairs and on seeing Priya, smiled an oily smile.

"Pretty little thing," he said. "And a virgin, I am sure."

That was when Priya realized where she was, in a brothel. Terrified, she ran towards the front door, but four hands snatched her and carried her upstairs. She screamed and screamed, and a door opened in the hallway.

"They have got you, I see," said a young woman dressed as if she were going to a wedding. "You have been a fool, but don't think about escaping. If you succeed, they will come find you wherever you are and make you wish you had never run away."

"Get back into your room," the man scolded. "You are forgetting your place."

The woman shrugged and went back into her room. Priya was thrown into a dark room lit by a small, dusty lamp and the door was locked. When her eyes adjusted to the dark, she realized the windows were boarded so no light came in. There was an earthen pot of water and a squatting toilet in the corner. Her bag and money were gone, and she began crying. After a while, she lay down exhausted on the stone floor and curled into a ball.

Priya had no idea how much time, how many days, she was in the room. Every day, a plate of food was pushed through the gap beneath her door. She ate nothing, determined to starve herself to death but she did not succeed. When the door finally opened, she was too weak to even protest. The man lifted her with his hands under her armpits and dragged her out. She was taken to a bigger, more airy room lit by harsh, blue tube lights.

"Do as you are told, and you will have a good life here," the man said.

"Wash yourself in the bathroom and come down to the kitchen to eat," the woman said. "If I were you, I would be grateful for a roof over my head and food to eat."

And, once again, Priya became resigned to her fate. She became a brothel woman and when she was not working, she re-dreamed her dreams because that is all she had left. At first, she wished she had never left home; marrying an old man was surely better than this but, with time, even that thought vanished, and she simply focused on her work, becoming one of the highest earners in the place.

Seeing her potential and intelligence, the brothel owners brought in a social worker, a man who knew there was little hope for the girls working in such places but was still willing to try and make their lives better. He went around teaching the girls from the books he read, hoping to widen their worldview, perhaps give them some hope. Most girls were disinterested in learning but Priya was drawn to the man like a thirsty desert traveler is to an oasis. She looked forward to her daily lessons with the man whose name she never knew. She was drawn to his unassuming manner, his slender frame, his fine and gentle features. Seeing her keenness to learn, the man took Priya to Rati Mandir. Priya never discovered how he had managed this with the brothel owners, but she was grateful to be in Rati Mandir. She still had to sell her body, but now she could pick and choose. She was trained in the arts, in manners and etiquette, in all the skills that elevated her from a prostitute to a courtesan.

That is how Priya became what she was—a corpse at night that has little say, a ghost during the day that floats from place to place without a thought or sound. In brief moments, she became the girl she once was with dream-filled eyes, but she discarded that image as one might a broken chair that cannot be mended.

And then, one day her eyes had fallen on Raj Nayak. He reminded her of the social worker who had helped her, and she was instantly drawn to him. Her heart sank when he walked away as she danced but he returned the next day to read her poetry, which puzzled her even though she loved hearing the way he pronounced his words in a sophisticated, upper-class manner. When he told her who he was, she knew she wanted to be with him, loved by him in whichever way he chose. He was the man in Nilgi who would have made sure she went to college. Seeing how attracted he was to her, fueled her own desire, something she had never felt before. She knew, instinctively, that she was safe with him and allowed herself to fall in love, head over heels. She knew their time together was short so she savored, cherished, preserved every moment knowing it would get her through life. She did not know, however, that he would leave her with a gift that would remind her of him, every day.

CHAPTER SEVEN

Daya was worried about Raj. He was back from a conference in the state's capital, tired and withdrawn, and nothing she did returned to her the husband she knew. Their love was no longer the all-consuming passion of their younger days. It had grown, matured and quietly sunk into their lives, to a place where, Daya believed, almost nothing and nobody could touch it. They had settled into a comfortable, sweet friendship that baffled everyone because arranged marriages were not built on friendship but a common purpose to keep populating the earth from the confines of a relationship approved and accepted by all. There were too many people in an arranged marriage which is why they almost never failed. Your spouse did not carry the burden of fulfilling all your emotional needs, so there were fewer opportunities for quarrels and arguments. It was also easier to fall in love after you got married; it was harder when you married to prove that your love was true.

But circumstance and their basic natures made Daya and Raj the best of friends. There was nothing they could not tell each other and, yet, there was a tacit agreement to give each other space and respect that the other might be unwilling to share some things. You were allowed your secrets and that, in fact, lent an element of mystery to a relationship that was mostly driven by practicality and responsibility.

"When you marry, make sure it is someone like Uncle Raj," Daya advised her brother's daughter who was seeing a boy the family did not approve of. Laughing, she added. "Don't marry someone like your father or you will spend the rest of your life being forced to watch the same three western movies again and again."

For the first time in her life, Daya was worried about Raj's reticence. He was uncharacteristically moody and was behaving in strange and bewildering ways and she wanted to know what was going on in his mind.

It was the beginning of winter, the season of pleasure after the rains ceased and before the summer sun began beating down relentlessly. Nature bestowed its best upon the village, making it paradise. The streams were full of water, guava and pomegranate orchards crammed with fruit, and groundnuts ready to be eaten. Children played truant from school, running through green fields, eating whatever they fancied. It was Raj's favorite season, but he seemed not to notice.

"I don't know what is eating at him," Daya confided to Sharada. "He's not engaged, not even with Jai and Rohan. Even when he is playing with them, holding them, his thoughts seem far away."

"He is dreading when Jai leaves for boarding school," Sharada said. "It is only a few months away and it is hard sending a seven-year-old off into the world without his parents. I keep telling you, it is not a good idea."

"No, that is not it. We decided to send Jai and Rohan to boarding school so they could get a stellar education. No one forced us to make that choice and we are comfortable with it. It is something else."

"He could be suffering from depression," Sharada concluded. "His father used to have bouts of it."

At night, when Daya reached for Raj, he kissed her softly, said he was tired and turned away. Initially, her pride was hurt but when they had not made love for more than two weeks, Daya became concerned.

"Won't you tell me what is bothering you?" she finally asked one night. "And please don't turn away and pretend you are sleeping because I know you are not. Is it something I have done?"

"No, Daya!" he exclaimed and engulfed her in his arms, squeezing her close. "It has nothing to do with you. Please don't ever think that."

"Then, what Raj? You have become so distant, you barely eat, and even the children are noticing."

"I just have a lot on my mind," he finally said.

"We want you back," Daya whispered and, finally, after weeks of rejecting her, Raj made love to her with a certain frenzy she did not understand but which she, surprisingly, liked.

SHORTLY AFTER, THE brief tension in Daya and Raj's marriage vanished as all attention turned to something else. Villages in the district were flooding during the monsoon despite the government's assurances that the recently raised-dam wall would not cause floods. The floods were the worst in the villages that had been ravaged by mines. People approached Raj for help and he started his battle with the government, trying to get it to compensate people for their losses. Priya, and his transgression, were cast aside, relegated to a place of less significance. Were not the sufferings of the people far more important? What were Raj's problems in comparison?

Raj's own guilt lessened as he realized that his affair had not diminished his love for Daya. He discovered that he could love two women in different ways, and with the same intensity. His love for Daya was happy, free, light while his feelings for Priya were tethered in sadness and resided in a dark corner of his mind. When he thought about Priya, his heart missed a beat but there followed a heaviness in his heart, a deep regret—not because of what he had done, but because she could never be a part of his life, at least not on a day-to-day basis. In the end, his hopeless love for Priya destroyed the peace of his love for Daya. Raj hid the battle in his mind well and Daya, with her big and trusting heart, never noticed it or if she did, dismissed it.

RAJ WENT BACK to the brothel a year-and-a-half later. By then, he knew he could not war with his memories any longer. He still loved Priya, he needed to see her. He had no idea where she could fit in his life; he just knew that he wanted her to be close. He knew what was at stake—he could lose Daya and his sons.

"She is not here," the woman, who answered the door of Rati Mandir, told him.

"Where is she?" Raj asked.

The woman, not Sarla, shrugged.

"I don't know. She left more than a year ago without a goodbye. She did not even return to attend Sarla's funeral. Sarla loved her like her own daughter."

"Sarla is dead?" Raj asked, his heart sinking to his feet.

"Yes. Poor thing, she suffered before she died."

Raj breathed in and out deeply to calm his nerves.

"Is there anyone who might know where Priya is? Her family has been looking for her for years and someone recently told them she was here. I often visit the city for work and offered to make inquiries. Priya's people are very poor and cannot afford a trip like this."

Understanding dawned in the woman's eyes and a sliver of empathy crept in.

"I really don't know where she went. She was pregnant, you see, and insisted on keeping the baby. Women with children aren't allowed to work here. Are you a relative?"

Raj shook his head, thanked the woman and left. He returned to his life where the memory of Priya became a soft sigh, a missed heartbeat, or a whiff of the jasmine attar she always wore.

And now, almost ten years after he had first met her, Priya had returned and Raj wanted to see her again. In fact, he was *desperate* to see her again.

CHAPTER EIGHT

It was three days since Raj's fainting episode and he was exasperated by how everyone was hovering around him, offering him food, insisting he rest, not walk, not even talk. He accepted Daya's attention and that of the household, but it did not stop there. Friends, like Samar and Usha, and villagers he had not even heard of, stopped by to wish him a speedy recovery. Old women with lemon-size buns put their knobbed hands on his head, blessing him. He appreciated—was even grateful for—the concern but his mind was occupied with a matter he could not discuss with anyone.

"I am going crazy," he declared on the morning of the fourth day. "I have to go to school. I have a lot to do."

"You will not listen to anyone!" Daya said and gave in. "You should come home for lunch."

Raj thought for a moment.

"Why don't you send me lunch with Guru?" he suggested,

hating himself for his ulterior motives. He had spent three days doing nothing except think of Guru; he wanted to resume the conversation he had been having when he passed out.

Daya sighed and agreed, and the driver took Raj to school where he tried focusing on his piled-up mail, waiting impatiently for Guru.

"Lunch," Guru said walking into the office at noontime, placing a tiffin carrier on Raj's desk. "I'll come back later to get the empty containers."

"Why don't you wait while I eat?" Raj said. "Make yourself a plate. I can't eat all of this."

"Oh no, dhani," Guru replied. "I don't like cauliflower curry. It reminds me of bones. Basu has made potatoes for the staff, but I will wait while you eat."

Guru sat on the floor cross-legged while Raj nibbled on the food.

"Are you all right now?" Guru asked. "You gave us quite a scare!"

"I am alright, son. The doctor did some blood tests, and everything is fine. I just need to pay more attention to my health, eat better and take breaks."

"Yes, dhani, you must," Guru said.

"And thank you for telling me about your father and your sister. You can tell me anything; your secrets are safe with me."

"That is good," Guru said, adding. "I did not understand a word the doctor said. He spoke only English."

"You would understand if you knew English. You should be in school."

"I am too old for school."

The idea slid into Raj as easily as a book into its cover.

"Guru, let's make a deal, shall we?"

"What kind of deal," Guru asked, his eyes lighting up, his head brimming with business ideas.

Raj carefully stacked the steel containers of the tiffin carrier.

"If you attend school, I will help you look for your sister."

Guru opened his mouth, but no words came out.

"I mean it," Raj insisted, keeping his voice from shaking. "I have connections and I can help."

"But why would you do that dhani?"

"So that you go to school," Raj said, marveling at how easily he could lie. "Education means a lot to me and I would love to see you learn to read and write. And we can find your sister. We both win."

"The other children will make fun of me if I sit in class with them," Guru protested. "I am older than all of them."

"I will make sure they don't," Raj promised.

"Thank you dhani," Guru said, bending to touch Raj's feet in gratitude.

Raj felt sick to his stomach. What he was doing was self-serving, motivated by a forbidden love for a fallen woman, but he could not stop himself.

Raj laid his hand on the coarse hair of Guru's bent head. For a moment he convinced himself he wanted to do this for the boy with the three belt marks on his back, even if he had not been Priya's brother. But he knew that was not true and closed his eyes, begging for forgiveness.

"First bring me a picture of her," he said, hoping Guru's Priya was not the woman he had loved. Still loved.

The picture Guru brought later that afternoon crushed Raj's last hope. The photograph was of poor quality, black and white, taken when Priya was still a schoolgirl. She stood among a group of girls, her classmates, dressed in a blue and white uniform, jasmine flowers in her hair and a young girl-smile on her face.

Raj had never known her age, but she must have been at least five years younger than when they met. Her apsara-eyes were the same, but they did not have the sad secrets he would later see. Her smile was open, her face relaxed. She had none of the qualities that had made her irresistibly, hauntingly beautiful to him.

"Will you really help me find her?" Guru asked again.

"Yes," Raj managed, his throat choked. "How old was she in this picture?"

"Sixteen. She ran away from home shortly after."

What happened to you Priya? Raj wondered. *How did you end up in a brothel? I wish I had asked you more questions when we met.*

"Can I keep the picture?" Raj asked. "So, I can ask around when I go to the city?"

After Guru left, Raj wondered at the horror of his life. To finally meet someone from Priya's family who had known her years before he did, but did not know what he, Raj, knew—that she had, indeed, ended up in a brothel. How could he ever tell Guru he had met Priya less than a decade ago and known her better, more intimately, than anyone in Guru's family?

Raj had given up all hope of ever finding her. He had forced himself to stop thinking about her. But things had changed so suddenly when he found out Guru was Priya's brother. At the very least, there was now someone who wanted to find Priya as much as he did. But how do you find someone who does not want to be found?

Three days later, Guru took his place among the third-grade students and Raj knew that his search for Priya had officially begun.

RAJ WAS IN his office at the vada, waiting for Samar. The government had officially declared its plans to raise the dam to its originally planned height but there were still no displacement and rehabilitation plans. Construction would begin at the end of the year, in less than eight months. Raj knew that Santosh was behind this; there was a lot of money to be made from a construction that would cost several hundred lakhs. No one would notice the few lakhs Santosh intended diverting to his personal account.

The next few months were crucial to stop or delay the dam's construction until the affected population was adequately compensated. It was important work that would save hundreds of thousands from destitution and poverty and Raj needed to stay more focused than ever.

Raj's mind, however, was elsewhere. It had been three weeks since Guru had brought him Priya's photograph. Unable to share it with anyone, he had been carrying his love and his guilt like a hunchback that grew every day.

He had promised Guru he would start looking for Priya but did not know where to start. Seeing Priya's picture had revived memories and he felt his world closing in on him. Suddenly, nothing made sense—the village, the houses, the river, the fields. Even people stopped making sense. Life was an illusion, Raj thought in his worst moments, and nothing really mattered anymore.

There was so much at stake. A carefully constructed life, his children, his wife. His reputation. He could not even imagine what would happen if the truth came out. He had started looking back at his life, thinking about all those times when things were uncomplicated and perfect.

Raj did not know what he would say if he did find Priya. He did not know what she would say to him. She may have moved on, forgotten him. She may be in love with the man she had a child with, if she did really have a child.

A light spring breeze, laden with the fragrance of marigold and the sounds of playing children, wafted in through the window. Raj knew they were building an effigy of Hollika, the demoness. The effigy would be burned in a few days, the night before Holi, the festival of colors. It signified the triumph of good over evil. Raj would have gone out to watch the children if he had not been so preoccupied.

He heard Samar talking to the children, telling them how to build their effigy. The children laughed, rejecting his advice and Samar walked into Raj's office a few minutes later.

"They don't know how to build it," he said to Raj. "The way they are doing it, it won't burn down completely."

"Let them do it their way," Raj said. "They will figure it out."

"Would be nice to make an effigy of Santosh and burn it," Samar said. "Actually, you can get away with it. I cannot because I am supposed to be a loyal government official."

"Let's save our energy for bigger battles. Still no information about displacement and rehabilitation?"

"None. And there will probably not be until a few weeks before construction begins."

"Why do you think that?"

"Because, right now, people have been appeased with a promise of a plan for displacement and there is nothing to protest. Certainly not the dam whose first stone was laid several decades ago. And definitely not a compensation plan that is not even out yet. Some written petitions have started coming in, spearheaded by community leaders, but they are just requesting to release a formal compensation plan as quickly as possible."

"With the height raised, all 86 villages will flood, even ones like Nilgi that sit on higher ground," Samar said. "Except the rich, people will have nowhere to go. I have experienced this firsthand when my village was mined."

"You never told me about that, I thought you grew up in the city."

"I did, after my parents died," Samar said. "I stayed with different relatives. My mother died from cancer, probably from the toxic fumes she was inhaling. My father died a few months later from malaria. The mining trucks had created large potholes where water stagnated, creating the perfect breeding ground for mosquitos."

"I am sorry, Samar," Raj said, placing his hand on Samar's shoulder.

"What has happened has happened, but it cannot keep happening. We have to think of a way to stop this."

They sat in silence weighing their options. It was a hard decision as Samar, a government employee, could not instigate dissension and Raj did not want to get involved with small demonstrations.. He wanted to save his influence and credibility for well-planned, well-attended protests that would yield results.

"I am meeting the leaders of the 86 villages and we can put together a strategy to organize a protest as soon as the compensation and displacement plans are made public," Raj finally said.

"That is one way to do it, but it will be hard convincing people that the displacement and rehabilitation plans, when they do come, will be inadequate."

"Perhaps," Raj said, a frown on his brow. "But we could use past experience, with the mining and the dam, to stage a protest now. We can say we want to be assured a solid compensation plan because past government behavior has been untruthful."

"That might work," Samar said. "We will need to get some testimonies of people from the destroyed villages. Guru is one."

"He is?"

"Yes. His alcoholic father drove the family, in a village already impoverished by mining, into destitution."

"I know his father is an alcoholic but didn't realize his village was badly affected by the mines," Raj said, a thousand emotions clouding his head.

"He doesn't talk about it but did tell me when he realized I was also a victim of the same project. I will meet with people who were affected by mining—they may have more incentive."

"Be careful," Raj cautioned. "Veera visited me and told me to warn you against getting involved in any protest. You are a government employee and could be jailed for treason."

"There is no such law!" Samar said angry.

"There is no law, but anything can happen under Santosh, and quelling dam protests is very high on his agenda. He may use you as an example. So be careful when you meet your friends."

"I will," Samar assured Raj.

After Samar left, Raj sat back in his chair and closed his eyes. Still another connection to Priya—she was a victim of circumstances that had driven her to the brothel and into his arms. He wondered why Guru had not mentioned the mining in his village and realized that it might have been an insignificant problem compared to others. Would it ever end? Would he continue finding wretched, unhappy things about Priya? Things that made him even more determined to find her, make her life better even if he, too, might have been the source of her unhappiness.

CHAPTER NINE

The cave's mouth was concealed by giant kikar shrubs growing out of rocky soil. A sheer sandstone cliff, at whose base the cave was, dominated the landscape; the muted pink of the stone reflected the sunlight casting the cave in deep shadow. The terrain was rocky, supporting the shrubs and the lone acacia tree, the only species able to survive in these parts. The kikar shed their thorns generously and large black ants nested in their tiny piles. Any man, woman, or child foolish enough to walk barefoot experienced the wrath of the thorns and the ants. The thorns dug deep into soles and when you sat down to remove them, the ants laid siege. It was not unusual for Shantur's doctors to be asked to remove a deeply lodged thorn.

At one time, the cave housed a small statue of Lakshmi, the goddess of wealth, but now there were only bats hanging from the damp ceiling and small animals scurrying across the floor. When the goddess had resided in the cave, it had been accessible by a dirt track on which only bullock carts plied. Then, the statue was stolen, and people stopped visiting the cave. The track was now a barely walkable path.

Local lore had that the cave extended back deep in the mountain, into the earth's bowels. Every few years, an adventurous soul decided to explore the cave, find out exactly where it ended, but a kilometer in the cave narrowed so only a small dog could get through. People said there was a large lake beyond, but no one dared blast through, reluctant to be robbed of this small fantasy.

On this chilly spring morning, the sun worked hard warming the cliff's face. A group of men and women sat with their backs to the warm rock. Their voices, swallowed by the deep silence, could be heard only when you came close. Then, a motorcycle's revving and spluttering invaded the stillness sending foraging partridges flying off in fright. Spotting the approaching motorcycle, the red wattled lapwings began their alarm call.

Did-you-do-it-did-you-do-it-did-you?

Heads turned towards the approaching vehicle. The rider turned off the engine when he was almost at the cave's mouth. He propped his silver Yamaha against a rock and swung one long leg over, removing his helmet as he walked towards the others.

"Namaste, I hope you haven't been waiting too long?" he offered by way of an apology. "Mahesh, thank you for getting everyone together. I couldn't have done it with the authorities watching. As it is, Veera has caught a whiff of my doings and warned me through Raj Nayak."

"He has caught more than a whiff," the young man named Mahesh replied. "He told me clearly that he was watching you."

"What exactly did he say?" Samar asked.

"He said if there was any kind of protest against the government, he would go after you. He is certain you are partly responsible for the rising tension between the people and the government."

"Sulimaga," Samar said swearing in the local dialect. "All he cares about is the kickbacks from Santosh. He has warned Raj dhani that I could be jailed for instigating people against the government."

"How can he do that?" a small, child-like woman in a pale orange salwar-kameez asked. "Surely, that is against the law?"

"Going by the books, I shouldn't be inciting people against the government," Samar said. "I can be fired for it but not imprisoned. But Santosh is all powerful in these parts and can do whatever he likes. Even jail me."

"Maybe you should stay out of this, Samar?" Mahesh said.

"I intend to," Samar said, scanning the gathered people. "I will just 'leak' information and you can use it as you wish. It will be hard to trace the information back to me as all the Displacement and Rehabilitation Officers will also have the same facts I do."

"It is public knowledge that the government plans on raising the dam's height, flooding 86 villages," the small woman in pale orange said. "We can protest that."

"That won't work," Samar replied. "The dam's construction began several decades ago and we cannot protest its completion at this stage. Besides, the government has said it will be releasing a compensation plan for displacement and rehabilitation."

"If we have nothing to protest, why are we even meeting?" Mahesh asked, impatiently.

"We do have things to protest. The displacement and rehabilitation plan the government intends releasing will be inadequate, I am certain, but we won't find that out until it might be too late. My guess is it will be made public a few weeks before construction is supposed to begin, and it will be impossible to organize a protest in the little time we will have. And we cannot protest something that hasn't happened and it may not be easy to convince people that the plan, when it will be released, will fall short."

"You are basically saying we have no case at all?" Mahesh said, worriedly.

"No, we do. We can start by petitioning the government to release the plan, say, within a month. If it doesn't, we will protest. We also remind the government, when we petition, to think back to its past behavior when no compensation was provided to the people affected by the mines and the initial phase of dam construction."

"That is a great plan," the child-like woman said. "Our first step is starting a petition."

"Exactly. Some leaders of villages have already started petitioning the government, but they aren't really strong enough. We need to use testimonials of victims, so our case is irrefutable."

"That is a brilliant idea," Mahesh said, slapping Samar's back. "That includes you and me. Anyone who was a child when the mines wrecked their lives will be willing to testify."

"Yes, that is our beginning point. But we should start planning a protest in case the government doesn't release the displacement plan by the given date. Can you muster enough support to do that? I am certain the government won't give us the plan by our deadline but what about people? What do you think?"

"I think we can convince enough people to plan a protest," an elderly man enveloped in a black, goats-hair parka said. "We did manage to prevail upon the government and force it to construct the dam at a lower level because there was no compensation plan. That wasn't an organized protest, but it worked. Young people now are so disillusioned by the way the country is run that they will protest almost anything the government does. The older people will take time; they have always accepted, with resignation, every atrocity by the authorities. But even they will join once the government fails to provide a compensation plan by the given date."

"When should we plan the protest?" Mahesh asked Samar.

"First of all, gather testimonials from victims of dam and mining projects. Use them to petition the government to release a concrete displacement and rehabilitation plan by, say, end of April. If the government doesn't meet the deadline, we protest. Santosh is hosting the state's Chief Minister in mid-May. There will be a rally at which the minister will speak. Our protest will be then—we will publicly bring to light past government indifference towards displaced people and its failure in providing a plan by the date we have demanded."

"When shall we meet again?" Mahesh asked.

"You have to decide that" Samar said. "I won't meet you until we start planning the protest in earnest. I will be in touch with Raj dhani and you can work with him to figure things out. I am safer leaking information through him. He is meeting with the leaders of the 86 villages to begin drafting a petition."

The people, united by their open hostility towards the government and a common determination to be heard, dispersed. Their grievances and fears had been fueled and validated and there was now a new urgency so they would not be, once again, deprived of the lives they had painstakingly built despite an indifferent, callous government.

Back in Nilgi, Samar doffed his activist hat and donned his underpaid government employee shroud. He gazed at himself in the mirror and realized the flushed man he saw there, with battle in his eyes, was very different from the one the world saw. To most people he was a boring employee living by government rules and guidelines that benefited no one except those in authority. Few knew his internal war between a staid, stoic displacement and rehabilitation officer and an angry, grieving, orphaned boy thirsting revenge on the government, to rip it apart, dismember it, so it was completely powerless.

RAJ'S RED MARUTI 800 bumped along the road connecting Nilgi to Shantur. At one time, more than three decades ago, it had been a tarred road laid even as the dam doomed to flood Nilgi was being built. It was another government project undertaken to fill the coffers of local politicians. After it was completed and people who wanted to get rich had become rich, the road had slowly deteriorated into a potholed dirt track with patches of tar. There was not much money to be made from road maintenance.

When it was first built, the road had brought the world to Nilgi's doorstep; it had also made it easy for people to leave it. The women began going to Shantur to shop, the men to carouse, and the young people to watch Bollywood movies in the town's cinema. All it had taken was a bunch of dust-covered, rattling buses to put Nilgi on the map, wake it from its sleepiness.

The women became bolder wearing bright, synthetic saris and plastic flowers in their hair. The men began drinking and beating their lovely, dressed-up wives at night. The children watched the changes in their homes and compared it to the drama of the Bollywood movie they had recently watched.

"Why are there more women than men in the fields?" Raj, in his teens, had asked Sharada.

"Because the men are too hungover to go to work," she had replied. "The bus has made it easier for the men to go to Shantur and drink. They spend all their wages on alcohol and the women have resigned themselves to working so they can support their children and drunk husbands."

Even today, despite the road's deterioration, people walked it, cyclists biked it, and motorcyclists transported entire families on it. Buses continued to barrel along all day, every day. Raj swore under his breath trying to avoid the potholes. The remaining tar seethed and boiled under an unusually hot spring sun that scorched travelers' bare feet and drove stray dogs to madness.

The smell of ripening jowar and freshly fertilized fields wafted into Raj's car through the rolled-down windows. He was on his way to address the meeting of the leaders of the 86 villages. Besides the leaders, several hundred people from the doomed villages were gathered in front of Shantur's Ganesh temple. There was dissension in the air that spring afternoon, a whiff of rebellion outside the temple. Vendors, dogs, and beggars mingled with the meeting attendees. The air was infused with the smell of marigold, jasmine, frying pakoras, roasting peanuts, the sound of ringing temple bells and squealing children. A cow stopped and emptied her bowels in a glorious heap by the temple entrance. How auspicious, people said, carefully stepping around the dung; the sacred cow shitting in front of the temple.

Ganesha, Shiva's elephant-headed son, sat cross-legged deep inside the innermost sanctum of the temple, a bronze figure with a bulging stomach and gentle eyes, surveying the mounds of sweets his devotees were piling in front of him. He was the sugar-loving god and if a child with a sweet tooth was told, "You are just like Ganesha," it was a compliment.

A makeshift podium decorated with strings of marigold and mango leaves had been set up outside the temple. The half dozen prominent leaders seated in plastic chairs on the podium stood up with folded hands when Raj walked up and took his seat with the others. He had wanted this to be an informal meeting but gave in when attendees, now seated on the podium, had insisted on this setup. He knew there was an ulterior motive; they wanted to use this opportunity to demonstrate their power and superiority. Basic human nature never changed.

Some attendees sat on blankets they had spread out. Others squatted on the ground or stood at the back, trying to get a glimpse of the important people on the podium. Cows, used to wandering around freely, looked on, with resignation, their space taken over by humans.

A portly man on the podium, the unofficial leader of the leaders, walked to the microphone and began introducing those on the stage. The ones he liked, he spoke of with respect and love. For the ones he did not like, he threw in an insult disguised as an endearing eccentricity.

"The qualities of this man are as vast as his ghee-fattened body," he said and everyone applauded. The subject squirmed in his seat and feigned amusement as he plotted his revenge.

The introductions went on for almost half an hour. At first there was an enthusiastic applause but as the sun climbed higher and higher in the sky, the applause became scattered, sometimes even inappropriate. Babies began crying, children played in the dirt, and the old dozed off.

Finally, it was Raj's turn to be introduced and the crowd visibly perked up.

"We are truly honored to have the venerable Raj Nayak with us," the leader of the leaders said.

The audience applauded politely.

Raj's qualities were extolled as if he was a stranger, "Mr. Nayak is very highly educated and has even been awarded an honorary law degree from Delhi University."

The people applauded loudly, even the ones who knew this was untrue. Raj winced and wondered if he should refute that statement but decided there was no point as everyone in the district knew him and his qualifications. When it was Raj's turn to speak, he took the microphone knowing he had probably lost his audience even before he had begun addressing it.

"Thank you for the flattering introduction," Raj said. "I am honored to be addressing this meeting."

A polite applause.

"We should be proud we have managed to gather here to fight

for our rights," Raj said. "We prevented the government from building the dam to its original height a decade ago because there was no compensation. We did that without organizing a formal protest, simply through petitions. The government promised us the dam at its reduced height would not flood our villages, but they lied and our low-lying villages have been flooding every monsoon. Now, they want to raise the height to the original level, and they are promising a compensation plan so we cannot protest."

A louder applause.

"We should have protested decades ago when our villages were being ravaged, first by mines and then by the floods caused by the dam. We didn't gather, then, because we trusted the government and believed it would do what was best for us. The government, however, let us down and here we are. This time we will not be taken advantage of and we will fight until every one of our demands is met."

A resounding applause as a new energy infused the cheering crowd.

"What are our demands, you might ask. We all know the government is going to raise the dam's height and the construction is to begin in a few months. If the height is raised, all 86 villages will flood in the backwaters. Our villages, our livelihoods, our fields, our cattle."

The crowd shouted in agreement.

"The government has promised us a displacement and rehabilitation plan before the construction begins. We need the government to give us the same amount of land we now have so we can move and start over. If it cannot give us land, we want to be paid market value for what we will lose in the dam's backwaters. We need a plan from the government as soon as possible and we have asked but haven't gotten a release date yet. This is not acceptable."

The crowd began to boo. Someone shouted, "The curses of a

thousand rishis on the government!"

"So, what will we do now?" Raj asked. "We will petition the government, demanding it release the displacement and rehabilitation plan by the end of April. In the petition we will include testimonials of victims of the mines and flooding to stress that we have been abused before, but we won't take it anymore. We will not take this lying down."

The crowd cheered and booed.

"This is also an opportunity to get rid of the caste, class, and religion distinctions that are holding us back from true progress. We have to make sure the lowest of low in our society, the untouchables, the lower castes, also get compensation so they can start a new life, shoulder to shoulder with the rest of us, even if they do not own land or house. It is the rest of us who have kept them behind."

A smattering of applause from the liberals and activists as the conservative upper classes and castes became uncomfortable, worried they were about to lose the social status they did not deserve. The men on the podium applauded the loudest. They had political aspirations and their biggest vote bank, the untouchables and marginalized, was squatting in the dirt.

"If the government does not give us the plan by the end of April, we will protest. We will mobilize all 86 villages."

"Hear, hear," a young man in the front shouted. "We must warn MLA Santosh, so he is prepared with his stash of whiskey and women as we protest outside his house. He will be too scared to leave."

"If we protest, we will do it when the Chief Minister is visiting Shantur for the engineering college's silver jubilee," Raj said. "We will gather in the college's grounds. Let's not get personal about Santosh."

"We don't care," someone else in the crowd shouted. "That

man needs to be castrated."

Before Raj could respond, there was a flurry in the crowd and several policemen, who had sneaked in without being noticed, charged with their lathis, waving them around and trashing whoever they could, whatever they could. Veera materialized from nowhere and climbed the podium.

"Leave at once," he said to the people in chairs. "Or we won't be responsible for what happens. This crowd needs to be tamed and you don't want to be caught in it."

One of the leaders caught Veera by the lapels, "Tell your police to leave us alone or we will not be responsible for what we do."

Veera shriveled and Raj strode towards him.

"Call your policemen off," Raj said quietly. "If you don't, I will make sure this story is written in tomorrow's newspapers. I will also make sure every human rights group is informed so they will make your life, and of those who put you up to this, difficult. They will be so ruthless that you will wish you had spared us."

Veera ran down to gather his men and leave but he did not have to. The crowd had cornered the policemen and chased them away.

It was quiet after the police left and the crowd slowly dispersed. There was a plan now, to implement, but Raj knew he had underestimated the power of the politicians, especially Santosh. He worried there would be riots and violence if the government did not do what it was being asked to do.

CHAPTER TEN

Santosh's biggest problem was that he was married to a tree. He had been married a few months and had several more months before he could divorce the tree and find another wife. He had divorced his first wife; his second wife had divorced him and the astrologer insisted his third marriage should be to the sacred pipal tree because three is an unlucky number. After divorcing the tree, he could move on to a successful fourth marriage.

His first marriage was arranged, like all respectable marriages, after the astrologer studied the horoscopes of Santosh, who was not yet a member of the state's Legislative Assembly, and his first wife and announced they matched. The astrologer would have said the same thing even if the horoscopes had not matched because the bride was Santosh's first cousin and their marriage had been intended since they were children. Santosh was reconciled to the match because it was beneficial; the bride's father was well-respected and fairly well-off.

The astrologer, to establish his authority, said the marriage must happen at once as the couple's stars would never be as perfectly aligned as now. The ceremony took place one blistering summer morning during the auspicious wedding season, under the shade of a red and white shamiyana decorated with marigold flowers and mango leaves. Santosh was twenty-five and his bride nineteen and the dowry was excessive—a scooter for the bridegroom, a black and white television, several steel pots and pans and a quilt for the marital bed the bride herself had sewn. The bride's parents were grateful to Santosh for marrying their daughter, a plain and mild girl with few prospects.

It was not that Santosh had much going for him; he was neither attractive nor did he have a steady income. After graduating high school at sixteen with a third class, he had tinkered in several jobs—grocery shopping in Shantur for the richer families in his village, mending leaking roofs, grazing other people's cattle in nearby pastures and even killing squirrels with his slingshot for their blood which was used by the village healer to treat a range of diseases. His flaws, however, were more easily forgiven because he was a man.

Bored wedding guests, busy fanning themselves with old newspapers and school textbooks, were paying little attention to the bride and groom and even that was gone when Raj and his parents arrived. The Nayaks were invited to almost every wedding in the district but attended just a few, sending a gift to the rest. But Santosh had gone in person to the vada with his green, palm leaf-shaped wedding card and begged the Nayaks to come until Raj's father relented. Wedding guests squatted or sat cross-legged on striped rugs spread on uneven ground but the Nayaks were given chairs alongside other important guests.

Santosh felt happy and jealous. People would now think his family was better than others because the district's most powerful family had come to his wedding. Santosh was happy about that. He felt jealous, especially of Raj, who was at least a decade younger than him and was treated with a deference and reverence that Santosh could only dream about. He would have been devastated if he had known he would never command that degree of deference and reverence no matter how rich and influential he became. If he did become wealthy, he would always belong to the nouveau riche.

On that hot day, though, Santosh knew nothing of his future and reveled in everyone's envy as he and his new bride sought the Nayaks' blessings soon after the ceremony was over. Raj's father handed the couple an envelope of cash and Santosh put up an expected token resistance before accepting the money. The Nayaks made an appropriate exit before the wedding lunch and Santosh wished he could do that someday, arrive and leave like a king, whenever he wanted, however he wanted.

The couple began their life in Santosh's parents' three-room house. The front room opened onto the street through a door tall people had to duck to get through. There were two plastic chairs, and a table and male guests were received here. Santosh slept in this room on a thin mattress he rolled out every evening and put away in the morning. The middle room was his parents. His father slept on an aluminum bed and his mother on the floor. After he married, Santosh's parents moved to the front room and gave theirs to the newly-weds. The last room in the back was a kitchen, looking out to fields through a small window. In one corner was a clay stove and soot from it had turned the whitewashed walls black. The bathroom was in another corner, marked by a low wall that separated it from the rest of the kitchen. There were two large brass pots of water, one cold and one hot. Village women queued up to draw water from the public well every morning. The bathroom wall hid only the feet and shanks of the bather from view, so everyone left the kitchen when the men took turns bathing. It was less complicated for the women; one carried on cooking and cleaning while the other bathed. Dirty water drained into the fields through a hole in the bathroom's floor.

Santosh's father was a poor tenant farmer who grew millets and sunflowers on land he leased from a landowner. His parents had used their meager savings to marry off their two daughters and had nothing left for Santosh to inherit except the humble house. Soon after the marriage, iron ore mines began laying land bare and farmers lost their livelihoods, succumbing to poverty. Some stayed on and some went to the nearest towns looking for work only to discover they had no skills besides farming. Slums mushroomed in towns, growing at an alarming rate as the mines forced more and more people to leave their villages. Santosh's father had to stop farming when the land he leased was forcibly bought by National Mining.

A grim cloud of poverty and misfortune enveloped the village and others in the district. Entire families perished from destitution and forgotten diseases that began reappearing, typhoid, cholera, and malaria. Santosh's family, too, would have met the same fate if it were not for his enterprising mind. The village's one grocery store closed, and Santosh took advantage of that. He rode his scooter, given to him by his bride's family, to Shantur twice a week. There he bought in bulk all the things' people needed—rice, salt, jaggery, spices, medicine, plastic combs, bhidis and arrack. He sold his merchandise to the villagers, saving them a shopping trip to Shantur, making a decent profit so he could run the house and deposit some money in a savings account at the Bank of India, Shantur.

Santosh's parents died within three years of his marriage and by then he had saved enough so he could move to Shantur with his wife where he rented a flat with a bedroom, an attached bathroom, living room and kitchen. He bought shares in National Mining, the company that had destroyed his village, and started working as a peon in the office of a local politician who had contested in every election for the last two decades and never won. Santosh wanted to figure out what he should not do in order to become a successful politician.

As National Mining's profits grew, Santosh's shares increased in value and he began selling them and investing in different lucrative businesses. He amassed enough wealth so he could buy a large house and hire a housekeeper who could cook, a gardener, and a driver for his Fiat car. He kept his scooter as a constant reminder of his previous poverty. By then, he had risen from the ranks of a peon to the personal secretary of the failed politician. He resigned from his job as it was not in keeping with his newfound status and wealth. Besides, he had learned enough and made contacts so could launch his own political career.

He had successfully shed his embarrassing, impoverished past and should have been happy but he was not. His wife was a constant reminder of where he came from and was becoming a hindrance, especially because she had not borne him a child. She had conceived for the first time five years after their marriage and miscarried before the end of the first trimester. There were two more pregnancies that ended the same way. Finally, the same astrologer who had matched the couple's horoscope was summoned.

The erudite man arrived at Santosh's new house at dawn carrying a bag of charts and drawings, settling himself comfortably in a corner of the kitchen. He studied the horoscopes and the stars, the frown on his face deepening as the morning wore on. The tension in the house rose and the cook brought him plates of delicacies and cups of tea. Santosh hovered, waiting for the verdict, and his wife prayed in the pooja room. Finally, after fifteen cups of tea and several plates of food, the astrologer looked up and announced that there was no reason why Santosh and his wife could not have a child as long as they did what he suggested.

First, said the man, the front door of the house was facing in the wrong direction, trapping negative energy. The door should be walled up and another one made at the side of the house. Santosh protested that the new door would result in guests entering the house through the kitchen. The astrologer shook his head in disappointment and said it was necessary if a child were to be born. He would also need to perform poojas in the house every Monday and Friday for three months and Santosh's wife should fast on those days. Santosh relented even though it would cost him a lot of money. Deep down he was thrilled he could afford all this.

The astrologer's advice was followed but nothing happened even a year later despite Santosh's wife continuing to fast after the three months were up. At that point Santosh wanted to throw his wife out but restrained himself because he was planning on launching his political career and a divorce would reduce his chances of getting elected. He had never been fond of his wife but now, he derided her in private and was the perfect husband in public. People, especially women, shook their heads in empathy and sympathy and held him in high esteem for sticking with his wife even though she had failed him by not producing a child.

Santosh aligned himself with the district's right-wing nationalists whose main aim was to unite the Hindus of India and establish a Hindu state. Santosh did not particularly care if India was a Hindu state or not, but Hindu nationalism had been growing rapidly and publicly supporting it increased the chances of him being elected to the state's Legislative Assembly. The politician he had worked for had been a liberal and against a Hindu state; it was what had prevented him from getting elected and Santosh was not going to make the same mistake.

For the next few years, Santosh served in the local Hindu nationalist organization, Naam Hindustan, meaning "Our India," which had several thousand members. Only a few hundred of the organization were active and most were "sleeping," the treasurer informed Santosh. Santosh became an active member attending every Naam Hindustan event. He rose before four in the morning and went to meetings held in Shantur's public gardens. The day began with yoga, discourses about Hindu philosophy, and training in unarmed combat. Very quickly, Santosh became indispensable. He could lead a discourse, not because he had mastered Hindu philosophy but because he had mastered the gift of gab. He was also a brilliant public speaker. Within a few years he established a reputation as a formidable nationalist and was elected as Naam Hindustan's president. He was well on his way to being elected to the state's legislative assembly.

Santosh was given a ticket to run for a Legislative Assembly seat in the elections of 1989. He campaigned as a pro-Hindutva candidate against his liberal opposition. He fed and fueled rising right-wing sentiment promising things he had no intention of delivering if he got elected. He promised Naam Hindustan land and resources for its activities. He promised to stop the killing of cows, sacred animals in Hinduism, for India's beef industry even though no cow had ever been slaughtered in Shantur district. He promised that every church and mosque would have to pay a hefty fee to the government if it intended to stay open.

On the sly, Santosh bribed the poorest with promises of a better life without actually telling them how he would do that. He distributed free liquor to men in dry villages and towns. If the men decided to vote for him, the women would most definitely follow.

The victory was marginal, but Santosh did not care; he knew he could only go up from there. He had guile, scrupulousness, and enough ego so he could stay in power for as long as he wished. He may not deliver all his pre-election promises but it would not matter as no one would remember. He would keep his popularity by presenting solutions to new problems he planned on creating; ending child marriage even though it was almost non-existent, funding workers' unions, and stopping dowry. While people in his constituency were focused on these problems, he could dig into the state's treasury and help himself to money on the pretext of different projects.

Santosh, now a member of the State Legislative Assembly, exchanged his cheap polyester safari suits with crisp, starched white pyjamas and kurtas. In the winter, he wrapped a cashmere shawl around his shoulders. On his feet were brown leather shoes. Behind his ears he dabbed sandalwood attar. When he looked at himself in the mirror, he saw how closely he resembled the liberal politician he had worked for.

He began surrounding himself with people who were loyal to him because they were as treacherous as he was—bank managers, accountants, CEOs of companies, and the police. He kept their secrets and they his and it worked out—he was re-elected again on completion of his five-year term and appointed agriculture minister despite his blatant corruption and inefficiency. This time, he played another card, promising people he would complete the dam, work on which had stopped more than a decade ago when funds ran out. When people protested the construction, refusing to leave until fairly compensated, Santosh decided to build a shorter dam that would not flood the villages. But, even the shorter dam began flooding villages, especially the ones most ravaged by the mines; the government refused to take responsibility.

Simultaneously, he began the construction of his magnificent, thirty-eight-room mansion with carved marble arches, indoor pools and a front door guarded by two pink sandstone lions.

He met Veera during his second term at the unveiling of the statue of Babasaheb Ambedkar, a man who had campaigned against India's social discrimination. Veera, who was there to ensure the safety of the important people, made it a point to meet Santosh, shake hands with him and ask to meet him in private. Santosh sensed that Veera could be an important ally and invited him home.

VEERA RODE HIS Vespa scooter down Santosh's driveway through manicured gardens, in which gardeners uselessly worked, to the teak front door. Veera, impressed by grandiosity, admired the extravagantly and tastelessly decorated house. He propped his scooter in the car port and walked in through the open front door. A servant saw him and led him to Santosh's office. Santosh waved the inspector to a chair across the desk where he sat, talking on the phone. He hung up after a few minutes, apologized and pointed to the tea and Glucose biscuits a servant had brought in.

"Have it, have it," he urged when Veera politely refused.

"Thank you for your time," Veera said, dipping the sugar biscuits in the sweet, milky tea.

"You said there was a matter you wanted to discuss?"

"Yes, it is rather a delicate matter...." Veera did not finish. Santosh's wife walked in carrying a silver plate piled with perfectly round gram flour laddus. She placed them on the desk and left.

"My favorite sweets," Santosh remarked.

"You are so good to her," Veera said. "People commend you on staying married to her despite the fact that she hasn't given you a child."

"It isn't easy, but I have learned to live with it. I have found ways to ease the pain of childlessness."

"Yes, yes, I know. And I can help you in that area."

"How?" Santosh asked.

"I know people who would love your company so you can be distracted from your problems. For example, I know this amazing woman who sings like a koel. Knowing your love for the arts, I thought you might want to hear her."

Santosh smiled. Veera was just the kind of person he wanted to know. He was being offered a woman and he needed that. He had had many flings, but it was tiresome finding a new woman, of the caliber he felt he deserved, every few months.

"I would like that very much, but I cannot have her perform here. My wife does not approve of my interest in the arts. Can I listen to this woman elsewhere? How about my old house? I often go there to work because it is so quiet."

"I will try my best to convince the singer to come to your old house," Veera said unctuously.

"I want to do something in return for your kindness. I will make sure no one interferes with the way you conduct business as a police inspector."

Santosh was offering to protect Veera from officials who could arrest him because he collected hafta, protection money, from Shantur's businesses. In return, Veera assured the businesses that they would not be harassed by the local gangsters. Everyone knew that the gangsters were part of the racket and received a share of the hafta but no one challenged this system knowing that the gangsters would pay them a visit if they did.

"Thank you," Veera said, standing up to leave. "I will call you once I have arranged things."

"You said there was something you wished to discuss?"

"No, no, that can wait."

After the Veera left Santosh realized that the matter the inspector wanted to discuss had been discussed. Veera would supply him with women if Santosh looked the other way.

IN THE BEGINNING Santosh was discreet about the women Veera provided him. As the years wore on, he became increasingly impudent and flaunted them, knowing it would not affect his re-election for his third term in the legislative assembly, not because people liked him but because the candidate of the opposition did not have the funds to run a successful campaign.

He was right and won again in 1999. Shortly after, he sent his wife to stay with her brother claiming she was mentally disturbed. He made it known that he was giving her a large monthly allowance to demonstrate his generosity, then filed for divorce and started over as a fifty-five-year-old free man.

Three years later, Santosh met his second wife, a fashionable city woman half his age, at a dinner hosted by her rich father. The girl's parents were thrilled even though they knew that their daughter was marrying a corrupt older man. They saw this as an opportunity to expand their liquor business, using Santosh's influence to obtain much sought-after licenses for new stores. The girl was taken with Santosh's pompous unapologetic attitude and aura of misused power that preceded him wherever he went.

A year later, the second wife dumped him and eloped with the boyfriend she had dumped to marry Santosh. The novelty of his power and position had worn off and she began noticing his paan-stained lips, henna-dyed grey hair, and bowed legs.

Santosh bore his second wife's deceit with obvious grief and despair. He rode the storm of sympathy and was re-elected once again for a fourth term in 2004. Shortly after, he consulted his astrologer and married the pipal tree before embarking on his fourth marriage. The astrologer took a personal interest in this marriage and found the perfect tree on the outskirts of Shantur. People said it was more than nine hundred years old and it was under one such tree that the Buddha had meditated and become enlightened. Strangely, for the first time in his life, Santosh felt small, inconsequential sitting below the deep shade of the pipal, imagining all it had witnessed for centuries.

In the meantime, while he waited to divorce the tree and embark on his fourth marriage, Santosh asked Veera to bring him better women than the ones he was being provided. Veera wrung his hands in despair because he had exhausted all his resources in Shantur. He started looking in nearby towns for a woman who was good mistress material and was sophisticated enough so Santosh did not mind being seen with her in public.

CHAPTER ELEVEN

Unlike most of the district's villages, Nilgi had escaped the devastation from the mines decades ago and, more recently, the annual floods caused by a partially constructed dam. Its people became increasingly confident that their village was indestructible. They added haphazard rooms to their houses, for the sons who married and moved in with their wives and for their daughters who were unlikely to ever marry. Some painted their houses in glorious colors. At one point, the villagers unanimously decided that every house in Nilgi should be the same color, cream, to match the vada's exterior. This unofficial decree was carried out but within a couple of years, the cheap cream paint bought in bulk began to chip and people decided to repaint their houses however they liked. Farmers continued developing their fields installing sprinkler systems, PVC pipes, and underground irrigation.

Then, electricity came to Nilgi, and the village thought it had arrived in the modern world.

Nilgi could not have been more wrong.

India slowly imploded, declining swiftly as every post-independence dream shattered to smithereens. It was partly because of a corrupt government and partly because of people's growing tolerance for corruption. Or perhaps Indians had been programmed that way because of centuries of foreign rule and did not think much of the atrocities heaped upon them by their elected leaders.

Electricity, too, slowly disappeared from Nilgi. Not officially, as Sharada the toothless roti-maker said about things that were not supposed to be the way they were. The government had not planned for India's exploding population and was producing less than half the needed power. As a solution, electricity was rationed to small villages. The government called the several hours of power outage, "scheduled power cuts," as if giving it an official name made it acceptable. As politicians became increasingly greedy and corrupt and the people more compliant, the scheduled power cuts disappeared, replaced by days of power outage.

Oil lamps, lanterns, and candles reappeared. In the beginning the villagers made excuses for the outages. Probably a tree falling on the power lines or a broken electric pole, they said, but when it worsened, they cursed the politicians, the officials and the electricity. When the dusty light bulbs in Nilgi lit up, women dropped whatever they were doing, grabbed sacks of *jowar* and wheat and rushed to the mill to grind the grain to flour. The men ran to their farms to turn on pumps and water their wilting crops. For the few hours when there was power the rhythmic chugging of the water pumps and grain crushers sliced the silence of the countryside. The silence returned when the electricity went off, broken occasionally by the sound of a bus or motorcycle bumping along the road to Shantur.

Now, the tar road between Shantur and Nilgi was full of

potholes, some so deep that a small dog or cat could easily drown in the water that collected in the monsoons. The buses still came every hour, but the ride was bumpy and uncomfortable, braved only by those who had no other way of getting to Shantur. Most villagers owned bicycles and motorcycles and two families even had cars. The bullock carts were still there even if they now preferred the dirt road of the past. The government refused to repair the road assuring Nilgi that it would certainly drown very soon when the dam's height was raised. What was the point of investing in a place whose days were numbered?

Nilgi's isolation was complete when the telephone lines, too, became unreliable. They went dead for several days so friends and family in far-off towns and cities, who had seemed close because of the telephones, retreated to their distant places again.

Then, cell phones appeared putting Nilgi on the map once again. With the availability of the Internet, people in the 86 villages to submerge began to understand and ask for their rights. Tensions rose when the government failed to release the demanded Displacement and Rehabilitation plan by the given date, April 30th.

It was time to officially protest.

Raj's anti-dam movement was ready for war.

THE MAY SUN beat down on Nilgi that summer of 2005. The village was silent as almost everyone, except the very old and frail, were in Shantur to protest. The Chief Minister was visiting to celebrate the twenty-fifth anniversary of the engineering college and would speak on the grounds before a large crowd. He would be flattered by the gathered people little knowing that most of them were there to protest the government's callousness towards the dam's victims.

"I thought they would give out sweets to everyone to celebrate the twenty-fifth anniversary," Reshma whispered to Guru and Bharati.

"Don't be silly," Guru replied. "The sweets are only for the people on the stage and the police guarding them."

"What are they guarding them for?" Bharati asked.

"Important people are always guarded because they are important and more likely to be harmed," Guru said.

"Harmed how?" Bharati asked.

"They are responsible for all the things that go wrong," Guru answered. "People feel angry and helpless, and someone might decide to harm them, even kill them."

"Well, it isn't such a bad idea if Santosh is killed," Bharati said. "Everyone says he takes bribes from even the poorest people. Everything in his kitchen is made of silver and he sits on a golden throne studded with gemstones."

"Hush, there may be some truth to that rumor but don't say it aloud," Guru clamped a hand on Bharati's mouth. "Are you crazy? If someone hears they might put you in jail."

"Thank you all for gathering before our venerable Chief Minister," Santosh began from the podium on the stage. "It is an honor that he is helping us celebrate the twenty-fifth anniversary of Shantur's engineering college. He has even generously donated two lakhs of rupees to buy computers."

Santosh paused for effect, expecting a loud applause, becoming uncomfortable when almost no one clapped.

"Without wasting any more time, I ask our Chief Minister to address us."

The Chief Minister, an ineffective, mild, old man stood up and an overly zealous engineering student, a teacher's pet, walked up onto the stage and garlanded him and went a step further, bending down to touch the minister's feet. The Chief Minister placed a withered, grandfatherly hand on the boy's head and ambled to the podium with the speech his granddaughter had helped him write.

"Sons and daughters of the Krishna river," he started. "I am honored to be invited to this celebration. When this engineering college was first opened, there were less than twenty students, all boys. Now, there are more than 200 students and at least one-third are girls. Educating our daughters is real progress."

The feminists and families who were educating their daughters applauded loudly.

"There are now five different engineering departments. Civil, electrical, computers, automobile, and mechanical. The graduates will go out into the world and make it better. The women engineers will be role models for not just their daughters but also their sons who will grow up seeing women thrive in professions that were once dominated by men. The only way to empower our women is by educating them."

There was thunderous applause and Santosh squirmed in his seat. The Chief Minister always made him look bad with his high ideals, progressive thinking and morality. It was why the chief minister was so ineffective; none of his projects, weighed down by ideology, got approved because he never pandered to his fellow politicians who were mostly like Santosh—corrupt and self—absorbed.

The Chief Minister carried on talking about all the progress the state was making. The Indian flag on the engineering college building billowed in the hot breeze. People began wilting and some started to leave. The Chief Minister would have continued but his secretary gestured to him to wind up. He ambled back to his chair and Santosh stood up again.

"We are ahead of almost every state in terms of development and economy," he boasted, making false claims. "Things will only get better going forward."

"We want to know what is being done for the people who will

be displaced by the dam," a man sitting in the front shouted.

"We are working on it," Santosh replied. "It is a complicated problem."

"It cannot be that complicated," someone else shouted. "All you have to do is make a plan for displacing and rehabilitating the victims."

"The people who will be displaced are not *victims*," Santosh said. "They will be the ones responsible for progress in the state. The dam will irrigate thousands and thousands of acres of arid land, improving the economy."

"How are you planning to irrigate the land when there is not a single canal to carry the water from the dam?" someone with a bullhorn in the back shouted.

Santosh began to sweat. He was not prepared for this.

"We have also heard rumors that you, as an agriculture minister, have done nothing to come up with a displacement and rehabilitation plan," the man with the bullhorn challenged. "Our contacts in the government tell us that you will be making a lot of money from the construction of the dam."

"You did not meet our deadline," another voice from the crowd shouted. "We asked for a displacement and development plan to be released at the end of April and this is mid-May. We have tried to find out the status of the plan and been unsuccessful. Every official and politician we have talked to has been vague."

"These things take time," Santosh hedged. "We want to come up with something that is perfect."

"You should have released the plan before ordering the completion of the dam," the man with the bullhorn said. "It is going to begin in a few months, right after monsoon, and we don't even know where we can move."

"This has gone on long enough," a woman's voice shouted. "Many of our villages are already flooding. When we approach you to help us, we are told that the floods are because *our* farmers have stripped the forests."

"The flooding is because the mines stripped all our forests and made many of us destitute three decades ago," the man in the front said. "People displaced because of the mines have still not been compensated and we don't trust you to take care of us now."

"And we know you had holdings in the mining company and became rich from it," the man with the bullhorn shouted. "We will not take this lying down. We will take action."

Santosh grew scared. He knew he was unpopular but, until now, had no idea how much people loathed him.

"Let's sneak to the back of the stage," Guru whispered, taking advantage of the crowd's rising anger. "The sweets are there, and we can take some. No one will notice."

"That isn't right," Bharati protested. "It is stealing."

"It is absolutely not stealing," Guru responded firmly. "Those sweets were bought from the taxes we pay, and we have every right to them."

Bharati could not argue with this logic.

Guru led Bharati and Reshma along the periphery of the crowd, towards the front as people began getting to their feet. Some threw their chappals at Santosh. The police, lethargic from the heat, became alert and started elbowing through the crowd hoping to intimidate. The seriousness of their expressions scared some away but most remained. As the crowd began moving towards the front, four policemen herded the people on the stage to waiting cars. Veera would have liked to get into one and be driven away to safety, but he could not while the mob grew increasingly agitated and began pelting the stage with stones.

The policemen who had infiltrated the crowd started beating the protestors with their lathis. They caught hold of four men and one woman and quickly walked them to their waiting jeeps, driving away from the screaming crowd. Veera took advantage of the distraction and dove behind the stage, squeezing himself between the baskets of sweets that would have been distributed after the speeches were over.

Guru, Bharati, and Reshma crept behind the stage, startling Veera.

"What are you doing here, sir?" Guru asked.

"What are *you* doing here, Guru?" Veera asked.

"We are running away from the mob," Guru replied. "We thought you would be out there."

"I came here to call for reinforcements," Veera lied, holding up his cell phone.

"We want to stay here until everything is quiet. Can we have a few sweets while we wait? We won't tell anyone that we saw you here and that you let us have the sweets."

The boy was sly, Veera thought. He was making a bargain—if he was allowed to have the sweets, he would not tell anyone that the inspector had been cowering behind the stage.

"Go ahead," Veera said. "They won't be given out now, anyway."

"Thank you," Guru said and turned to the girls who were behind him. "Come, take some sweets."

Veera saw a slight girl step forward, her hand reaching out timidly as Guru gave her a peda. He froze, then turned away quickly, his cell phone to his ear, pretending he was calling someone.

"I will be right there," he said into his phone, rushing out to the front of the stage. The ground was almost empty, and he felt cold in the furious May sun. He got on the scooter he had parked in a side street and rode home. It was only after he had thrown up twice in the toilet that he could think clearly.

Veera had been foolish in believing the little girl would remain in his hometown, but here she was in Shantur, where he had moved years ago. He was lucky she had not recognized him—but he could not count on it. He needed to act fast but did not know how. She probably lived at the vada, but how could he confirm it without being seen by her again? And even if he managed to find out, discreetly, where she lived, what should he do next to protect himself?

THE FIVE ARRESTED protestors—one woman and four men—were detained in the police chowki that night and released the next morning. It was an intimidation tactic the police had successfully used before, but it backfired this time. The anti-dam activists gathered outside Santosh's house that afternoon and burned his effigy shouting insulting, threatening slogans.

"We will burn you like this effigy."

"You dishonored our woman comrade by keeping her in a cell without giving her a chance to defend herself."

Santosh's secretary called Veera who said he was ill and sent a dozen police to guard the MLA's house. Santosh took refuge in the storeroom at the back of his house until the protestors left late in the evening.

A dangerous line had been crossed.

SLEEP ELUDED RAJ that night. He tossed and turned and finally gave up and went to the terrace outside his room. A sultry sky met with a simmering earth, trapping the hot, dry summer breeze. No woman had ever been arrested in Shantur district before, and it made everyone, even those not involved in anti-dam activism, furious—including Raj.

But he was also preoccupied with a phone call he had made that morning to Rati Mandir, the brothel where he first met Priya. He remembered that Priya had told him the girls were not allowed to go shopping in the bazar and bought their saris from traveling salesmen.

"I have saris from Kashmir, embroidered silks," he told the girl who answered. "Sarla bought saris from me when she was alive. You probably never met her."

He despised—hated—himself for all the lies he was weaving. It did not become his status as a benevolent, respectable landlord, but he had never made sane decisions when it came to Priya.

The chatty girl said she had never met Sarla but her niece, who lived in the city, came at the end of every month to collect her share of profits from the brothel—Sarla's beneficiary. Apparently, everyone who had known Sarla said the niece was the opposite of her aunt: mercenary, vulgar, unkind.

They talked about Sarla and other things and by the end of the conversation Raj knew the name of the niece and where she lived. He breathed a sigh of relief after hanging up; the girl had not asked his name or suggested he come to Rati Mandir to show his new saris. His elation at having found someone who knew Sarla and might have known Priya faded quickly. Suddenly he was not sure if he wanted to find Priya, even if the chances were still slim.

Now what? Raj thought. *Should I go to the city to find Sarla's niece? Or should I stop here and tell Guru that all my leads have dried up?*

The more he tried to push Priya to the back of his mind, the more he thought of her. Unbidden thoughts came to his head, sometimes hopeful, sometimes despairing. By the time it was dawn he had decided to go to the city and meet Sarla's niece.

Raj despised himself even more and in his most ironic moments he marveled at his ability to string lies, make up stories and cheat the only person who knew him in and out: Daya. That she did not even suspect the extent of his infidelity made him wallow in self-disgust and weep at his weakness. Until he met Priya, Raj had thought himself immutable, incorruptible but he had been disabused of that haughty notion. To make matters worse, he truly felt that his love for Priya was not just lust. It was much, much more and he was still unable to establish where it belonged.

The next day, he told Daya he had to go to the state capital for some dam-related official business. When she asked him what exactly he would be doing, he told her he was meeting with some human rights and environmental activists to understand how best to pressure the government. And because he had come up with the lie, Raj did make appointments to meet with some prominent activists who did not tell him anything he did not know but made him feel less of a liar than he was.

CHAPTER TWELVE

The rubbish, the unpleasant smells, the wretchedness of the place distracted Raj from the task at hand. Piles of garbage flanked the street like sentries guarding the filthy secrets of the shacks that lined it. Secrets were revered here amidst the poverty, desperation, and dirt; it meant you knew how to survive against all odds. It was the largest slum in the city and whatever could not be contained in the asbestos-roofed aluminum shacks spilled on the street.

Children squealed, sloshing around in rivulets of dirty water flowing down the street as if it were a mountain stream. Old women in their tattered saris and ill-fitting blouses rambled, muttering the finest obscenities under their breath. Unmarried girls and women flirted, lounging outside the doors of their shacks, fragrant princesses in their rose gardens. Drunk husbands let out a litany of verbal abuse at their wives who were getting their children ready for school. Cats mewed from behind garbage dumps and street dogs snarled over discarded food.

Raj reached into the right pocket of his pants and pulled out the picture of Priya Guru had given him. In the picture she was a child, so different from the picture Raj had of her—a beautiful woman with wild, loose hair, her skin glowing, smiling but not happy. She had been sad when Raj took this picture of her, just before he bade her goodbye. His picture of Priya was more recent than the one Guru gave him but he could not use it; it was intimate and incriminating.

There were no cars on the street, only motorcycles and bicycles, and Raj walked carefully sidestepping the garbage piles. He stared at the piece of paper with the name of Sarla's niece, Mamta, and the slum. He had thought that would be enough to find Mamta but the slum was huge and he wondered how he could find her. Raj's heart sank.

"Excuse me?" he said to a passerby.

The man stopped.

"Do you know a woman called Mamta? I was told she lives here."

"There are at three Mamtas on this street. Which one do you mean?"

"She is Sarla's niece," Raj said.

"Oh, that Sarla. She ran Rati Mandir."

"Yes, yes, that's the one."

The man looked carefully at Raj's expensive clothes, his neatly combed hair. People were always full of surprises, he thought. Who would have thought such a respectable-looking man would even know about Rati Mandir?

"That would be Mamta Ghule," the man said. "She lives in the house there. The one with a blue tarpaulin hanging in front."

"Thank you," Raj said.

Raj felt conspicuous walking towards the shack the man had pointed out. The blue sheet hid the front door and there was no bell or knocker. As he wondered what to do a half-naked child shot out the door.

A woman emerged, shouting, "Don't you dare run away, you rascal."

Seeing Raj, she stopped.

"And who are you, sir?" she asked, her voice changing, her hips leaning against the door's frame, her ample bosom thrust out.

"Are you Mamta?" Raj asked, his heart pounding. "Sarla's niece?"

"Yes, that's me."

"I am here to enquire about a girl your aunt knew."

The sly, flirtatious look left her face.

"What kind of enquiry? Are you a policeman? My aunt is dead, and I have nothing to do with her business."

Raj knew Mamta was collecting her share of profits from Rati Mandir but let the lie pass.

"No, no, nothing like that," he said, despising himself for another lie. "I am looking for a girl who worked at Rati Mandir. Her name was Priya, and she ran away from home many years ago. Her family lives in my village and they looked for her for years, then gave up. Recently, someone told her parents that she used to work at Rati Mandir. The family is poor, and I come here often with work and offered to follow up. When I went to Rati Mandir, I was told that Priya had left almost a decade ago when she became pregnant and the one person who really knew her, Sarla, is dead. One of the girls said you might know, and I came here."

"How do I know this isn't some sort of trap?" Mamta asked. "The police have been coming down hard on anyone connected to the city's brothels."

"I assure you this isn't a trap. The family will pay anyone who has information about Priya."

"I don't know any Priya, but you can come in and we can talk,"

Mamta relented.

Raj followed Mamta in. The shack was surprisingly clean and spacious. Rice was cooking on a kerosene stove and two little girls dressed in school uniforms were braiding each other's hair.

"These are my two older ones," Mamta said. "You saw my youngest running out."

Raj smiled at the two girls and sat down on the chair Mamta dragged from the corner of the room. He accepted the glass of milky tea Mamta gave him, wondering if it was safe to drink. Not wanting to offend Mamta, he took a sip, discovering it was sweet and fragrant with cinnamon and cardamom.

"How much?"

"How much?" Raj asked, confused.

"How much money will the family give for information?"

"It depends on the information, but I am certain it will be over four thousand rupees."

"That is it? My husband died from drink leaving me with three kids. I have to think about our survival. Four thousand rupees won't even cover a month's rent!"

Raj looked around at the shack that cost more than four thousand a month. He took another sip of tea.

"I can try and convince the family to give more but they are poor. If you do give them information about Priya and they find her, I am sure they will give more."

"Alright," Mamta relented. "I don't run a charity. Do you have a picture of her?

Raj pulled out Priya's photograph and showed it to Mamta.

"It is the girl at the right end of the back row," he said.

"The one with the long braids?"

"Did you ever see her in Rati Mandir? Your aunt and Priya were close. She may have mentioned her to you?"

"I hardly saw my aunt when she was alive," Mamta said. "I saw her a lot when she was sick and dying. By then she was rambling, and I wasn't paying much attention to what she was saying. If she had mentioned a pregnant prostitute I would remember."

Raj winced. It was still hard for him to hear Priya called a prostitute.

"Are you sure Sarla didn't say anything?"

"You sound like you want to find her more than her family," Mamta said, narrowing her eyes.

"Ours is a small village and we share each other's pain and misfortune," Raj said.

"Tell you what?" Mamta said, waving her girls off to school. "I will call if anything comes to mind."

Raj hesitated, then wrote down the number of his office in Nilgi's school.

"I am here in the morning, most weekdays. I could also call you now and then to check."

"I am not rich enough to get a phone," Mamta said sarcastically. "So, I will have to call you from a public phone. Long distance calls are expensive, you know."

This time, Raj understood what she was saying. He pulled out two hundred-rupee notes and gave them to her.

"This should cover the long-distance call if you have something to tell me."

"Yes, of course," Mamta said, suddenly losing interest.

Raj knew he was being dismissed and left. He was not sure Mamta would call if something did occur to her and he had no way of reaching her except to return to the slum. Another lead that had gone cold. Suddenly, all hope of finding Priya drained from him and he felt despondent. He resolved to go back to Nilgi and put his heart into all the things he had to do. He had been disengaged since finding out that Guru was Priya's brother.

THE CLOUD OF smoke and dust bounced along the road to Nilgi. When the dust settled, a scooter and the rider became visible. Veera was on his way to see Raj. It had been three weeks since the anti-dam protest in Shantur, and Veera would have liked to see Raj sooner, but he had been unavailable, visiting the city on business.

On that hot June morning, the semul trees dotting the landscape around Nilgi were in full bloom; they had lost their green foliage, and scarlet blossoms which would turn into cottony pods covered the leafless branches. The trees had bloomed two months later than they normally did, and scientists bemoaned climate change. June was the beginning of monsoon and grey clouds should have started gathering, but the sky was a clear blue as far as the eye could see.

Children played on Nilgi's cobbled streets, where the smell of woodsmoke and spices settled into the heat. Stray dogs sat in front of houses, waiting for food scraps. A few disgruntled people waited outside the tailor's shop while, inside, the sewing machine went at a frenzied pace. Sundays were the worst for the tailor. Clients came by demanding he finish making their garments, which should have been delivered to them weeks ago. It was the way of things. If you were a tailor, you never delivered on time; and if you were a client, you pretended to be furious even if you were not.

The crowd parted for Veera. He had never been popular, but public approval of him had sunk to an all-time low since the Shantur riots.

"Traitor," a man called after Veera as he turned on the empty road leading to the vada.

"Ass-licking low-life!" someone else shouted. "Just because you are Santosh's chamcha doesn't mean you are safe."

Veera sweated from the threats and the heat. If the crowd knew the extent of his crimes, they would devour him alive. Whole. He propped his scooter in the vada's front yard and walked inside.

Guru seated him in the living room, served him cool, salty buttermilk and went to get Raj.

"Namaste," Raj said. "Why the urgency to see me?"

"I am here to apologize for the arrests in Shantur. That should have not have happened."

Raj was taken aback. It was the last thing he had expected.

"I know you are surprised," Veera pressed his advantage. "But I have been thinking and feel guilty. I have a lot of power but am still the servant of the people."

"Your power comes from associating with Santosh, not from your status as the police inspector of Shantur. That is hardly a powerful position."

"I understand, but I have pressure from the top to do certain things."

"Like making arrests without adequate reason? That was merely a move to intimidate the anti-dam protestors, but it will backfire in the long run. People are furious. You and your MLA have managed to dig yourselves into a bigger hole."

"That is why I am here, to make amends" Veera lied. "I have been foolish and selfish and want do right by the people. I am on their side."

"Why the sudden change of heart? And does Santosh know about your new loyalties?"

Veera took a gulp of buttermilk and the white mustache stayed on his cherubic, treacherous face.

"He can't know," he finally said. "If he knows he will make my life hell and simply find someone else to force his agenda. There is no benefit to anyone knowing that I have decided enough is enough and that my loyalty should, must, lie with the people."

"Raj dhani," a voice said from the doorway and before Raj could respond. "The tailor sent this for you."

Bharati held out a brown package.

"Bring it here," Raj said holding out his hand. "It is a kurta the tailor has been making for a few months now. Congratulate him, will you, for finishing it."

Bharati giggled and walked in to give Raj the package.

"Here, do you want some chocolates?" Raj asked picking from a bowl of Cadbury eclairs on the center table. "Do you want some, too, Reshma?"

Reshma, who had been hovering at the door, was forced to come to Raj.

"Yes, dhani," she said, holding out a small hand, palm upwards.

Raj gazed at her for a few seconds, his heart muscles clenching. She was so dainty and fragile, beautiful, and quiet. Reshma took the candy, then turned away shyly. Her gaze fell on Veera, and Raj, watching her, saw the faraway look leave her eyes for a split second. He thought he saw recognition but was not sure as the distant look re-entered her eyes, like the quickly drawn shutters of a house that wants to keep its secrets.

"I better leave," Veera said as soon as the girls left.

"Are you all right?" Raj asked, looking at Veera's pale face.

"I am fine. I have been having some stomach problems these past few weeks."

"You should get tested. There are all kinds of infections going around this summer."

"I will," Veera said, getting up. "And remember what I said: I am here for the people."

Raj stayed in the living room for a long time and wondered if he should believe Veera. Could this be some kind of trick, so people began trusting Veera while he continued to work with Santosh to push the politician's agenda? It bothered Raj—but not as much as seeing Reshma. Every single time he saw her, she reminded him of someone, but he could not say who.

VEERA GOT ON his scooter, distraught that he had not been able to see Reshma alone. It would be hard, she was always with that good-for-nothing boy and the ugly servant girl. He put his hand into the cloth bag slung over the scooter's handle. The cheap plastic doll had been easy to find. Almost every stationary shop sold it, but Veera could not understand how any little girl could like such a toy. The face was pink and pudgy, the eyes set apart, each pupil looking in a different direction. There were two choices for hair—yellow or black—and Veera had picked black because the doll the girl had been playing with had black hair. He was surprised he even remembered the doll. Or the girl for that matter. He had barely glanced at the girl—whose name was apparently Reshma—when he visited his town's brothel.

He rode his scooter out of the vada's front gate and stopped for a few seconds, wondering what to do next. He had brought the doll to lure Reshma but hadn't had any opportunity. He was not ready to give up and return to Shantur. But what could he do? The road was deserted and he clasped his head in his hands, squeezed his eyes shut and looked down.

"Are you all right, policeman?" a soft voice asked. Veera's head shot up. He saw Reshma standing by his scooter and the blood pounded in his head.

"Yes, yes, tangi," Veera said, forcing himself to remain calm. "Your name is Reshma, isn't it?"

"Yes."

"That is a very pretty name," Veera said, thinking fast. "I once knew a girl by that name."

"Where is she?"

"I don't know. She disappeared. But, whenever I saw her, she used to be playing with her doll. Do you like dolls?"

Reshma did not answer and Veera looked around. The road was still deserted.

"In fact, I have a doll exactly like she used to have. I liked it so much that I bought one for myself. Can you believe it? I like dolls."

Reshma's face was still expressionless. Veera pulled out the doll from his bag and held it up.

"What do you think? Do you like it?"

Veera saw Reshma's lips trembling and, in that moment, he knew that she had not forgotten her past. She had simply pushed it to the back of her mind because it was very painful. Who knew when something might trigger clearer memories and she would remember *him*? She may not associate him with what had happened but she might remember that she had seen him. And what if she did know, somehow, his role in the whole sordid mess? So far, he had gotten away without arousing suspicion.

"Reshma, Reshma," Bharati called, coming out of the vada's gate. "I've been looking for you. Don't you want to…"

Bharati's voice trailed off when she saw Veera dangling the doll in front of Reshma.

"What are you doing?" Bharati yelled at Veera. "Don't you see she is terrified? I don't think she likes that doll."

Bharati put her arms around Reshma and led her away.

"Don't worry, don't worry. It will be all right. He is a mean man showing you that horrible doll."

Veera stayed where he was, shocked. How low had he sunk that a servant girl felt no compunction raising her voice and chastising him? It was hot out, but he was suddenly cold and yet, the coconut oil in his hair melted and ran down in rivulets over his forehead.

That night, Veera could not sleep and he did not try. He needed to stay awake, think logically, fix the problem. Everything was fixable, his mother had taught him and he wished she was still alive. *She* would have understood him, understood what he had done and why he had done it. She would not have judged him. But she was dead and he was frightened—terrified. Outside, an owl

142

hooted. Stray cats fought, their cries vicious, sounding like a child screaming in pain. The summer sun rose, quickly getting rid of the brief coolness of the early morning hours. And Veera had a plan.

RESHMA REFUSED TO eat and refused to answer questions for the rest of the day after seeing Veera. She lay awake for most of the night, dozing off in the early hours of dawn. Then, she woke up, bathed and dressed, and came into the kitchen as if nothing unusual had happened. And the shutters came farther down over her eyes.

CHAPTER THIRTEEN

Veera's delusions of grandeur were not his alone. They had been inspired, fired, stoked and re-stoked by his widowed mother. He was her only child, her son, her golden boy who could do no wrong. She blamed the teachers when he failed school exams. She accused the boys in Veera's class of conspiring against him when they excluded him. *They are jealous of you*, she told her son and he believed it. When she died suddenly from a heart attack, Veera had been completely lost. He was a twenty-two-year-old man who had barely passed his exams for his bachelor's degree, but believed he was smarter, better, superior. He did not see what the rest of the world saw—a pathetic, bumbling fool with the shiftiest eyes this side of the Krishna.

After his mother's passing, Veera felt a desperate need for a wife, someone who would take care of him and boost his confidence. He began propositioning girls—and they rejected his advances without hesitation. Even children made fun of him. He became furious. His mother was not around to confirm his worth and he directed his anger at the world. In the end, there was only one place he could find what he wanted, feel needed and even loved: he turned to the town's brothel.

The brothel stood at the end of a dirt path forking off the single street of shops in the shabby town. The building rose in all its ugly cheerlessness—a boxy, concrete, two-storied structure with eight small windows. The ratio of prostitutes to clients was high as few townsmen visited the brothel for fear of being found out. Most men desperate for company went to nearby towns where no one knew them.

Veera, with no hesitation or reservation, frequented the brothel openly and with considerable arrogance. In that space, which was hell for some and heaven for others, he found a buxom lover with green eyes and black hair. She stated her unworthiness, and he went ahead and fell in love with her. When she presented the person she loved: a scrawny, worm-ridden young girl picked off the streets of Mumbai, Veera bedded them both. He was sure he was doing the women a favor and they confirmed it.

He should have been happy, but his attention wandered to the four women he had been forbidden to see. They were mistresses of wealthy, influential men and seldom left their rooms with the shutterless windows that let only the mosquitoes in. Veera, enamored and impressed by this arrangement, wanted to emulate the men who kept them, who came and left discreetly in the dark.

He wanted someday to be able to have a mistress like this but, for that, he had to become rich and powerful. It was the only way he could punish all the people who had rejected him, dismissed him, but there was no opportunity for bettering himself in his drab town, yet another victim of the mines and dam. He thought about it and finally decided to move to Shantur, the district capital, and become a police officer.

Veera fell short in education and ideals, but he was street smart and devious and rose to become an inspector within a few years. There was almost nothing to police in Shantur. The worst crimes were minor transgressions in broad daylight: a beggar running away with food from street vendors, cattle trespassing, grazing on someone's front lawn, or a customer paying less than the marked price for an article without the seller noticing. Grocers often contaminated their goods: pebbles in rice, watered down milk, or hydrogenated oil sold as ghee—but it was never brought to the attention of the authorities because it was not a large town, everyone knew everyone else, and no one wanted to be labeled a troublemaker. Traffic rules were constantly broken but went unpenalized, accepted as minor inconveniences and not worth making a fuss about.

Government officials were underpaid and expected to take bribes, but Veera discovered to his dismay, that there was no one to bribe and no money to be made. His heart was set on a small house in the outskirts of Shantur, a new development where the houses looked alike, and a new car. There was no way he could get either with his salary, so he turned to alternatives. There was a group of gangsters in a nearby village and Veera enlisted their help. He asked them to harass small businesses in Shantur and collected weekly money—hafta—from them in return for protection from the gangsters. The gangsters got a share of the hafta from Veera. To establish their power, the thugs set upon anyone who failed to pay or was behind on their hafta.

Things went smoothly for Veera for the first few years, until Shantur's new graduates became idealistic and confrontational, threatening to expose him to higher authorities. Fueled by the dissension of the youth of Shantur, people started becoming increasingly intolerant of his corruption. Veera began despairing he would never get his house or his car. Was he so unlucky that he could not even have these basic things after all his hard work?

That was when Veera realized that he needed contacts in high places to continue doing what he was doing. He turned his attention to Santosh who, like him, was devious and corrupt. Santosh's flings with women were well known, but nobody had the guts to talk about it openly. Veera plotted in his mind concluding that he could strike a mutually beneficial deal if only he could meet Santosh in private.

He got his chance when Santosh unveiled a statue of Babasaheb Ambedkar in Shantur. Veera was in charge of protecting the dignitaries and keeping the enthusiastic crowd at bay. He positioned himself by the makeshift stage where the V.I.P.s sat, startling the police who worked under him with his sudden willingness to take on the arduous task of ensuring the safety of the most important people.

Veera made sure to shake hands with Santosh and got invited to his home where he and the politician struck a mutually beneficial pact. The real purpose of the deal was unclear by the words exchanged, and only the two men knew what it meant. Veera would supply Santosh with women in return for shielding him from the idealistic, zealous citizens who wanted to arraign the inspector for his corruption.

Initially, it had been easy to hire women for Santosh because he was appropriately discreet. At some point, Santosh became the object of people's empathy and pity for being a saint, sticking with a wife who had not given him any children. That was when Santosh began asking for better educated, attractive women he could show off in public. He flaunted the women Veera arranged for him, discarding them before they became too comfortable and demanding.

Veera was under great pressure, and it became worse when Santosh finally divorced his wife. Freed from the responsibilities and expectations of marriage which he had never taken seriously to begin with, Santosh demanded a long-term mistress, someone he could be with for a few years—or at least until he tired of the relationship. Veera had almost exhausted his cache of women attracted to the possibility of a better life with Santosh.

Just as Veera was giving up his dream for a house and car because he could not hold his end of the bargain, Santosh decided to marry again. The new wife, an attractive, wealthy city girl, made it clear that there could be no women at the fringes of their marriage even though she almost never graced her husband's bed.

Veera was relieved that he did not have to find women for Santosh. At the same time, he was worried his services would not be needed anymore and that Santosh might decide he did not have to protect Veera. His worry amounted to nothing when Santosh's second wife left him in the middle of his campaign for re-election to the legislative assembly for the fourth time. Santosh won his seat in a landslide victory fueled by a sympathy vote. Shortly after, he married a pipal tree, and renewed his demands. This time, Santosh told Veera, the woman had to be a young, beautiful, well-informed courtesan who appreciated being seen with an influential and accomplished man such as himself. What Santosh implied, but did not say, was that he had no use for the inspector if his needs were not met.

There was not one woman who fit that description in Shantur and Veera grew increasingly despondent. And just like that, an idea slid quietly into his mind. He thought of his town's brothel and the women there who were long-term mistresses of influential men. He was certain he could convince the owner to let go of one of these women for a generous payment. Veera was good at striking such deals and visited his hometown for the first time in fourteen years. This time, he was returning as a man with influence and status and surely no one would refuse him especially after he mentioned who the girl was for.

CHAPTER FOURTEEN

That June mid-morning, the usual weekday silence did not descend on the streets of Nilgi. The children were out of school for the annual Ganesh pooja where the elephant-headed god was called upon to set the school year off to an auspicious start. A clay model of this tender-eyed, potbellied, sweet-loving Hindu deity sat on a wooden platform outside the school, surveying the piles of sweets in front of him he would never eat. The children eyed the mounds of laddus, barfis and dhoklas longingly, waiting for the puja to end so they could have them.

Despite the gloom of the sunny, unending summer, Nilgi was exhilarated—that evening the traveling circus, camping outside the village, would put on a show. The circus performed throughout the district on listless summer evenings when people were desperate for entertainment after spending most of the day indoors to escape the heat. The traveling stopped in early June when the rains came but there were no rains this year and the summer went on and on and on much to the delight of the circus and despair of the farmers.

Samar was sitting at the front of the grocery store on one of the chairs meant for customers and visitors. A box of groceries Usha had asked for sat at his feet while he chatted with the grocer. It was just the way of Nilgi. Business transactions were opportunities for socializing and Samar had initially complained about the inefficiency of the system until Usha pointed out that exactly the same thing happened in their home village. Now, Samar looked forward to visiting the stores in Nilgi even if a task took much longer than it should have.

"What now?" the grocer called seeing Guru walking down the street with Reshma and Bharati. "You were here just a few hours ago."

"Basu wants more rice and onions," Guru replied.

"Is that true?" the grocer asked the girls. "Is he using this as an excuse to get out of work?"

"It is true Basu asked for rice and onions," Bharati replied, giggling. "But it wasn't urgent."

"What are you doing so dressed up?" Samar asked Guru.

"I attended the Ganesh puja in school," Guru said.

"But you don't even like school," Samar said.

"I don't but Raj dhani said I must. He says I might imbibe some knowledge just by being in the vicinity of the school."

"Ah, I see," Samar said. "Is he still teaching you?"

"He goes for tuitions with Raj dhani every day," Bharati said. "He also sits in on some classes and studies in the evenings."

"Really?" Samar said, impressed. "What have you learned so far?"

"Just recognizing alphabets and numbers. Dhani says it is enough if I can read and do some math."

"It isn't such a bad idea to get an education, you know," the grocer said. "I could have done so much more if I had only finished high school."

When people told him knowledge was power, Guru took it with a pinch of salt. The politicians and bureaucrats of today were wealthy and powerful, and most had not even finished high school. Guru did not believe education led to success but let Raj educate him in return for his help in finding Priya. It had seemed an absurd deal in the beginning. What was in it for Raj, Guru had wondered, and given up when he could find no intention besides the fact that Raj considered education very important.

"Come here," the grocer beckoned the girls.

Bharati and Reshma, hovering in the background, came forward knowing they were getting candy. The grocer did that, handing sweets to the children passing by.

Samar watched Reshma's small hand close around the rock candy and something clenched in his heart as it always did when he looked at her. There was something familiar about her that forced him to dig into his terrifying past looking for someone she resembled. He came up with nothing but could not stop wondering where this gorgeous little girl had come from.

"You are not listening to me," Guru's voice broke into Samar's thoughts.

"Sorry," Samar said.

"I want to start my own photo studio. I was explaining my business idea. I want to buy a camera and take pictures," Guru said when he had Samar's attention. "There is no photo studio in Nilgi. Will you give me a loan?"

"Of course, not," Samar said. "That is thousands of rupees and you might not even succeed."

"I will succeed more than the studio in Shantur," Guru said.

"How?" the grocer asked.

"Well, if people are not dressed up for the picture it means they care less and should be charged less. If they are dressed up, it means they care about their picture and I charge double. The photographer in Shantur has a standard rate. He doesn't understand that it is more work photographing someone who *wants* to be photographed."

The girls giggled, the grocer laughed, and Samar looked at Guru in astonishment.

"You may actually pull that off, you monkey!" Samar said. "You may not need an education for your studio but you will need math to do your own accounts, so no one cheats you."

"Reshma will be my accountant. She is good at math and has already agreed."

"But she will get married someday and leave," Samar said. "She may marry a man from another village, or her husband may be wealthy so she doesn't have to work."

"I am not going anywhere," Reshma said in a small voice. "I will marry Guru and live here."

"You can't marry me, silly. I am like your brother."

"Yes, and brothers are there to protect you," the grocer said. "Especially if your husband is mean or unkind, Guru will set him straight. Right Guru?"

"I will never marry. I will never go anywhere. My mother told me to never marry. She said most men were unkind and not to be trusted."

The leaves rustled in the silence that followed. They all turned to Reshma, the girl from nowhere who had revealed nothing of her past until now. Her hands flew to cover her quivering mouth, her eyes filled with fear.

"Your mother?" Samar asked gently.

Reshma remained rooted to her spot, her face crumbling as tears rolled down her cheeks.

"Come here, darling," Samar said picking her up. "Where is your mother? Will you tell me?"

152

"No," she screamed, raining blows on Samar. People crowded around and Samar carried her to his house to avoid a public scene. It took the combined efforts of Guru, Bharati, Usha, Samar and the grocer to calm her and force her to lie down on the sofa. A few minutes later she turned to look at everyone. The turmoil in her eyes was replaced by calm, deeper and more unnerving than before, like the quiet before a big storm when even the earth stops moving and unheard sounds become suspended in ether. Except, the people gathered in the living room of Samar and Usha's house did not know this was the calm or that a devastating storm would follow.

At that moment, the sun came out from behind a cloud, a single ray entering through the slats of the closed window shutters, falling directly on Reshma's face. Samar, with his back to the window, saw the light fall on a tiny, tear-stained face and he looked at it carefully for the first time, feature by feature. He saw the red, puffy nose, the swollen eyes, the high cheekbones. He saw these features individually and as part of a familiar face. In that moment, he knew who Reshma reminded him of, who her father was. The air left his lungs and he sat down heavily on a chair. Questions crowded his mind like demons. Why? Who? How? Should he even try finding the answers? And even if he did, would it be worth knowing the truth?

"Hey Shiva," he said to himself like a dying man. "Hey Shiva."

THE CIRCUS BROUGHT a new energy to the languid village, and people gathered in the maidan behind the vada late that afternoon. They were dressed in their best, clothes they wore to weddings. Bright colored nylons, silks, and cottons with sequins, elaborate embroidery, tassels and gold zari work that reflected the sun's rays, creating an intricate, kaleidoscopic pattern that baffled the eye.

Sweat from the heat and the unbreathable fabric of clothes ran down in salty rivulets and disappeared into the dry, parched earth. There were no puddles.

People sat, squatted, and stood at the periphery of the square maidan. They jostled for the best spots, cursed their errant gods and yielded to no one. At times like this it was to each his own. Friendships and loyalties were put on hold until the show ended.

Veera was at the back of the crowd, dressed in civilian clothes and dark glasses. Not many people in Nilgi knew him and, for once, he was happy to blend unobtrusively into the crowd. The villagers who knew him paid him no attention; he was even more ineffective without his khaki uniform. He told the few who greeted him that he was there to watch the circus and get the blessings of Shantima, the saint in saffron who went where the circus went and placed herself on the outskirts of the village where the circus was performing. After the show, people thronged to Shantima so she could bless them and keep them on the right path.

Veera gazed up at the vada's back balcony, suspended over the northern edge of the maidan. The Nayaks, their friends, and staff watched from the balcony. He felt a pang of jealousy knowing he would never sit alongside the Nayaks because he was not part of their inner circle and would never be. Unlike the dressed-up crowd, Raj and Daya, Samar and Usha and the vada staff wore simple everyday clothes and sat on blankets spread on the floor, watching through the wrought iron rails of the balcony.

Reshma sat on Samar's lap, Usha next to him and Veera saw Daya reaching over to pat Reshma's head. He felt the familiar fear rising in him but was distracted by the cheer that went up in the crowd as the performers entered the maidan. The ringmaster walked in front, bellowing indistinguishable words into a megaphone.

Despite the commotion, the air was still, motionless, and

the brown dust rose in a haze through which acrobats, jugglers, magicians, talking parrots, and performing monkeys, moved in dream-like images. An old man pointed to a dancing bear and was told it was not possible because the government had outlawed using bears for entertainment. The old man shrugged and continued watching the bear, dancing with its forelegs up. It did not matter if it was a dream, a hallucination, or a mirage.

Samar watched the woman in an ankle-length sari tightrope-walking, holding a long pole horizontally in front of her chest. There was a tense silence as people prayed she would not fall. When she reached the end of the tightrope there was a cheer so loud that it shook the ground and made steel vessels on kitchen shelves rattle.

Samar registered none of what was happening. He was preoccupied with Reshma, who had not spoken since the breakdown that morning. Usha, next to him, was quiet and he knew she was holding back tears. They had been so sure they could adopt Reshma, certain she was an orphan—only to discover she was not. Word spread fast in Nilgi and now everyone knew Reshma had a mother.

As if that was not complicated enough, Samar and Usha knew who the father was. They did not know what to do—what the right thing was. If Samar revealed Reshma's paternity, there would be a huge scandal with no guarantee that her life would improve. If Samar said nothing, he and Usha could adopt Reshma, and her life would certainly be better. Still, was it right to withhold such significant information, driven by a selfish desire?

Samar and Usha left before the last act where bare-chested men walked barefoot through a pit of blazing coal, showing no pain, emerging on the other side with not a blister on their soles. They left Reshma with Guru who had been hovering worriedly around her all day. Usha wanted to see Shantima to ask her about the future, and what to do about Reshma. Samar had a deep derision for gods and saints, religions and prophecies, but had agreed to go with Usha because she was distraught. Deep down, he hoped the depraved saint could actually read the future and reassure them that Reshma would be their child.

Shantima sat under a banyan tree outside the Hanuman temple surrounded by roots creeping downward. In her saffron robes, she looked like a flycatcher held hostage in a rusty iron cage. On either side was a devotee, young men who had renounced everything so they could serve her selflessly. Shantima's intentions were benevolent. She wanted to awaken the innate goodness in people through magical powders, prayers, fasts, and sacrifices. She explained futures with an ambiguity so they could be interpreted in different ways and made her devotees even more confident in her abilities. Shantima wanted nothing in return and did not even touch the money and gifts people brought her. Her two assistants gathered everything into cardboard boxes and put them in the trunk of Shantima's car. No one asked what happened with the collections. To doubt Shantima would release the wrath of the gods.

Usha brought her head down to touch Shantima's feet and discreetly placed an envelope by her side, saying, "You don't accept gifts, but this comes from my heart. It isn't much, just three thousand rupees, but we hope it will help you in your good work."

Samar cringed at Usha's obsequiousness and realized she had mastered it after spending so many years begging the gods for a child. Three thousand rupees was a generous amount, a third of his monthly salary, with which you could buy a favorable prediction of the future. Samar felt Usha's exasperation and folded his hands in a namaskar. They would have to kill him before he bent down like Usha.

"We are childless," Usha said. "We have been trying for years and been to doctors, prayed, fasted, made sacrifices, but nothing has worked."

"I can understand your pain, my child," she said. "I can see it in your face. Go on, tell me everything. I am your Shantima."

"There is a little girl who came to Nilgi a few months ago. We thought she was a beggar and sent her to stay in the vada. She has never mentioned a parent and we assumed she was an orphan. My husband and I have grown very fond of her and would like to adopt her."

"But there is a problem," Shantima concluded. "I can see it."

"Yes, there is a problem. Today, we discovered that Reshma, the girl, has a mother. We don't know if her mother is alive or dead because Reshma refuses to talk about it after the outburst. We don't know what to do. Should we try coaxing more information out of Reshma and look for her mother? Or should we let it be because it seems she doesn't want to be reminded of her past?"

Shantima looked down, a frown on her brow. She stayed there for several minutes and when she gazed up, the frown had left her face and there was a clarity in her eyes.

"I can't tell you what the right path is because that is your decision to make. Our destiny is predetermined and there are several paths to it. If you are fortunate your path will be happy and joyous. If you are unfortunate, it will be strewn with problems and disappointments."

Samar barely hid his disdain for such vague prophecies that determined nothing and only added to the confusion and distress he and Usha were feeling.

"I understand, but which way we decide to go is also determined by what we want," Usha pressed. "If we don't look for Reshma's mother, we can go ahead and adopt her. If we do go looking and find her mother, she will never become our daughter."

"That, too, will be revealed to you when the time comes. I am seeing some things in your future, but the picture is still nebulous as this new development happened today, just a few hours ago."

"Can you at least tell us if there is a chance that Reshma will be ours?" Usha begged.

"Don't force the future to come now, my child," Shantima said, placing a hand on Usha's bent head. "But I do see a girl in your future and also that Reshma will end up with loving parents."

"Thank you," Usha said. "We only ask that you don't mention our intentions to adopt Reshma. The whole village knows she may have a mother but not that we want her to be our daughter."

Shantima nodded, looking past at the line forming behind Samar and Usha.

Samar and Usha walked home in silence realizing they were where they had started though Usha would never admit it and Samar would never mention it out of love for her. He sighed, regretting the three thousand rupees they had just burned at Shantima's feet. He thought of all the toys and clothes he could have smothered Reshma in with that money and then caught himself, with a knife piercing his heart, because he may never be able to spoil her as his daughter.

Veera, too, went to the Hanuman temple to meet Shantima after the circus was over. He brought generous gifts to all the saints and astrologers he visited so they could confirm his worth and status in society. Today, though, he needed to hear that his past would not rise up to destroy his future. He did not know how to do that without going into specifics, but he had to try. He stood in line to see Shantima, grateful there were several dozen people in front of him. It gave him time to think. What should he say? Engrossed in his cesspool of gloom, he did not pay attention to the two women standing in front of him until they mentioned Reshma's name.

"Imagine, we assumed she was an orphan," one woman was

saying. "And all this time she never corrected us."

"Something in her past must be terrifying," the other woman replied. "She has not spoken of her mother since this morning and Basu told my husband that everyone in the vada has tried getting more information out of her and failed."

"Sorry, ladies, I couldn't help overhearing what you were saying," Veera said. "Were you speaking of that girl who works in the vada?"

"Yes, yes, we are talking about Reshma," the first woman said. "We all thought she was an orphan but found out, today, that she may have a mother. She said something this morning."

The ground beneath Veera's feet gave way and he felt like he was falling through an abyss. This was much worse than he had thought. He was sitting on a ticking bomb and had to act fast.

CHAPTER FIFTEEN

That first year after Raj was born was etched in Sharada's memory as if it had happened just a few weeks ago. By mid-April, spring's coolness was a distant memory and Raj, four months old, began to smile. The days lengthened; the sun infused everything alive with a lethargic surliness. For the first time in her life Sharada had a purpose—taking care of Raj—and she felt none of the discomfort from the heat.

Back then, before the mines and floods devastated the district, even the brutal summers were magical. People rose when it was still dark outside to get their work done before it became unbearably hot. They stayed indoors or under the shade of trees as the afternoon sun beat upon the little village by the Krishna. In the heat, the dirt road connecting Nilgi to Shantur became a shimmering river, winding its way around hazy trees and curious rocks. Sometimes, a lone traveler, usually a salesman or vendor, was seen walking down the road. The people of Nilgi shook their heads at such foolishness, offered the traveler buttermilk spiced with garlic, cumin and salt and warned him of heatstroke.

Summer's soul was the mango, and it was only the obsession with its progression from flower to fruit that made the heat bearable. Within weeks, white sprays of flowers turned to green fruit, causing branches to bend with the weight. Women ground the raw fruit into a spicy chutney with green chiles and coriander; children ate it with salt until their teeth hurt from the sourness. Farmers argued good-naturedly about the superiority of the mangos from their trees.

FIFTY YEARS LATER, the summers had lost their magic. They were no longer verdant, seething with life. They did not come on time and did not leave on time. It was June, the beginning of monsoon, but there was not a single grey cloud in the sky. Progress had brought cars, tractors, motorcycles and scooters which bumped along the pot-holed tar road. The tar melted into a black, viscous liquid burning the bare soles of walkers who could not afford shoes.

From above, the district was a moonscape of bare hills, derelict villages, patches of struggling fields, clumps of hardy trees. Most farmers had fled, and their fields lay fallow, the topsoil taken first by the mines and then intermittent floods during heavy monsoons, made worse when the dam wall was raised. The fruit orchards, too, were gone and the few remaining trees bore mangos, pomegranates and guava only sometimes. There were hardly any children on the streets and nothing to look forward to except the hope that, somehow, fortunes would turn, and things would go back to being what they once were, before the mines. The sad thing was that an entire generation had been raised in these ruins and knew nothing of the magic and charm of the past.

Nilgi was the only proof that a far better past had existed. The fields and forests around it were untouched, the orchards prolific. The bells in the Hanuman temple rang all day, every day, as devotees paid their respects to the monkey god. Children still ran through the fields and the adults had so far dismissed that their village would drown in the dam.

Until now.

Ever since the government had declared its intention of raising the dam wall to its originally-planned height, Nilgi had started feeling vulnerable. All these years, it had been an empathetic watcher of the disaster caused by the mines and the erratic floods. On occasion it had even participated in the mild protests against the mines and floods, but things were different now.

Sharada tossed and turned on her thin floor mattress in the kitchen. It was a brutally hot, still, June night. Not even a leaf moved. Nilgi was quiet, lethargic, and tired but unable to sleep comfortably. Sharada dozed off for a few minutes, then woke up drenched in sweat. She splashed herself with water from an earthen pot she kept by her head. The cool water made the heat bearable, but only for a few minutes.

Beside her, Reshma was sound asleep, breathing evenly. Sharada adjusted the thin blanket Reshma had kicked off. It was hot, but the child could still catch a cold. Reshma stirred in her sleep, turning her back to Sharada and her top rode up, exposing her back. Even in the dark, Sharada could make out the white birthmark on Reshma's back. Its location, its size, its shape worried her. She was now quite sure who the father was. Reshma's resemblance to him was obvious if you cared to look for it—and Sharada cared to look for it. She did not know who to discuss it with. It was such a delicate matter and what if she was wrong? She hoped she was wrong.

SHARADA AMBLED DOWN the street in the silence of dusk. She walked carefully, hunched over her walking stick. Looking at Sharada from behind, it seemed she did not have a head. Over the years, her back had bent to such a precarious angle that if it were not for her walking stick, she would have definitely toppled over. Still, she swatted away help from well-meaning passersby muttering she was capable, even now, of making a hundred rotis a day. Her rotis were her pride and joy; after all she had made them every single day for fifty years.

This evening, she had stuffed a dozen rotis in the folds of her sari for Samar and Usha. They loved her rotis and it was important to bring them something because she was dropping by unannounced to entrust them with the secret she no longer wished to be the sole keeper of. Sharada was unsure if Samar and Usha would *want* to know, but she needed the help of people smarter than her— assuming they believed her. Once again Sharada wondered if she was going senile. But, no, she was not because before leaving the vada she had insisted Reshma take a bath and scrubbed her back to confirm, once again, the presence of a white birthmark the size of a thumbprint, its edges uneven and exactly like the one on the back of a man Sharada had known as a little boy.

Sharada wished she did not know what she knew because she was not someone who liked to gossip, relay bad news, or find pleasure in the misfortunes of others. She hesitated for a second, then raised her hand and knocked on Samar and Usha's door.

"Namaskar Sharada maami," Usha said. "Come in, come in."

"I hope I am not intruding," Sharada said, glancing at the two places set at the dinner table.

"Of course, not. We are getting ready to eat dinner. Please join us."

"Are you sure?" Sharada asked. Normally she would have accepted the invitation without hesitation but, today, she was looking for an excuse to leave so she did not have to disclose her secret.

"Yes, I am sure. I have made brinjal curry."

"I have brought you some rotis," Sharada said, removing them from the folds of her sari.

"Samar, dinner is ready," Usha called. "Sharada maami has brought us rotis."

Sharada flinched. She did not understand how these modern women shamelessly said—shouted—their husband's names. Her husband was long dead but Sharada did not say his name out loud. In fact, she did not even say it quietly. To her he was always avaaru, the formal, more respectful, version of "he."

"Your rotis melt in the mouth like butter," Samar said. "How are things at the vada?"

"Fine," Sharada answered, mixing a small ball of rice with dal and kneading it so she could swallow it without chewing. She had resisted dentures for years.

"How is Reshma?" Samar pressed. "We haven't seen her since the circus."

"She has been mostly home, more withdrawn than before, complaining of a stomachache, but I know she is avoiding everyone after her outburst."

"I guessed that," Samar said. "I wish she would tell us more about her mother, at least if she is alive or dead."

"Had she said anything to you?" Sharada asked.

Usha shook her head.

"I feel Reshma puts up all these walls because she wants to forget something in her past, something that may have been traumatic," Sharada said. "Her silence is unnatural for a child her age."

"Her mother is probably dead," Samar reasoned. "Otherwise, she would not be here."

"What if she came here looking for someone?"

"What do you mean?" Samar sat up straight, staring at the hunched woman in front of him.

"Well, I don't know exactly," Sharada said, her courage deserting her. "I am just an illiterate old woman, but I do wonder why Reshma chose to come to Nilgi of all places. Did something bring her here? A relative?"

Samar gazed at Sharada without blinking. He stopped eating, and washed his hands in his plate signaling he was done.

"Is there something else, maami?" he finally asked. "We want to adopt Reshma and if there is a chance of that not happening because there is a relative on the scene, we would like to know. That is only fair."

Sharada's uncertainty collided with Samar's persistence. It hung over the vinyl dining table for a moment before collapsing like a deflated balloon.

"There's a birthmark on Reshma's back," Sharada finally said.

"Yes, there is," Usha confirmed.

"Well, I am not sure it is a birthmark," Sharada hedged.

"It is a birthmark," Samar asserted. "What about it, maami?"

"Don't rush her," Usha scolded. "She is trying to tell us something that is hard for her. Right, Sharada maami?"

Samar threw Usha an impatient glance and remained silent.

"I know someone who has the exact same birthmark as Reshma," Sharada said,

There, the words were out.

The silence thickened. Fear, confusion, questions settled like a rock sinking to the bottom of a pond.

"Who?" Samar asked after a few minutes.

"I don't know if I should say more," Sharada said, nervous. "I knew him as a boy and may be remembering things wrong."

"Who?" Usha persisted. "If someone else has the exact same

birthmark as Reshma, they must be related."

"I can't say the name out loud," Sharada said, twisting the end of her sari with her fingers. "When you say things, they come true even if they are not."

"Can you write the name?" Samar asked, hiding his exasperation. "You can write a little?"

Sharada nodded and Usha brought her a paper and a ballpoint pen.

The toothless roti-maker hunched lower, peered at the paper and wrote each latter painstakingly in the dim light. Samar and Usha stood up and looked over her shoulders like children.

"Are you sure?" Samar asked when Sharada finished writing. Then, tapping the two words Sharada had written, he added. "If that is Reshma's father, it is a huge scandal."

"He may be a relative, not her father," Sharada said.

"He is the father," Samar said. "Reshma has always reminded me of someone but I couldn't think who until that day when she became hysterical. The walls she has built around herself crumbled and I knew exactly who her father was. I just didn't want to believe it."

"You already knew?" Sharada asked. "Have you told anyone?"

"No," Samar replied.

"He could be a relative," Sharada tried again.

"No, maami, he is the father," Usha said, forcing the words past the lump in her throat, her dream of becoming Reshma's mother slipping away.

"If our secret comes out there will be a huge scandal," Samar said again.

"I know," Sharada replied, defeat in her voice. "That is why I waited for months before coming to you. I noticed the birthmark on the day Reshma came here."

"The question is, where should we go from here?" Samar asked.

"We may never be able to adopt her," Usha burst into tears. "She is *our* child. We have already decided that, Samar."

"I am sorry I have made matters worse," Sharada said, wiping her own tears with the end of her sari, feeling sorry for Usha and Samar, devastated for Reshma's father. "I should have carried the secret to my grave."

"Sharada maami, you have not done anything wrong," Samar consoled, placing a hand on her shoulder. "You only confirmed what we already knew. We have been racking our brains trying to decide what to do. It might be best to not be hasty and think this through."

Samar tore the paper Sharada had written on into two, then four and lit a match to it.

Usha and Sharada nodded. They all knew they were buying time so they could find a way to refute the obvious truth—burn it like the piece of paper on which it was written.

IT WAS THE end of June and the rains should have come four weeks ago, but the sun was becoming stronger, bolder, establishing its dominance as summer went on and on and on. It was perhaps the longest, hottest summer in living memory. Surya, the sun god, shone in all his godliness, sucking the moisture from grass, water from rivers and streams, vigor from people and animals. Trees drooped, sunflowers refused to turn their heads towards the sun and the Krishna was reduced to a trickle. Summer lethargy stayed on, stealthy and gleeful.

The falling water level of the vada's well worried Sharada.

"I have never seen so little water in our well," she said to Raj and Daya. "The well drying is bad luck."

"Oh, you must not believe in these superstitions," Raj said, quelling his own rising anxiety. "It is a harsher summer than usual, but it also means more rain when the monsoons arrive."

Raj was right on both counts. There had never been a hotter summer or a more ravaging monsoon than the one that followed.

Power cuts, now, were scheduled for the hottest hours of the day when fans and air coolers were most needed. The village streets were deserted after lunch. The adults stayed inside and tired children sat in schoolrooms barely registering their lessons and, for once, the teachers did not care because even they found it hard to remain coherent in the brutal heat. On the streets stray dogs fought for the deepest shade. Cattle grazing in the hills gathered under the sparse shade of acacia and kikar bushes. The trees smiled their tired smiles at the scorching earth below.

Raj was in his office waiting for Guru, his diligent, trusting student to arrive for his tuitions. He did not know how much longer he could assure Guru that Priya could be found. He had visited the slum, spoken to Mamta weeks ago—that trail had dried and he felt helpless but could not bear to tell Guru, see the disappointment on the boy's face. If he told Guru, it would make Priya's disappearance permanent and Raj was not ready for that.

After every lesson Guru asked, "Any more news, dhani?"

"No, not yet" Raj always replied. "But we must be patient. Just focus on your studies."

The one good thing that will come from all this is that I will have turned an illiterate into a literate, Raj consoled himself. *At least I will have taught Guru to read and write.*

The sound of rustling papers as Raj went through his mail in the school office was magnified by the after-school silence. The sun had set but the heat stayed on, only slightly more bearable. A fan blew the hot air around and every few minutes Raj dipped a muslin cloth in a bucket of water by his desk, wrung it out, and placed it on his head. The heat sucked the water out of the muslin in minutes, cooling Raj—somewhat.

The phone rang, breaking Raj's concentration, and he picked up the receiver with an abrupt, "Raj Nayak here."

"Namaskar, namaskar," a woman's voice trilled.

"Yes, who is this?"

"Why, sir, don't you remember my voice? This is Mamta, Sarla's niece."

Raj stopped breathing for a moment. He gripped the receiver.

"Mamta, of course. I was hoping you would call."

"I have some information for you," Mamta shouted. "Can you hear me?"

"Yes, yes, very clearly."

"I was lying in bed trying to sleep the other night and all kinds of thoughts came to me. You know how you think about things in the middle of the night? It happens to me a lot since my husband's death."

"I know exactly what you mean," Raj said, controlling his impatience.

"I started thinking about my aunt Sarla. She was so delirious in the last few weeks of her life. Poor soul, she never hurt anyone. She took care of all the girls."

Raj closed his eyes and counted to ten.

"In her delirium she kept talking about her daughter, Ritu. She talked about Ritu's daughter, her granddaughter. She smiled when she spoke about teaching Ritu to bathe her baby, feed her, care for her. She said those were the happiest days of her life. I thought my aunt was hallucinating. Ritu committed suicide years ago, she never married or had children. Her death broke my aunt, poor soul, and she was never the same again."

Raj leaned back in his chair, counted to ten again.

"But that night, when I couldn't sleep, it occurred to me that my aunt wasn't talking about Ritu. She was talking about Priya and confusing the two."

Raj sat up straight, alert.

"Why do you think she had her confused with Priya?"

"Because I knew my aunt was very attached to one of the girls who worked for her. The other girls were jealous and made snide remarks about Sarla's "daughter" who had to quit working because she was with child. You said the girl you are looking for, Priya, left Rati Mandir when she became pregnant. It all adds up."

"What else did your aunt say?" Raj asked, his knuckles white from gripping the receiver.

"First, I want to make sure I get the four thousand rupees you promised me for information even if it doesn't lead you to the girl."

"I promise I will send you the check first thing tomorrow," Raj's hands were clammy.

A small pause and then, "I wanted the money first, but you seem reliable so I will take a chance. My aunt, bless her soul, repeatedly mentioned a town Ritu moved to, to have the baby."

"What was the name of the town?" Raj asked. "Do you remember?"

"She wasn't clear, but she said it was four kilometers from a bigger town, a district place called Shanti or something like that."

"Was it Shantur?" Raj asked, his mind processing the information faster than he could say the words.

"I am not sure. Is there a big Ganesh temple there? My aunt said she took the bus from this small town where Ritu lived to the district capital to worship at the Ganesh temple."

Raj's head grew light, his body heavy. He felt his head detaching from the rest of him and floating away like an over-ripe cotton pod.

"Sir, are you there?"

"Yes. I think the town is Shantur. Did your aunt say why Priya—no, Ritu—went there?"

"To work in a brothel that took pregnant women," Mamta said.

"So Priya worked in a brothel in a town four kilometers from

Shantur? Are you sure?"

"No, I am not sure," Mamta said impatiently. "My aunt was delirious and dying and kept telling the same story again and again. I am only guessing she meant Priya because her daughter had never married or had children."

"I understand," Raj said. "Did she say why this particular town?"

"So here is the interesting part. She went there to be close to her daughter's father who lived in a village nearby. Now, don't ask me the name of the village because I don't remember."

RAJ WAITED FOR a day to gather his thoughts before heading to the town where Priya might be. It was the only town near Shantur large enough to have a brothel, and if Mamta was right, Priya worked there while raising *their* daughter. Why had it not occurred to him that Priya's child was his? All those years ago when he had gone looking for her the woman at Rati Mandir had told him Priya had insisted on keeping her baby because she loved the man who had fathered it.

It all made sense. When Priya was forced to leave Rati Mandir, she had come to a town close to Nilgi knowing that he, the father of the baby, lived there.

Still, Priya had never contacted him. *Why not?* Raj wondered. *Because she did not want to ruin your life,* a voice answered. Somewhere deep in her heart, Priya was content that he, Raj, was close.

Raj drove to the town where Priya was, parked his car on a side road and walked to the brothel. It was late in the evening and people were indoors, getting ready to eat and go to bed. There was a power outage and Raj was glad. He was dressed in inexpensive clothes and hoped no one recognized him.

He wondered how he could think so clearly despite the chaos in his mind—he was still not sure if it was a good idea to see Priya, but he had never succumbed to reason when it came to her. He still loved her and believed she did, too, but doubts assailed him. What if she had stopped caring for him? Worse, she may have started despising him for saddling her with a child after the novelty of love wore away.

He could not get his head around the fact that he, a respectable landlord, had fathered a child with a prostitute more than two decades younger than him.

Nothing odd about that, Raj thought.

It reeked of scandal.

Raj was not sure if he wanted his secret revealed but he had to see Priya and their child. He did not know what the future held, but it would not be strewn with jasmine petals. If it all came out, Daya would be devastated, his adolescent sons would never forgive him. He did not want to lose any of them and should have felt shame and remorse but despite digging deep he felt none. He still loved Priya. He still loved Daya. He had always believed there was only one true love but when Priya had thrown back her veil and their eyes had met, Raj had known it was not true. He had realized it was possible to love two women and the thought had shaken him, forced him to leave the safety of his predictable morals and beliefs. Oddly, over the years the idea that he could love two women had strengthened him and he was counting on that strength to help him decide what he should do.

The brothel was a garish green glowing neon in the dark and he stepped in through the open door. Inside, it smelled of incense and Dettol and Raj waited in the unmanned front room with its tattered sofa and two oil lanterns. The walls were bare, peeling, and he was glad he could not see the dirt and stains.

The woman I love is working in this hovel and my daughter is being raised here, he thought squeezing his eyes shut so the tears would not run down his cheeks.

He wondered if he should call out when a man appeared chewing paan. He raised a short, fat arm in greeting, walked past Raj to the door, leaned out and spat the red paan juice. onto the street.

"What kind of girl do you want?" he asked, his voice thick, his lower lip pulled up to prevent the paan juice dribbling down his chin. "We have all kinds."

"I am not here for that," Raj said. "I am looking for a woman named Priya and her daughter. I was told they live here."

"Priya? No one by that name works here. Definitely no one with a child."

"Are you sure? The child is about nine."

"Oh, are you asking about Champa? She had a daughter."

"*Had?*' Raj's throat constricted.

"Yes, had," the man confirmed looking at Raj with interest for the first time.

"Where are they? Did they leave?"

"No, no. Champa was murdered last year. She died of a head injury. Someone threw her against the sharp corner of her bed. The police began a half-hearted investigation that they soon dropped because Champa was of no consequence or importance. Are you not from this area? Everyone knows about this murder. I am lucky I still managed to keep my business after all that bad press. I used all my savings to bribe the police."

Raj had read about the murder but not connected it to this particular brothel. Another dead end, he thought. Priya was not here.

Then it hit him like a thunderbolt. Was it possible?

"Can you identify Champa if I show you her picture?" he asked. "Her family is from my village and very poor. She ran away from

173

home many years ago and we discovered she might be working here."

"I don't force girls to work here," the man said, his voice belligerent.

"I am not saying that" Raj replied. "I just want to find out if you have seen this girl. I am doing this..."

"Yes, yes, I heard you. Sure, show me the picture. Champa was beautiful. I will never forget her face."

Raj pulled the picture out of his pocket and held it under the dim light of one of the lanterns.

"This picture was taken when she was a schoolgirl, before she ran away from home."

The man ambled over, took the picture and gazed at it closely. He frowned, then tapped the spot where Priya stood with her schoolgirl braids and uniform.

"That is her."

Raj looked at where the man was pointing. It was Priya. Priya was Champa. Champa was Priya, the murdered prostitute. His world reeled, shattered. It fell apart and stopped existing.

"And the child?" Raj heard a distant voice asking. It was him but it was not really him.

"She ran away the day after her mother was killed. Listen, I have told you everything I know. I am already in trouble with the authorities after the murder and don't want some friend of Champa's showing up, causing more trouble."

"I promise no one will make trouble," Raj said, impulsively opening his wallet and handing the man two crisp five-hundred-rupee notes. "It will be closure for Champa's family knowing she is dead. But what about the child? Any idea where she might be? What was her name?"

"We never looked for her. The authorities said they would but never did. There was nothing for them in this investigation."

"What was the child's name?" Raj repeated.

"Oh, Champa called her Reshma."

"Reshma?" Raj was not sure he could take much more.

"Yes, Reshma. The child was beautiful. She would have been a great addition here. What a pity she ran away."

CHAPTER SIXTEEN

Behind the Hanuman temple, the Krishna river, which should have been overflowing its banks by now, gurgled like a stream over a rocky bottom. Raj sat on the sandy shore in the shade of a rocky outcrop, watching the endless flow of water. *How is it possible?* he wondered. *To keep going hour after hour, day after day, year after year. When can you say you are tired and disappear into the ocean forever?*

"The Krishna river is anya, inexhaustible," Raj's mother used to tell him when he was a child. "It is immortal, it will be here long after we are gone."

He had been sitting there all day, under the outcrop that hid him from the world, hid the world from him. Raj came to this spot to think, sometimes to not think. Things became clearer, easier when he was here. Sometimes he stayed for a few hours, other times for an entire day. In the background, he heard the temple bells ring when someone came to pray. It was a soothing sound from his childhood and had always calmed him, until now.

This last week, since discovering that Reshma was his daughter, Raj had spent almost every day under the outcrop. Daya had become worried, and he had fielded her questions, saying he was growing increasingly concerned the anti-dam movement was losing its passion and fury. The government had failed to release its compensation plan and showed no signs it would. After the riots in Shantur, people had become enraged but also wary of public protest, fearful they might be arrested without reason. The drought added to the weary acceptance of injustice.

Santosh, after winning a fourth term in the legislative assembly, had become even more brazen. Under him, the government had become more complacent than before, dragging its feet because the monsoons had not come and when they did it would be a short season with negligible chances of flooding. It gave officials another year to find the funds to pay people in the 86 villages.

In some ways, it was a blessing there were no rains, but the district was facing devastation of a different kind—drought. Water and food shortage, increasing poverty, civic unrest and a heightened distrust of the government, disease and death. It did not matter if it was too much rain or too little, the outcome would be similar. The situation was uncontrollable but what was happening to Raj, what could happen to his family, was worse than death.

He had behaved dishonorably. He was ridden with guilt. If he had not made Priya pregnant she would have carried on working in Rati Mandir, a safe and clean place. She would not have been forced to move to a shabby brothel that allowed women with children—and she would not have been murdered. He was wholly responsible for Priya's death, Reshma's birth and, for making his daughter motherless.

By now, stormy monsoon waters should have turned the Krishna brown and muddy. By now, fields and forests should have become a lush, wet green. By now, the birds on the useless electric wires should have been soaked and shimmering. By now, the monsoon damp should have seeped into everything.

By now.

Instead, Nilgi was a bristling, brown patch of earth on which the sun shone triumphantly. There was not a grey cloud; the defeated soil cracked, fell apart without inhibition.

The crops in the fields wilted, the cattle grew thin and the little milk they produced tasted of the bitter parthenium weeds they were grazing on. The grass was brown, dead, long gone. Shrinking puddles dotted the bed of the Krishna, islands of water that birds swooped down to drink from.

The scum of birdlife congregated in Nilgi. Crows gathered around rotting piles of garbage. Vultures circled the clear blue sky waiting for the scorching heat to suck the life out of yet another animal and, when it happened, swooped down and feasted. The happy, twittering sparrows were gone.

The water in the vada's well was gone, not even a puddle remained. The sandy soil at the bottom, never directly exposed to the sunlight, now flirted with the Surya, the sun god, not realizing it was a self-destructive, dangerous liaison. People came to the well every day to gaze anxiously at the exposed bottom. Perhaps the village superstition was true, that the drying of the well signaled doom. No one had ever elaborated on the nature of the doom, but few doubted it. People now understood the basis of the superstition. Only a severe drought could drain the well.

The drought became the only subject of conversation, the theme of nightmares in Nilgi. People measured the growing cracks in the ground with their eyes; farmers added up their losses from failed crops.

People accepted the drought and it thrived. It reveled in the awe and fear it inspired. Clear blue skies, somber thoughts, dead fields, and a dried river marked its success. It stayed because it was unwelcome.

Solar-powered fans whirred in the vada doing nothing except blowing the hot air around, yet the sound was comforting. The heat had numbed the senses and the body felt cooler just listening to the blades going round and round. Anxiety made the heat claustrophobic.

RAJ NOTICED NONE of this. His claustrophobia came from a different, deeper, darker place. It was his self-created hell, one he was completely responsible for. Bad news never came by itself, shamefaced. It came in twos and threes, skipping delightedly. One brief conversation with a fat, paan-chewing man and Raj's life had been turned upside down. Now, his life was a series of "what ifs."

What if he had not been mesmerized by the kohl-lined eyes of a dancing girl?

What if he had not returned to find out if the promises in those eyes were real?

What if he had not fallen in love, returning again and again to explore the promises in those eyes?

What if he had not walked away when she had asked him to leave?

The list of Raj's transgressions was too long and terrible.

Raj realized that he had not looked hard enough for Priya because, deep down, he did not want to find her. He turned the damning facts he now possessed over and over in his exhausted, guilt-ridden mind. He wondered if Reshma had found her way to Nilgi after Priya's death because she knew her father lived there. Had Priya told Reshma about him?

These days, when Raj ran into Reshma he stopped to talk to her. He looked at her features for traces of Priya and him and found them. She had Priya's eyes and dainty chin, his mouth and skin. He understood, now, why his heart had clenched every time he saw Reshma. He searched her face to see if she knew about him, and realized she dealt with him the way she dealt with all men—with indifference, shyness and a little fear. The only man she seemed comfortable around was Samar, and Raj suppressed an unexpected twinge of jealousy.

Practically speaking, Raj was off the hook. If Reshma had no idea of her paternity, the secret could remain a secret. She was safe in Nilgi, Raj argued with himself, and he could keep an eye on her, make sure she was cared and provided for.

But how, an angry voice challenged. *How can you provide for her without revealing that you are her father?*

After the initial shock and grief of Priya's murder waned, Raj emerged from his self-created hell where he had been cowering. He stepped into the battlefield where rationalization warred with conscience and fear with integrity. Unable to decide what to do and knowing inaction was dishonorable, Raj reached out to the only man in Nilgi he completely trusted and who was likely to understand and forgive him.

ON THIS HOT, dry monsoon morning Raj tried to sit still at his desk in the vada's library, waiting for Samar. He had left strict instructions that he not be disturbed and Daya assumed the meeting had to do with dwindling anti-dam activism that she held responsible for Raj's recent listlessness and lack of appetite. She decided to mention it to Samar so they could find a way of taking some of the burden off Raj without him realizing it.

Raj, unaware of the strained expression on his face or his

shrinking body, gathered his flailing courage, forcing himself not to think about how Samar would react when he revealed his secret. Every action had an equal and opposite reaction and the reaction to his action had already occurred: Priya murdered, Reshma orphaned. It could not get worse.

Raj heard Samar outside, talking to the cowherd tidying the cattle stalls.

"Namaskar," Samar said stepping inside.

"Come sit down, Samar," Raj said. "Close the door."

Samar had not seen much of Raj since the day of the circus when he had realized that Raj was Reshma's father. He had been avoiding Raj, uncertain of his feelings, whether he still had the same love for Raj after discovering that he had fathered an illegitimate child. Now, Samar breathed a sigh of relief. Nothing had changed, though he now knew even Raj was capable of transgressions, just like anyone else.

"Is something wrong, dhani?" Samar asked, looking at the broken man behind the desk. "You look ill."

"I have to talk to you about something important before I change my mind," Raj said pouring Samar a glass of sherbet. "I did something many years ago and it has come back to haunt me."

Samar's heart sank. He stared at Raj, concerned and confused.

Hey Shiva, Samar thought. *He knows Reshma is his daughter.*

"I had an affair ten years ago and fathered a child," Raj said calmly.

Samar turned to stare at the wall, then forced himself to look back at Raj.

"I met Priya, a courtesan and the mother of my child, in the city and we fell in love. My love for Priya did not diminish my love for Daya and I only felt an occasional pang of remorse. But, now, I know things that not only make me a man who has cheated on his wife, but also a murderer."

"What are you saying, dhani? None of this makes sense."

Outside, the cowherd apologized to the calf about the dried grass. The calf mooed in agreement, accepting the apology.

"Your mother may find some good grass in the hills today," the cowherd continued. "Then you and I will have some thick, creamy milk to drink."

The calf mooed again, rubbed her nose against the cowherd's back, making him laugh.

"We are lucky to be here and not in the heat outside. But, see, there are some grey clouds over the hills. Maybe it will rain."

A breeze blew the few dark clouds away as the cowherd gazed at them hopefully.

More cracks unfurled in the parched ground while Raj talked to a shocked Samar.

The sun sucked the remaining water from the vada's well.

A flock of black crows fought over a mouse carcass in a rubbish heap.

Raj finished his story, listed his mistakes and the war in him raged.

Samar looked at Raj as if he was seeing him for the first time. There was a hint of admiration in his gaze. Raj's story was the stuff of soap operas. Priya, the murdered prostitute. Reshma, the illegitimate child. Guru the brother and uncle. Raj the father, the virtuous landlord.

The play was just beginning to unfold. Samar knew there was more to come.

"Of course, Reshma may not be my daughter. I assumed I was that man Priya loved whose baby she did not want to abort. It could be she loved someone else."

"She is your daughter," Samar said. "There is no doubt about it."

"You *knew*?" Raj asked, stricken.

"Yes."

"How?"

"Dhani, Reshma looks so much like you. She also has a birthmark on her back like yours. That is how Sharada maami knew she was your daughter."

"*Sharada* knows?" Raj repeated.

"She knew the day Reshma arrived here. She told Usha and me recently, but we had already figured it out for ourselves."

Raj squeezed his eyes shut.

"Samar, this is an unforgiveable mistake, and I will have to pay for it in this life and several lives after. But what is done is done and the only thing within my control is that I can make Reshma's life easier, be her father. Guru needs to know, too."

"That will hurt not just you and your family but also Reshma. She will always be the illegitimate child of a prostitute and people won't let her forget it."

"What else is there to do?"

"This may sound selfish, but it may be best that Usha and I adopt Reshma and move from here. Start over somewhere else."

"But surely Guru deserves to know? And surely Reshma should know I am the father."

Samar shrugged.

"I have disappointed you, Samar. You looked up to me and I've let you down."

"Everyone makes mistakes, and I am more sad than disappointed. I am heartbroken that Usha and I may not be able to adopt Reshma, but it is your decision to make.

Raj nodded.

"There is one more thing, dhani. If this gets out, you will lose the trust of the people whose rights you are fighting for. The dam protest is already losing its momentum and you won't be able to lead it effectively. The government will get away with drowning the lives of hundreds of thousands of people without paying a single rupee in compensation."

Usha was livid. She wept when Samar told her what he and Raj had discussed. Unlike Samar, she was unable to forgive Raj. She held him responsible for everything, especially that she may not be able to adopt Reshma.

"He was selfish and continues to be," she cried. "His desire to disclose his deceit is also about him. He wants to do it so he can feel good that he has done the right thing. How can you forgive him? He will disrupt more lives and get away with it because he is the landlord."

"Usha, you are overreacting. People make mistakes and god knows Raj dhani has been punished enough. An affair should not lead to so much horror. I do believe he loved Reshma's mother."

Raj, that night, met with his other, newer demons. He shook their hands, invited them in. The demons sniggered, swept in, ousting the older ones living in his mind. The new ones were better, ruthless and all-consuming. They led him down a dark tunnel at the end of which there was no light. So, into the darkness he went, towards his own destruction. Towards the destruction of an indestructible village and the obliteration of a way of life which, until now, had withstood the ravages of the outside world. The newer demons told him to publicly declare that Reshma was his daughter and Guru her uncle. They insisted he confess his affair. They did not care how this would affect the future of Reshma or him or the anti-dam movement. They wanted to dominate.

He wondered what Priya had thought of in her last moments. Did she have that desperate, glazed look in her eyes when they had made love and she was on the brink of unraveling, shattering into a million pieces? Had she closed her eyes the way she did when she accepted the inevitable surrender of her body, heart and mind to him? Had she bitten her lower lip silencing her cries, except her last cries were not of pleasure but of terror and pain. Had she thought of Reshma and him? Had she hated him, loved him? Had she forgiven him?

The imagined last look in those kohl-lined eyes haunted Raj. The terror in them terrorized him. He, alone, was responsible for the terror of those last few moments. Sex sent the world into a self-destructive frenzy. Love was the soft sigh of contentment.

THE FOUNDATION OF Daya's life as a Nayak was Raj's unconditional, unwavering love for her. She had basked in it, built her dreams in it, happily sacrificed her occasional pride to keep it sacred. Daya knew, too, that she loved Raj more than he her. It was not that his love was not enough, it was just that hers was bigger than everything—her, him, their marriage. There was no ego in it and, over the years, no expectation either, partly because Raj continued giving her what she needed and partly because her needs became only what he could give her.

Now, for the first time since she had stepped into the vada a new, diffident bride, Daya felt unsure. About a week ago, Raj had gone out one late afternoon without telling her where or why. He did that sometimes, especially if it was a matter that did not concern her or if it was something, he did not want to worry her about. In the past, Raj's secrecy had never bothered her, but that afternoon, her mind was not at ease. There was something in Raj's demeanor that worried Daya and when he returned late that night she saw how he looked and grew alarmed.

"What has happened?" she cried, rushing to him. "Are Jai and Rohan alright?"

"Yes, yes," he said, and she noticed his unfocused gaze as he stared past her at something terrible, hellish.

"Something is wrong. Please tell me."

"Nothing, Daya. Nothing. Go to sleep. I will join you soon."

She barely slept that night and woke up the next morning to find him gone. Sharada told her he had gone to the Hanuman temple. Daya knew Raj went there to clear his mind when he was worried, but grew concerned when he kept returning to the temple day after day.

Raj's continuing reticence, the pain in his eyes, the sudden, uncharacteristic restlessness that caused him to pace all night on the terrace of their bedroom frightened Daya. When she asked, he always gave her the same vague answer that he was anxious about the drought, the dam, and the future—but she knew he was keeping something from her. She had never been a nag and did not want to start now, certain he would only withdraw more.

Sharada tried consoling Daya, reminding her that there were times when Raj had been withdrawn, just like his mother used to be, but that did nothing to ease Daya's mind. She remembered the last time things had been like this, ten years ago, after Raj had visited the city. The tension in their marriage then had vanished in the face of growing unrest because of the dam. People's problems had diminished the problems in their marriage. This time, however, nothing seemed to distract Raj. He was still working for the people, trying to get them the compensation they deserved but his heart was not in it, of that Daya was sure.

He spent most of the day in his study, often skipping meals, and did not come to bed until well past midnight and when he did, he turned his back to her. The distance between them grew and she sensed something terrible was happening, even wondering if Raj was sick with something dangerous, like cancer. He had no appetite and was growing thinner every day.

Unable to figure out the reason, Daya pushed her own worries to the back of her mind and focused on Nilgi and its needs. She told herself, though she was not convinced, that Raj's recent behavior was because of the rising tension between the government and the people. The wellbeing of the village was the responsibility of the Nayaks and though Raj was still trying to help the villagers during the drought, he was not as effective as he should have been. Daya took over that responsibility, helping Raj as much as she could. As he began slowly emerging from whatever private hell he was living in, she realized that he would perhaps never go back to being what he once was.

CHAPTER SEVENTEEN

The heat ignited tempers, quarrels lasted longer, grudges were nursed, and everyone fretted. They came to Raj and the village elders to settle their squabbles, ask for advice and for comfort. There was nothing else to do anyway. No water for the fields, no crops to harvest, and no money to be made. The only thriving business was the arrack shop where the worst men spent their days drinking, adding to their considerable debts.

It was four weeks since Raj had confessed to Samar and he still did not know what to do, what the right thing was so Reshma's life could become easier, better. He forced himself to focus on bigger problems—the anti-dam movement that had ground to a halt because of the drought.

After discussing with Samar, Raj decided to call another meeting of the leaders of the 86 villages to gauge the temperature, where people stood on the matter. Only a couple of dozen leaders showed up and the meeting took place outside the Hanuman temple. Raj realized that people were so exhausted coping with the drought they had no energy for anything else. Plans for the real future, the one that would be determined by the dam, had to be postponed for now.

"Let's revisit the issue when things get better, after the rains start," Raj said. "Meanwhile, I will keep the pressure on by continuing to write to the chief minister and other officials who are sympathetic to our cause. We need to remain on their radar."

The first raindrops hit the earth that droughty evening as Raj made his way home from the Hanuman temple. There had not been a single cloud when the meeting began but now, the sky was black and seething, hanging low over Nilgi like a shroud over a corpse. The village emptied on the streets dancing, weeping, cursing the sun. Prostrate farmers kissed the earth, women wept into the ends of their saris and children became dizzy running in circles, singing the rainsong. Even before Raj reached the vada, the skies opened in merciless fury.

VEERA CROUCHED IN the shadows of a banyan tree outside the Hanuman temple watching Reshma playing with a group of children. The meeting was over, and everyone had left but the children stayed on squealing in delight as it began to drizzle.

"Let's go home," Guru said. "It looks like the beginning of a thunderstorm."

"I want to play in the rain," Reshma said. "Let's get wet."

"I don't want to get wet," Bharati protested. "I hate it."

"I have to light the lamps at the vada," Guru said. "The power is gone. Let's go, Reshma."

"Let me stay," Reshma pleaded. "I promise I will leave before the rain gets heavy. It is hardly a drizzle."

"Okay," Guru relented. "Don't be too long."

Veera fingered his beard. He had been hiding there, behind the temple where he could see everyone and no one could see him, for several evenings. He had almost lost hope of finding Reshma alone, so when he saw the children leaving her, he held his breath, hoping she would not follow them.

Reshma was dancing and Veera could not help but watch her. There was no music but she was keeping rhythm with the rain. She twisted her body towards the sky, she twirled round and round until Veera felt dizzy just watching. She raised her face to the raindrops and closed her eyes, letting them hit her face. As the rain grew heavier, her dancing became quicker and, at one point, she laughed. Veera, from the deepest recesses of his mind, dug out the picture of a young woman who looked exactly like Reshma, just more mysterious, more unapproachable, more desirable. He felt a twinge of regret at what he had to do and, taking a deep breath, stepped out of the shadows.

"Ram, Ram, Hare, Hare," he chanted, deftly moving the beads of a rosary with the fingers of his right hand. He walked towards the temple, eyes partially closed, climbing up the steps and sat down cross-legged in the verandah. He adjusted his robes, placed his cloth bag on the floor and opened his eyes, pretending to notice Reshma for the first time.

"You will get wet, child," he called. "Come, take shelter here."

Reshma stopped dancing, looked at Veera, hesitated, and started walking towards the temple. Veera prayed she would not recognize him. At first, a disguise had seemed like something out of a Bollywood movie, something dubious that would not work. But the idea had grown on Veera and he had discovered, with amazement, that he was quite the actor. He could change his voice. He could change his expressions. With the saffron robe and a stick-on beard he had found in a shop that sold costumes discarded by a drama troupe, he looked like a saint, a man worthy of respect. It helped that the men and women who came and went as saints were, themselves, also acting. Veera was just like any of them. He felt sure he had acquired an air of grandeur and holiness, just being in disguise.

"Why are you alone, child?" he asked. "Come sit here until the rain stops."

Reshma looked at Veera carefully, then sat down a few feet away from him.

"I was passing through and it started raining. I hope it stops. I have to be at the next village soon."

"Why do you have to be there?" Reshma asked. She knew she should bow down and touch the saint's feet but felt too shy. Guru had told her many holy men and women made wishes come true.

"Oh, people there want me to bless them so it will rain. But it has already started raining, so they may not need me. Or they might be thinking that the mere act of my walking towards their village has brought rain."

Veera laughed and Reshma smiled. She liked this man. He seemed so gentle and kind.

"Where are you from?" she asked.

"A village very far away. Across the three rivers. You will not have heard of it."

Reshma nodded.

"Here, are you hungry?" Veera asked. "I have some laddus to give people. Do you want one?"

Veera reached into his bag and took out a laddu made with gram flour, jaggery, cashews and raisins. Reshma took the lemon-sized ball in her small hands. She had been told to never accept food from strangers, but saints were not strangers.

"Eat it," Veera coaxed. "It is very good."

Reshma took a bite and then stopped. She looked at the rain, now coming down in torrents.

"I should go before it gets worse," she said.

"You must finish the laddu. It is an offering from the gods and should not be wasted."

"I will eat it on the way," Reshma said, running down the steps.

Veera watched Reshma disappear with distress. He had put pesticide in the laddu without really researching how much was needed to kill a small child. He wished he had tested it on a stray dog. He prayed Reshma would eat the entire thing.

Reshma was sick by the time she reached the vada. She went straight to the bathroom and threw up.

"What's wrong?" Sharada asked, as everyone rushed toward Reshma.

"I don't know. I suddenly started feeling ill."

"Did you eat something?"

"The saint at the temple gave me this," Reshma said holding out her hand.

"It may be spoilt," Guru said. "Throw it away. And why did you accept food from a stranger? You are lucky it was a saint."

They all shook their heads in sympathy. The poor saint, he did not know his laddus had gone bad. He needed to be warned but Reshma did not know his name or where he was from so nothing could be done.

THE RAIN WOULD not stop once it started. Now that it had been allowed to come it kept coming. It was not the gentle monsoon drizzle turning occasionally into a brief downpour but an incessant, vicious gushing of water from the sky.

The dry earth soaked up as much water as it could, as fast as it could, but the rain fell so heavily that most of it made its way to the river carrying with it Nilgi's rich, black regur soil, stripping the earth of its last layer of defense. Now, people stayed indoors to escape the torrential rain and street dogs and cats fought for shelter under protruding roofs and cowsheds. The birds disappeared and the fish in the river became confused by the sudden, strong, erratic currents. The trees, brown and drooping from the drought, now wilted under the onslaught of a long-awaited monsoon. They could not hold their heads up high and gave up.

Raj, too, drooped like the trees. He could not hold his head up high, and it was not because of the grey rain. He was a man broken and demoralized by his past. The love he had carried for Priya all these years, put on the pedestal, and nurtured now made him feel naked and exposed. The results of his actions were ever-present in the form of a taciturn little girl who carried the burdens of the world in the beautiful eyes she had inherited from her mother. Every time Raj looked at Reshma he thought he saw accusation in her eyes, and he became convinced she knew he was her father. Why else should she come to Nilgi, a village that led to nowhere?

Raj's paranoia was not entirely baseless. In a weak moment, unable to counter Reshma's curious questions with more lies, Priya had divulged the name of the village where her father lived. She told Reshma that when the time was right, they would go to the man who would make them both happy and they could live like a normal family.

The plan pleased Reshma who did not have much else than her dreams and she proceeded to imagine a perfect life with her waiting-to-be-claimed father. When Priya was murdered, Reshma's first instinct was to block out everything she had seen, pretending it had happened to someone else. Her second instinct was to run away to a village called Nilgi where her father lived. She followed both instincts, fleeing to Nilgi after systematically blocking out the life she had lived until then.

GURU CONTINUED COMING to the school for his lessons with Raj. The earnestness with which he studied drove Raj's guilt deeper, increasing his self-loathing. *How low will I sink? His sister is dead, his niece is right before his eyes and the boy knows none of this because I don't have the courage to tell him.*

Raj walked to the window and watched the rain fall in opaque, aqueous curtains that shredded as soon as they hit the earth. Children were trickling in, wading through the muddy streams gushing through the streets, drenched despite their umbrellas and flimsy raincoats. He saw Reshma walking through the school gate and sighed with relief. Reshma was by herself and Raj saw his youngest child, her pink knee-length dress drenched to red, her long braids wet, strands of hair whipping across her face as she tried holding her umbrella upright with her thin arms. Raj's heart constricted. He felt a stinging in his eyes and turned away from the window before he did something foolish like running out and gathering her in his arms.

Raj turned and watched Guru trying to comprehend a two-page story in a fourth grade textbook. He sat cross-legged on the floor, bent over the book, brow furrowed, his tongue sticking out from between his teeth.

"Morning classes will begin soon," Raj said. "Shall we continue tomorrow?"

"I cannot understand some of the words in this story," Guru said, then added reluctantly. "I can stay longer if you want me to."

"No, Guru, that is enough for today. You have already been here two hours. We will continue tomorrow afternoon."

Guru gathered his books. Raj wondered how to broach the subject of Reshma.

"I have an idea. Why not bring Reshma with you some afternoons? She, too, needs help and you are both reading and writing at the same level. You can help each other."

"Am I so behind?" Guru's face fell.

"No, you have had a very late start. Learning is easy when you are a child. What do you think of this idea? Studying with a friend is more enjoyable."

"I will ask her," Guru shrugged, and Raj despaired at the nonchalance.

Reshma came to her father's office the next day, dressed in her pink dress, a midget under the large umbrella Guru held over them,

"She agreed to come," Guru said, triumphantly. "Remove your shoes by the door so you don't dirty dhani's floor."

Guru helped Reshma put her slippers away, straightened her clothes, wiped the raindrops on her face with the edge of his shirt and hustled her inside.

"Shall I place our mats side by side?"

"Yes," Raj said unable to take his eyes off Reshma, a tiny sparrow in a cheap polyester dress with *her* eyes, *her* chin. *Her* delicacy, grace and uncertainty.

Her. Priya.

What have I done? I gave her nothing except false hope and misery and she gave me a beautiful child.

The sun chose that moment to peek out and flash a tentative, victorious smile before the clouds smothered it and continued emptying themselves into the exhausted earth.

Raj fell to his knees, opened his arms wide and said, "Come here my child, my daughter."

He saw the confusion in Reshma's eyes, the alarm in Guru's. He saw his own shocked face reflected in the glass doors of his bookshelf. He wondered if Reshma would take his word, if Guru would despise him, and whether Daya would ever recover if she found out. He wondered if the earth would start rotating clockwise because he, Raj, had just turned it upside down, inside out.

Yet, he felt no regret as he began explaining, making no excuses for himself.

THE KRISHNA SWELLED rapidly, and the dam wall held back the water creating the most magnificent lake in which egrets and flamingoes roosted and crocodiles frolicked. This year, the backwater lake expanded quickly, submerging the villages and towns it usually did and others it had never before. People began evacuating following government orders, but Nilgi resisted because it was on higher ground and watched over by Lord Hanuman. Samar began worrying in earnest when the rain refused to ease, and the lake's water level kept rising. During a regular monsoon the backwater lake surrounded Nilgi, sparing the newly constructed elevated tar road connecting it to Shantur. This year, Samar was certain Nilgi would flood, but when he mentioned it to the villagers their faith in Lord Hanuman's ability to protect them wavered only slightly.

The power, lost when the rains began, had still not been restored. The phone lines died, and newspaper delivery stopped. Bus service dropped to one roundtrip to Shantur a day and eventually, that too was terminated. The government communicated to Samar that it was not responsible for Nilgi as it had sent several notices for the village to evacuate. With the government washing its hands of it, Nilgi's isolation became complete.

Samar, knowing that Nilgi's flooding was inevitable, sought the help of Raj and the village elders and came up with a plan. People were told to move their non-essential belongings to the upper stories of their houses and share their space with those who did not have higher floors. As soon as the lake began flooding the single approach road, the village would evacuate in buses Raj had hired.

At first, the people of Nilgi refused to accept the inevitability of floods, and Samar sought the help of the village elders again. He begged them to go from house-to-house cajoling people to start packing. Raj made it known that the ground floor of the vada was being packed and moved to the upper story. He sent word that Daya and he would not leave until Nilgi evacuated. Finally, when the lake water was still a couple of feet below the access road, people began packing their homes.

"Take only what you need," Samar said. "We will be back soon."

"Back to our damaged houses and fields which we will have to fix with no help from the government," an old farmer said, spitting spitefully.

When it was not packing, Nilgi watched the slowly rising waters of the lake, dreading the moment when the road would start flooding. Samar said they could leave now, before it became worse, but no one took him up on his offer. Some insisted there was still hope, and Samar decided not to crush their optimism. He calculated that evacuation should begin when the water was a foot below the road. It would take five hours for the village to empty, much longer for the water to rise that last foot and begin submerging the village. They would be fine, he told himself, though Lord Hanuman was giving way to Lord Krishna and everything was the way it had never been.

CHAPTER EIGHTEEN

Guru and Raj were taking a break from packing his office into cardboard boxes to move to the vada. Raj sat on a frayed jute mat with Reshma in his lap. Guru stood by the window, gazing at the uncertain future, refusing to look at Raj.

It had been four days since Raj revealed to Reshma that he was her father and Guru her uncle. Disbelief, love, rage, horror, and sadness whirled around in a bottomless pit as a young man became an uncle and an orphaned girl discovered she had a family. Raj, finally, had claimed his third child, but the future could not be discussed because the floods had postponed it. It would have to be addressed later when the river calmed and they returned to Nilgi.

"You have to be quiet for now, keep this a secret," Raj murmured into Reshma's shikakai-scented hair as she snuggled in his lap. "Do whatever you are told until the floods recede and we can return. Once we are back, I promise I will find a way for us to be together. Do you understand?"

Reshma turned her face up, looked into Raj's eyes, and nodded her head. She had just found a loving father and doting uncle and did not want to ruin things. Her dream life was within reach and she knew how to keep a secret. The only outward sign of her distress was the chalk she had suddenly started eating, which she could not get enough of. She was scolded for it but when she did not stop, people let her be, assigning the new habit to the stress of leaving a village she had come to less than a year ago and now considered home.

They sat in silence as the rain pelted on the roof, the sound echoing through the empty classrooms. The school had been closed but the children were helping their families pack and the streets were bereft of their happy cries. A musty smell permeated the air from the abandoned, tattered books that were being left behind because they were not worth saving. At some point, loose pages from the books would float briefly on the surface of the backwater lake until the current took them away.

"The driver is here to get us," Guru said.

"I will make everything right," Raj assured again. "Don't worry."

He kissed Reshma's cheek before putting her down on the floor. His eyes met Guru's, asking for forgiveness. Guru looked away and busied himself with getting Reshma ready to leave. Deep down, Guru knew that if blame was to be assigned, his drunken father would have to shoulder most of it. Priya had run away from the marriage he was forcing on her and had, by some terrible misfortune, ended up a brothel worker. If anything, Raj had provided her a ray of hope, a patch of sunshine and a daughter borne from love. But, for now, Guru wanted to be unforgiving so he could deal with his own guilt and grief.

PILES OF BOXES lined the periphery of the vada's living room, filled with centuries-old things that were of no use but were being saved because they held the memories of ancestors long dead. Daya sifted through heaps of what could only be described as junk, rescuing whatever she considered valuable. A leaky brass cauldron. A chipped Wedgewood dining service with a pretty rose pattern, testimony to the many banquets the Nayak's had hosted for their British rulers. Raj's grandfather's harmonium, most of the keys missing. A toy bullock cart, the paint all gone.

Daya protested mildly when Raj got rid of things ruthlessly, but he paid her no heed. It was strangely cathartic, purging his life of all that was irrelevant, unnecessary. He felt light, left only with what was important.

"What should I do with this, dhani?" Basu asked, pointing to broken wicker rocking chair. "The rooms upstairs are getting full."

"Throw it out," Raj said

"Guru," Basu called. "Come here and give me a hand. You can go back to packing the kitchen later."

Then, turning to Raj, Basu said, "He was out all morning in the school doing god knows what!"

"He was helping me pack my office," Raj said. "Reshma was there, too."

GUILT AND PANIC coursed through Raj, leaving him winded. His actions had elevated Guru's status and his own was about to be crushed, destroyed completely. Guru was his daughter's uncle and that made them relatives. So far, the Nayaks had held on to their respectability by keeping a distance from people, not mixing freely with the common folk. That distance was now gone, and Raj did not know how Nilgi's society would be rearranged once the secret was revealed.

Raj forced his mind back to packing. After Nilgi was evacuated, Daya and he would go to her brother who would be thrilled to have his sister visit for longer than her customary two days. The household staff had been placed with different families in nearby towns. Raj was sure it would all work out even if the villagers were reluctant to go. When the water level rose and began flooding Nilgi, as Samar promised it would, they would be grateful they had evacuated. Raj hoped things would get back to normal in a few weeks once the floods receded.

IT WAS AUGUST 15, 2005, exactly fifty-eight years since the British left India. Enough time for India to have undone some of the damage caused by centuries of British dominance and oppression, redefine itself as a free country and recover what was taken, given, lost and wrested. It was also enough time to allow itself to be conquered and subjugated by a different, equally obvious, and more lethal oppressor—the corrupt politician.

The democratically elected, power-hungry, fraudulent politicians had successfully bred religious fanaticism, material greed, social irresponsibility, and a selfishness even the British could not have surpassed. The enemy now lay within, but Independence Day was still celebrated throughout India with the same fervor as almost six decades ago. Flags were hoisted, the national anthem sung, and self-righteous patriotism was allowed to sneak in. As the day wore on children dismembered the paper flags their parents bought them and adults deconstructed the romantic vision of a free India they had allowed themselves to build to mark the day.

This year there were no celebrations in Nilgi or the surrounding villages and towns. Some were drowned, others waiting to be drowned and no one was concerned with the day they were liberated from the white people who bathed once a week and ate cadavers for their meals. The few anglophiles, who remained obsequious to the British, believing that India had benefitted from colonization, secretly bemoaned the day the British left.

SANTOSH PACED IN his office, tracking the pink marble floor with his muddy shoes. A devout Hindu, he had ventured out in the heavy rain to visit the Ganesha temple. He could be accused of many things but his faith in god was true and immutable. It was his faith that had given him everything he desired. Power. Wealth. Women. When he sat behind his heavy teak desk on his magnificent chair with its maroon velvet upholstery and gold trim, Santosh felt untouchable, out of everyone's reach.

Today, for the first time since he had won a seat in the state's legislative assembly sixteen years ago, Santosh felt real gut-wrenching fear, as if some terrible undeserved tragedy was about to befall him. Not one to look back, he suddenly found himself ruminating on his past, his dishonesty and avarice. Still, he felt no remorse because he had done what almost every politician did.

That pesky landlord, Raj Nayak, had organized an anti-dam movement that had made Santosh's life difficult. People had demanded a compensation plan by the end of April which the government had failed to release. It was now August. Even if he wanted to, Santosh could not provide compensation because there was no money in the state's coffers to pay people. As the state's agriculture minister, Santosh managed to get all the corrupt politicians on board, assuring them that there was no urgency to oblige the anti-dam requests. Only the Chief Minister, the idealistic old coot, insisted the people's demand be met.

What he had not bargained for was the fury of the people, their aggressive resistance of the project, and the risks they were willing to take to get justice. Santosh had not taken the plea for the compensation plan seriously until the riots when the Chief Minister was visiting. That first sign of brazen dissension aroused an unfamiliar frisson of fear in Santosh.

The next protest, that had happened outside his house, where his effigy was burned, had terrified him. He became aware of the quiescent power of the people, the things they could do after being treated unjustly for decades.

The drought had been a godsend, distracting everyone from the dam. With no rain, there would be no floods, and the government would have more time to come up with the funds to move and settle people. The drought had pushed the anti-dam movement to the back of everyone's mind. The idea of flooding became absurd, even fantastical, and Santosh relaxed. He had at least another year to appease the people with a good rehabilitation plan—move funds around so there was money for compensation.

That relief had been short-lived, because of the heavy rains that followed. Every town and village in the low-lying areas flooded and people were fleeing and those who had not been warned were dying in their villages. Once the floods receded, there would be outrage, possibly violent protests.

For the first time in his adult life Santosh had no woman to help ease his stress. Things had been hard since his marriage to the pipal tree. His status did not allow him to be with common prostitutes and that rat of a man, Veera, had failed to provide him a worthy woman. There were rumors that Veera was now in Raj Nayak's camp, but Santosh had not managed to confirm it. All his attempts to meet with Veera, to gauge the mood of the people, had failed. Santosh cursed the inspector but there was not much he could do. The last thing he needed was to antagonize anyone who could help him, and Veera could help him when things returned to normal, and he would have to face the anger of the people.

From above, it was a humungous lake from which coconut trees peeked and only buildings of more than two stories rose. The rest was underwater, a serene, watchful, wasted kingdom waiting for more villages and towns to join it. Nilgi, from its temporarily unassailable position on higher ground, waved a friendly hello to the flooded villages knowing it would soon meet the same fate.

As Nilgi prepared to evacuate, the rain fell less furiously and the clouds beyond the hills began dispersing. The sun glinted every once in a while through the grey skies, offering hope. If the rain had ceased upstream, Nilgi could still escape flooding. Then the devastating news came in, more than twenty-seven dead in three villages unprepared for evacuation. The water was still rising.

The entire west coast was hit by severe monsoon. Mumbai stood in seven feet of water and life had come to a standstill. Moving south, some inland cities like Pune, Kolhapur and Satara had escaped flooding but the rest of the Deccan plateau, especially villages along major rivers, were flooded. The newsreader went on to discuss Independence Day celebrations and the latest violence along the India-Pakistan border, but no one in Nilgi was interested in politics. They were still trying to accept that their village, always before watched over by Lord Hanuman, was finally about to flood. They no longer felt smug.

So, it did not matter that the rain stopped and the sun came out later that day. The lake kept growing because of the rain upstream. Samar went to the approach road every half an hour, sat on his haunches, and assessed the rate at which the water was rising.

"We should evacuate tomorrow," he told Raj. "Can you ask the bus company to send their buses tonight so we can start loading them?"

"There is no avoiding it?" Raj asked as he rose to call the bus company.

"I will spread the word, tell everyone to get ready. Families with children leave first, then the old and everyone else will follow after."

"They will be ready to leave now even if they resisted so far. Those flood fatalities have shaken them. This is real, it is happening."

"Yes," Samar said. "Even those who were not active in the anti-dam movement are ready to join. There is a sudden restlessness among the people. Let's hope nothing douses their determination."

"I know what you are thinking. When news of my affair gets out, people will stop trusting me. They will need another leader. Maybe you should quit your job and take over? I can afford to pay you a salary."

"Let's discuss it when all this is over."

"Samar, there is something else we need to discuss."

"I know what it is. The secret is out, Reshma and Guru know."

"How did you guess? I wanted to talk to you but there was no time, with everything happening."

"There is no point in worrying about it now. There will be time to talk about it when we all return."

A perfect rain-washed, clear dawn gazed at Nilgi the morning after Independence Day. It was hard to believe it would flood—possibly by the end of the day—and harder still to leave a village that had withstood every natural and manmade disaster. A line of buses were parked on the approach road, watching with their large hyena-eyes people balancing boxes, trunks, gunny bags and children. The loading of the buses had started shortly after midnight.

"When can we return?" an old farmer asked Samar. "A week?"

"I can't say for sure," Samar responded. "It won't be long. Think of this as a forced vacation."

"What good is a vacation away from home?" the man mumbled

into his walking stick, shuffling towards the waiting buses.

Samar watched the rising water. He had lists of families and was organizing them into buses based on their destinations. Guru was making sure people were not separated from their luggage. It was going as planned.

"How many more buses to be loaded?" he asked Basu, who was helping children and old people.

"Half are ready, and the rest will be in a couple of hours," Basu replied. "Perhaps we can start evacuating as soon as a bus is ready rather than waiting to dispatch them all together as we planned?"

"I think that is a good idea," Samar said.

"The water is rising quicker than we expected?" Basu asked.

Samar nodded, putting a finger to his lips. The villagers were already distressed and the last thing he needed was them panicking.

"Reshma!" Guru's voice broke through the chatter of people organizing their packed lives into the line of buses. "Where are you? We have to leave soon."

"Where is she?" Samar said, worried. "She knows it is time to go. She should be here."

"I haven't seen her at all today," Guru said. "Don't worry, I will find her. She was upset at having to leave and must be in one of her hiding places."

Samar watched Guru speeding off with a frown. He knew that Reshma had been spending a lot of time with Raj and Guru, which is how Samar had guessed that Raj had revealed his secret. Samar was resentful Raj had not discussed it first with him, despite warnings that if the truth came out Raj's leadership of the anti-dam movement would suffer. More than that, Samar and Usha were upset and hurt because, now, adopting Reshma had become impossible. Samar forced himself to not think about the future. There were more urgent matters to deal with.

CHAPTER NINETEEN

Half the village had left on the hyena-eyed buses preying on the spoils of the flood, and the rest were ready to leave when Guru finally discovered Reshma under a hibiscus creeper on a nearby knoll. She was lying very still, her pink dress stained yellow by the pollen drifting down from the red blossoms. Her feet were crossed, her mouth open, her eyes unseeing. By her right hand was an open bag of blue rock candy, most of it strewn like pebbles in damp earth.

Guru knelt before her, frantically rubbing the pollen off her face, arms, and legs. Perhaps underneath the pollen, the body may not be Reshma's after all. His tears turned the pollen to yellow paste as he told himself the pink dress was very different from the one Reshma wore. Finally, the features emerged—the almond-eyes, the pointed chin, the high cheekbones. There were red bruises on her neck suggesting she had been strangled but Guru registered none of that. With his hands covered in yellow pollen-paste he staggered backward.

A terrible cry of pain rent the air, cutting through it as cleanly as a sharpened blade might slit a throat. The people gathered by the waiting buses, preparing to depart, froze at the inhuman sound. Heads swiveled before everyone began running towards it.

Samar dropped the trunk he was hoisting and ran towards the dreadful cry, now a series of subhuman howls.

Basu clutched his file of lists of people and buses and followed at a brisk pace, panting.

The bus crowd followed, postponing its departure.

As if in slow motion, Samar felt his suddenly weightless body drifting to where Reshma lay. He pushed Guru aside and fell to the ground on his knees. His hands clasped Reshma's face and he brought his mouth down on hers, blowing into it in small, quick gasps. He stopped after a few seconds, bringing his ear to her nose.

"She is still alive," Samar exclaimed and began blowing into Reshma's mouth again.

HYSTERIA IS SORROW'S failure just as pleasure is pain's vanquisher. Hysteria makes unbearable grief tolerable just as the pleasure of climax makes pain bearable. It was near hysteria that saved Raj that day, bringing some order to a disorderly universe. The truth had come out in bits and pieces when Samar carried a sleeping Reshma, her head tucked in his shoulder, into the vada. Raj came running from his room upstairs when he heard the commotion in the living room.

"What happened?" he cried, touching Reshma's back.

"She is fine," Samar said. "Someone tried to strangle her, but Guru found her just in time."

"Call the doctor, Samar, please," Raj said.

Raj heard Samar talking to the family doctor in Shantur but

the words did not register as he lay a sleeping Reshma down on the sofa.

"Doctor says she should rest," Samar said. "He will come see her as soon as the water goes down."

"Thank god," Raj said, kissing Reshma's forehead.

Daya stared at Raj, confused by the passion of his feelings. She put the cold compress Sharada had brought on Reshma's forehead.

"Surely, he is overreacting," she said, looking at Raj not expecting an answer. "She is only a poor orphan girl we have taken in."

"She is not an orphan," Guru said, ignoring Samar's beseeching look.

With that, the story came out, and Raj was buried alive in the hell of his making, which he hardly noticed. He did not see Daya dropping into the wicker rocking chair, unhinged by shock and pain. He did not see Sharada's sick look as she held a glass of cold water to Daya's lips. Or the stunned silence in the room as everyone grappled with resurrecting the Raj they respected and loved, trying to reconcile that image with the pathetic man on the floor.

SAMAR THUMPED THE rear of a bus, a signal for the driver to leave. He had left Raj sitting by Reshma. In normal circumstances he would have asked everyone at the vada to leave as the water was rising quickly but these were not normal circumstances. He would have liked a shot or two of whiskey as well, but there was too much to be done and he needed all his faculties to make sure the village was evacuated. He glanced gratefully at Basu who had left the unfolding drama at the vada to help with the evacuation. There was plenty of time to untangle the mess of their lives after Nilgi was safely evacuated.

Basu and Samar gazed at the last bus as it rattled off along the access road which was already under a few inches of water. Samar looked at his watch. The discovery of Reshma under the hibiscus creeper, about four hours ago, had turned the world of Nilgi upside down.

Reshma almost dead.

Raj inconsolable.

The truth exposed.

Daya on the verge of a nervous breakdown.

Guru shattered, guilt-ridden that he could have somehow kept Reshma safe.

Usha and he hopeless, their dreams of adopting Reshma shattered.

There had been disbelief all around as a drowning village became untethered. People had been reluctant to leave, some out of concern, but most wanting to watch the unfolding story of Nilgi's adopted child—that side of human nature that delights in the misfortunes of others, using people's losses to elevate its own flagging spirits. But even they realized that the sordid mess would not stop the village from flooding and left on the assigned buses.

Basu deserved credit for getting the people on the buses. He convinced them to leave with their misgivings and gossiping tongues, sure that everyone in the area would know about Raj and Reshma by the end of the day. Random strangers would talk about people they had never met, trying to establish a connection with the players in the drama.

Her uncle is the boy who comes to Shantur every Sunday to buy vegetables, see? That skinny boy....

Samar had informed Veera, expecting snide remarks about Raj, and been taken aback at the empathetic response.

"I am so glad she is still alive, poor child," Veera whimpered, his voice unsteady. "Has she said anything about who attacked her?"

"No, she hasn't."

"She may have blocked it out. It can happen after a traumatic event. How is Raj dhani? He has never done anything wrong. He is not the first man to cheat, and he won't be the last. Such bad luck that he strayed a little and it turned into this."

"When can you be here?" Samar asked, deciding not to analyze Veera's unusually kind response.

A long pause and, "I am neck deep in work filing autopsy reports of the people who have died in the flood, but I will send a policeman and detective to Nilgi within an hour. I promise I will get personally involved, investigate the matter thoroughly."

That was more than three hours ago and there was no sign of the policeman and detective. Only a few had remained back at the vada, waiting for the police to come, look at the crime scene and begin an inquiry.

Raj stayed because he was the father, Daya his devastated, wronged wife. Guru, because he was Reshma's uncle, and Bharati because she was Reshma's friend. Sharada, the toothless roti-maker, stayed because she had once been Raj's nanny and cared for Reshma since the day she arrived in Nilgi. Basu stayed because he did not want to abandon Raj and Daya at a time they probably needed him most. Samar and Usha stayed because they could not bear to leave Reshma in her fragile state.

Few words were exchanged among the group in the vada's living room. There was a lot needing to be said and, yet none of it was urgent. It could remain unsaid for years and it would not matter or change a thing. It was all so surreal. The only thing that was real was the slight, pollen-covered body of a little girl who refused to wake up from her gentle, safe dreams. Guru looked at Reshma and remembered how pollen made her sneezy and itchy. Yet, her body was covered in it now and she lay still.

"Maybe call the doctor again?" Sharada said. "He said to let her rest but she has been asleep too long."

Raj stood up and looked at Daya, forcing her to return his gaze. He saw no accusation in her eyes, just pain and grief, and it made him feel worse. A tear ran down his cheek and she looked away as he picked up the phone and dialed the family doctor again. Raj spoke quietly for a few minutes and, looking relieved, hung up and said, "It is not unusual to sleep after a traumatic event, but we should wake Reshma up in a couple of hours if she continues to sleep. You should all leave while you can. I will stay here until the police come and answer their questions. They can talk to all of you later."

"How can we leave?" Samar said. "If the police don't come on time—or worse not come at all—you will be stranded here with Reshma. Maybe call Veera and find out what's going on? The water is already flooding the approach road and we need to be out of here."

Raj dialed Veera and was told that a detective and a policeman were already on their way.

"I told him Reshma was asleep, but we would wake her up when the police came," Raj said. "He insisted that was not important."

"Why not?" Samar asked.

"He said statements from a child so recently traumatized are never recorded or taken seriously."

A POLICEMAN AND a detective arrived on a motorcycle, as it was now impossible for cars to drive on the approach road already under a foot of water. Samar had sloshed through the streets to meet them at the knoll, still unflooded, where Reshma had been discovered. The detective took photographs and notes, picked some of the strewn blue candy with gloved hands, dropping them into a plastic bag while Samar described how Reshma had been found and resuscitated.

"I need to speak to the others," the policeman said. "Where are they?"

"At the vada."

"Raj Nayak?"

"Him, too, though I am not sure how he can help. He was at the vada when all this was happening."

"We will see," the policeman said, an oily smile lighting up his face.

Samar's heart sank. It was as he had feared. The authorities, at Santosh's beck and call, were using this opportunity to destroy Raj's reputation so people would begin questioning his integrity and intentions. The anti-dam activism would fall apart without Raj's leadership and politicians like Santosh would be off the hook. Samar was angry and hurt by Raj's deceit, but he also felt sad for him. It was not uncommon for powerful men to father illegitimate children and be forgiven, but Raj would never be allowed to forget his sins because his reputation so far had been impeccable, and he was held to very high standards.

"You will have to leave your motorcycle here," Samar said. "It won't get through the flooded streets to the vada."

"Let's hurry," the detective said. "Or we will be stuck here."

"Yes," the policeman replied with no intention of hurrying. This was a high-profile case involving the most respected man in the district and he was going to milk the situation for all it was worth. He had been surprised and flattered when his superior, Veera, handed the case to him.

"I have too many things on my mind right now," Veera had explained.

"Yes, sir," the policeman answered noticing the tired, pinched look on the inspector's face.

"Any idea who might have tried to kill her?" the policeman now asked, sipping the tea Sharada brought him.

"No idea at all," Daya said, putting her cup down carefully on the center table. The pain Raj had brought her would never go away, but she was not going to let a mere policeman have the upper hand. She could denounce Raj all she wanted in private, but she would stand by him in public, make sure he was not demeaned and diminished. "Nothing like this has ever happened in Nilgi."

"Who was the last person to see her?" the policeman prodded, tapping his baton on his palm as he had seen his favorite movie star, Amitabh Bachchan, do when he played a police officer in a Bollywood movie.

"I saw her go out early this morning," Bharati said. "She was obsessed with the rising water level and went to the access road several times a day to check. I assumed she was going there, probably with Guru."

"I didn't even know she was going," Guru said. "Which is strange because she always told me everything."

"I wish I had gone with her," Bharati said, rubbing her tear-stained face on her sleeve.

"Don't blame yourself," Sharada consoled, drawing Bharati to her side. "We need to be grateful she is alive."

"I may have been the last one to see her before she was strangled," Raj said. "I asked her to come to the knoll by the river, her favorite place, so I could say goodbye and give her a bag of the candy she loved."

"Did she tell you what she was going to do after you met with her?"

Raj shook his head.

"I assumed she would return to the vada."

"So, you asked her to come to the knoll where someone tried to kill her after you left?" the policeman asked, softly.

A silence that lasted a second too long as everyone realized where this line of questioning was leading.

"What are you trying to say?" Daya sat up in her chair.

"I am not saying anything," the policeman said. "What do *you* think I am trying to say?"

Raj dropped his face into his hands, Samar closed his eyes in consternation, and Guru rubbed his tired eyes. Usha held back her anger only because Sharada laid a hand on her shoulder. It was the worst thing Daya could have said, trying to protect the only man she had loved, still loved, despite his deception.

"We would like to talk to Reshma," the policeman said. "Can you wake her up?"

"She is supposed to rest," Samar replied. "And it will be traumatic for her if you start grilling her right now. In fact, Veera told me statements from recently-traumatized children are not to be taken seriously."

"We need to speak with her as soon as she is able," the policeman said, standing up. "I will file the case with the information we have gathered and contact you with developments. If anything occurs to any of you, please let us know."

"How are we supposed to do that?" Samar asked, belligerent. "We cannot leave now because you took so long getting here. The water level is too high for a car to get through, power has been gone for several days and we have two cell phones partially charged by a solar battery. Shall we come with a handwritten letter in a fishing boat?"

"Don't worry, we will work all that out," the policeman backed down. "Just remember that obstruction of an investigation is a crime in itself. The truth will come out no matter what."

With that last warning and in classic Amitabh Bachchan style, the policeman left. This was the first time he felt like a hero and he was not about to relinquish that feeling.

"WE ARE TRULY stranded," Samar admitted.

The ground floor of the vada was flooding and they had moved upstairs where there were two rooms, a storeroom, and a bathroom.

"We have enough supplies and can stay here comfortably for a few days," Sharada said.

"And I can cook on the kerosene stove, but our groceries will last a day or two at the most," Basu said. "What do we do after that if the water hasn't receded?"

"I joked about getting out of here in a fishing boat, but it may be a good idea," Samar said. "I know a man with a coracle in Shantur who we can pay to bring us whatever we need."

CHAPTER
TWENTY

From the vada's tower room, Guru positioned the .22 caliber rifle in the crook of his right shoulder and, closing his left eye, pressed his cheek against the polished stock to look through the telescopic sight, adjusting the focus so he could see the bobbing coracle, dodging the tops of trees and buildings poking from the water. The rifle was a Remington, one of Raj's prized possessions, inherited from his father who had hunted in nearby forests. He had killed a panther that attacked him—a story the people of Nilgi told and re-told embellishing it every single time so it became a myth, an unbelievable narration that never failed to awe. Guru inhaled deeply as he had seen Raj do, held his breath so not a muscle twitched, aimed at the fisherman in the coracle and pulled the trigger.

No shot rang out because the rifle was not loaded. Raj, who never let anyone touch the rifle had handed it to Guru saying his eyesight was weakening and Guru should use it to watch the lake through the telescope. Each time Guru looked out, he pulled the trigger just as he had seen Clint Eastwood do in the western movies Raj watched.

At first Guru thought Raj had given him the rifle to assuage his own guilt, but quickly realized that was not the case. The tragedies in Raj's life were so many that no one, not even Guru, had the heart to punish him for his affair. Daya, though not speaking to Raj, had begun treating Reshma with increasing love and affection.

The fisherman must have sensed Guru pointing the rifle at him because he grinned and waved. Guru waved back and his face broke into a smile, the first one since Reshma was found. He held onto it like a dying man to his last breath and carried it inside to the others, but no one noticed and he tucked it away, hoping to use it another day.

The fisherman Samar had found was the only one who continued going out into the turbulent, uncharted waters of the backwater lake with his coracle to snare the best rohu, katla and bass. He brought supplies and prepared meals from a restaurant in Shantur so Sharada and Basu did not have to cook for nine people with a small kerosene stove and limited groceries.

Luckily, the water tank, above the tower room, was still quite full so there was running water. The area around the tower was flooded and impossible to get to, so Guru fashioned a raft with driftwood and straw, rowing it from the upper floor of the main house where they were stranded to the tower room for his water-vigil.

Guru watched the coracle coming closer and noticed that the water had receded in some parts, exposing bits of land. He would ask the fisherman what he thought. He wanted to be stranded, so he could continue living the way he was. Decisions, choices, heartache awaited outside. As Reshma's uncle he would have a new status at the vada. He did not want anything to change because, deep down, he still loved and respected Raj and it would be hard to live under the same roof as his equal. He had always wanted the limelight, to be the center of attention, but not in these unfortunate circumstances where there were no winners.

It was five days since evacuation and a sad, strained silence had sunk into the vada. A terrified coldness had entered everyone as they wondered what else awaited. They, each, tried going back to being who they were before Reshma was found under the hibiscus creeper, and failed. Something had changed in all of them, their loyalties were shifting, and their beliefs were being questioned.

Reshma had woken from her deep sleep that day with new, even more horrifying secrets in her eyes. When questioned about the attack she went into such violent hysterics that she could not be calmed.

"What will you tell the boys?" Daya asked Raj when she saw how he held and comforted Reshma, even though she, herself, had begun treating Reshma with the tenderness she reserved for her own sons.

Those were the first words she had spoken directly to him since the truth had come out. Raj looked at her with such anguish that she let the matter drop. Daya had not said anything to him since. If she wanted to say something to Raj, she did it through Sharada and Usha even though they were all in the same room. She ignored his replies, pretending she had not heard them.

They slept on floor mattresses at night, the women in one room and the men in the other. Raj, unable to sleep, went to the terrace every night to look at the pitch-black backwater lake, beautiful even though it held homes, farms and orchards hostage. On his way to and back from the terrace, he stopped at the door of the room where Daya slept and heard her soft sobs. She hardly cried and when she did it was always in private and for grievous reasons like the death of her parents. Raj's heart ached but there was nothing he could do.

"WHAT NEWS KAKA?" Guru asked, unloading a basket of fruit, a tiffin carrier with hot food, and bars of soap from the coracle the fisherman had rowed through the front door of the vada, right up to the bottom-most exposed step of the stairway leading to the top floor.

"The water is receding," the fisherman replied. "You may be able to get out soon."

"Have the rains stopped upstream?"

"Yes, they have,"

"Did you bring the cough syrup?' Samar asked coming down the stairs. "Sharada maami's wheezing is getting worse."

"Here," the fisherman said, pulling a bottle from his pocket.

"Guru, can you take the medicine upstairs and give mami a dose right away? I will unload the rest of the things." Samar waited for a few minutes, making sure Guru was out of earshot.

"How are things in Shantur?" Samar asked. "You know what I mean?"

"Yes. Getting worse every day as the news is spreading further and further in the district. There are still loyal people who will forgive Raj dhani, the Nayaks, for this transgression but it is rapidly becoming a political issue."

"That is what I feared. What exactly is happening?"

"MLA Santosh is using this as an excuse to invalidate anti-dam activism. He is rallying people against the vada, saying it is a traditional, obsolete set-up that gives one family the most power. He is telling them they shouldn't trust and believe a man like Raj Nayak who has cheated on his own wife with not just any woman but a prostitute."

"That is nonsense," Samar responded angrily. "What has one

got to do with the other? This is just a ploy to distract people enraged by the floods, deflect the pain of the families who have lost their loved ones to it. A personal transgression should not be used to undo all the progress we have made. Is there a way to keep people's faith in the anti-dam movement? Raj dhani may not be able to influence people the way he did."

The fisherman thought for a moment.

"It is interesting you say that" he said to Samar. "In all this, Veera has been very understanding and supportive. He is telling everyone that Raj dhani's good intentions for the people should not be doubted because of this. In fact, he checks in with me every day after I return to Shantur. He asks after everyone, especially Reshma and if she has revealed anything about the attack. He is investigating the case with uncharacteristic seriousness and wants to talk to Reshma after the floods recede."

Raj, walking down the stairs to pay the fisherman heard his name and stopped to listen. In hindsight, he should not have because he discovered he had caused more damage than a mere scandal and had no face to show the world. At a time when he was most vulnerable, the exchange between Samar and the fisherman broke him completely, annihilating the last bit of hope he had about saving his reputation.

The flood had merged the past, present and future. The waters carried an intact past into a scarred future, obliterating the present on its way. The present simply stopped existing—the past was flawed memory, the future, imagination. In the past was a little girl with faraway eyes, a beautiful woman whose life held no purpose, joy or meaning and a man deranged by grief. In the present was a group of people trying to make sense of a world that was suddenly spinning anti-clockwise. The future enfolded the little girl with faraway eyes and waited for more tragedy.

DAYA, BIG OF heart and generous of spirit, let herself fall in love with Reshma without inhibition, though she tried to keep their burgeoning relationship a secret from Raj. She wanted Raj to suffer—live in his guilt—but they were all living together in such a small space that he could not help but notice the growing tenderness between his wife and daughter. It made him happy, but it also made him feel deep shame at having cheated on a woman as good and honorable as Daya.

"Eat some more," Sharada was cajoling, placing a ball of rice and dal into Reshma's mouth. "You need to eat if you want to grow up and become beautiful."

"Here, let me feed her," Daya said, taking the plate from Sharada. "Open your mouth Reshma. If you finish your dinner, I will give you two bourbon biscuits."

Reshma's eyes lit up and she finished her plate of food. Daya watched, her heart overflowing, not because Reshma was Raj's daughter, but because the child had come such a long way since arriving in Nilgi less than a year ago. She remained reticent, unwilling to reveal her past, but the trapped look had left Reshma's eyes, and she smiled more often, allowed herself to be loved. Daya, in her saddest moments, thought of Reshma's life at a brothel, living with the memory of a murdered mother and then, the failed attack that could have taken her life. Daya put herself in Priya's shoes and forgave her, a thousand times over. No woman deserved such shame and humiliation.

Later that evening, Raj, from inside, watched Daya sitting cross-legged on the terrace, Reshma's head in her lap, as she put her to sleep. He walked out, sat beside Daya and placed his hand over hers. Daya tried pulling her hand away but he held on to it tight.

"You will wake her up," she protested.

"She is asleep. And it doesn't matter if she hears us."

In the dark, Daya turned and looked at Raj, fully, for the first time since they were stranded.

"I don't deserve your forgiveness, but I am so sorry, so deeply sorry I hurt you so much. Please, Daya, will you at least try? For your sake and the sake of Jai and Rohan? Their lives will never be the same but I, we, need to protect them as much as we can. I cannot right this without your help."

In the dark, Daya began sobbing and he let go of her hand.

"This is hard for me, Raj. Was anything between us ever sacred? Was I a fool to believe our love was untouchable?"

"No, no, my darling. This isn't your fault. It is me. I am weak. I strayed. I cheated."

"It is harder that you loved this woman, that she wasn't a fling. I need some time to gather my thoughts, examine how I really feel," Daya said. "Right now, I think Reshma needs our attention. She has suffered and suffered. We are adults, we can deal with our problems later."

"I am forever grateful to you for accepting Reshma…."

"I would do this for any child," Daya said, standing up.

THAT NIGHT, AFTER everyone was asleep, Raj got up and walked to the door at the top of the stairs. He turned around and looked at the sleeping forms of those he loved, the people who had determined the trajectory of his life without being aware they were doing so. Only his sons did not know of his deceit, and he was not ready to see the hurt and betrayal in their eyes, face their rejection.

He walked down the stairs slowly, feeling his way in the dark, careful not to make a sound, and on reaching the lowest unflooded step stripped down to the swimming trunks he was wearing underneath. He folded his clothes, placing them in a neat pile, then swam out through the front door of the vada and into the village. The Krishna embraced him, warm and welcoming. The moon smiled down from a clear sky and Raj smiled back at it. As a boy, on hot nights, he had slept under the stars on the vada's terrace. There was always a gentle cooling breeze, just like now, with an entire village asleep on roof terraces. Now, all that seemed so far away, and he felt like a different person in a different village, now drowned in water.

Raj was a strong swimmer and tackled the choppy waters with swift, sure strokes. Suddenly, he felt happy. Things were still strained between him and Daya, but her initial hostility seemed to have disappeared. Others were also coming around. Still, he would have to face the derision of the outside world, his children's anger. The last thing he wanted was for his sons to be reminded of what he had done every single time they looked at him. They deserved better.

He himself had been so wrapped up in his own grief that he had hardly spoken these last few days. There was a time he had worried that people would find out about his affair but now he did not care. All he could think about was that last look in Priya's eyes as she was murdered, the fear in Reshma's as she was being strangled. The look in Daya's eyes when she discovered his deception. His eyes clouded.

Raj swam furiously through the water towards the Hanuman temple, tears blurring his vision. He saw an owl perched on the collapsed rooftop of a dissolving mud house and a school of fish flashed past through the doorway of another house. He knew the stone houses would be fine. Even disaster discriminated, destroying the poorest ones, sparing the richest. The owners of the mud houses would have to rebuild their homes while the wealthier stone houses were still standing, requiring just a few repairs. It was all so unfair.

The Hanuman temple was not close, and he was getting tired,

but he wanted a glimpse of his beloved place, where Nilgi's energy was concentrated. A swimming tour. He laughed out loud at how bizarre it all was as he swam through the main street past the tailor's shop, the grocery store. He went past houses in which people he had known his entire life lived, towards the temple, along a path he had walked a countless time. He swam through fields of jowar and maize, groundnut and sugarcane. He swam around a spot where he knew a rock protruded from the ground though it was now at the lake's bottom, unlikely to trip him.

He was at the temple now, half-submerged, its whitewashed walls gleaming underwater. The silent banyan trees swayed, their trunks below the surface, their canopies spreading out like giant algae. A whole new world had been created in the spot the village held sacred. Now, Lord Hanuman—who should have protected Nilgi—was defeated, drowned in water. There were no people under the banyan trees outside and no monkeys screeched, no birds fluttered, and no squirrels scampered..

Raj turned over on his back so he could look at the clear sky. The full moon beckoned; the stars sang. He took a deep breath, ducking under the surface. It was lovely there because he felt nothing, heard nothing, saw nothing. He lost himself in the eyes of the woman who had built her world around him. He drowned himself in the eyes of another woman who had the world in her eyes, the whole world.

A FRANTIC SEARCH began at the vada the next morning when Raj's clothes were found at the bottom of the stairs. Guru, from his tower room, scoured the waters for signs of human life and found only water birds, cormorants, snake birds, and egrets. Tops of trees and roofs of houses peeked out of the water, sunning themselves.

"I am going to call the surrounding villages," Samar said. "He may have swum too far."

Daya looked at Samar with defeat in her eyes, holding a scared Reshma in her lap, and he knew she had already accepted the inevitable truth. Still, Samar called local people and authorities telling them Raj had gone swimming last evening, like he always did, and not returned. The current had been strong, he explained.

Mid-morning, Veera called to say that a body had been found on the banks of the backwater lake, directly opposite the Hanuman temple. They were sure it was Raj Nayak.

Samar hung up, opened his mouth to explain what had happened, then closed it realizing there was no need. The details did not matter because the only truth was that Raj was dead.

"He will be buried near Shantur," Samar told Daya. "We can arrange a boat if you want to attend the funeral."

Daya shook her head, a disconcertingly silent Reshma in her lap.

"He always wanted a daughter," she said. "And I used to tell him he would have to find another woman willing to give him a daughter. He used to laugh and say that was tempting. It was a joke, just a joke. I never thought it would really happen."

They all looked at Daya, calm and logical, knowing the dam would burst one day, but just not yet, because it was inconvenient. The last thing they all needed was Daya falling apart.

"I wish I had talked to him; told him I forgave him because I do forgive him. He was more than this, much, much more. I should have told him it was alright, that we could rebuild our lives together, face the world together."

"We are all guilty of that," Sharada said, rubbing Daya's back. "Yes, what he did was wrong, very wrong, but life punished him enough. We didn't need to punish him."

A silence filled the room because there was nothing left to say or do except wait for the water to recede so they could step out into the real world carrying with them their combined, isolated pain.

THE 86TH VILLAGE

THE WATER HAD receded, completely exposing a ravaged land. Debris was strewn everywhere, bits of aluminum, wood, abandoned furniture, a kitchen stove, and soggy newspapers creating a pattern in muddy soil. Red tiles from roofs of collapsed houses were embedded in the waterlogged earth. Carcasses of animals no one had thought to evacuate now posed a health risk. A stench permeated the air as people slowly returned to their homes to clean up, mend what could be saved.

THE GROUP STRANDED in the vada were far from relieved. They were afraid of walking down the stairs, because that would mean returning to the life they had abandoned ten days ago. There were new losses to grieve, new things to fear, and tenuous relationships to nurture. They had to find a new equilibrium in a precariously tilted world.

Daya had walked up the stairs a happy, married woman with two sons and was descending a shattered widow, holding a new daughter in her arms.

CHAPTER TWENTY-ONE

A semblance of order had been restored to Nilgi. The streets were cleared of debris and animal carcasses, the stench driven away by the incessant burning of sandalwood, jasmine, rose incenses and fragrant coal.

Authorities had tried to implicate Raj, make him the prime suspect in Reshma's attempted murder, but that line of question had fizzled out when no one supported it, especially the people of Nilgi. Nilgi had known Raj since he was a baby and shocked as it was by his affair, the thought that he could physically harm any person, let alone his own child, was fantastical, absurd, impossible. Guru's accounts of the tenderness between Raj and Reshma further corroborated Raj's innocence, The villagers forgave Raj because they still loved him—and because they did not have the time or emotional space to carry the burden of his dishonesty.

Interestingly, Veera seemed the most reluctant to pin the attack on Raj. He maintained he was taking the case seriously though he, himself, never interrogated anyone, instead sending junior policemen to take statements. When Reshma remained reticent, stoic, unwilling to answer questions, Veera instructed she not be questioned. Even if she spoke, he said, it would be hard to believe a child so recently traumatized.

In the end, the case was dropped because it was inconvenient. The police, unused to real work, were disinclined to launch a full-scale investigation. A thorough inquiry meant giving up their afternoon naps and mid-morning visits to the bank or market to shop for groceries.

People blamed Veera for dismissing the case, but there was nothing to be done as he had been transferred to a faraway village where his mother's family still lived. To stop gossiping tongues, Veera explained that he was a lonely bachelor and wanted to be around relatives. The junior, inexperienced officer replacing him had no intention of reopening the case because it was a difficult one and he did not want failure to mark the beginning of his new position as inspector.

There was also another problem: Raj's innocence meant there was still a murderer at large. People worried about it for a while and, realizing it achieved nothing, stopped ruminating over it, pretending it was not really a threat. It gave them a false sense of security which was ironic because there was an even bigger concern. Raj was dead and the anti-dam movement had fallen apart without him to lead it. The district would not survive another flood like this one if the government did not pay compensation and relocate the 86 villages. Nilgi felt cornered, helpless.

SANTOSH STUFFED A third gulab jamun into his mouth. Veera, sitting across from him at the dining table, watched the layers of fat underneath the MLA's chin. He had always been fat, bowlegged, but now he was seriously obese. The stress of dealing with an enraged public had made Santosh ravenous and he had eaten non-stop these past few weeks.

Santosh had been furious when Veera, who had been at his beck and call, showed a puzzling reluctance to join the crusade that would drag the Nayak family's name through mud, discrediting them. He did not understand this sudden shift of sentiment in the inspector who had once been willing to do anything to undermine the Nayaks.

Furthermore, in failing to provide the kind of woman Santosh demanded, Veera had hastened his own downfall. So, when Veera asked to be transferred out of Shantur, Santosh was only too happy to oblige.

"You should thank your stars I am not stripping you of your uniform and sending you to the middle of nowhere," Santosh said. "You have not fulfilled any of your duties."

"Sir, I am sorry," Veera said. "I have been trying to find you the right woman but there is nobody worthy of you in these parts. You have gone from strength to strength and the woman has to be special."

"What about Raj Nayak?" Santosh asked, somewhat appeased. "Why this sudden affection for him?"

"Sir, my feelings for the family haven't changed. I just can't bring myself to disrepute the Nayaks by spreading a rumor that Raj Nayak tried to kill his own daughter. He was no murderer, and we have no evidence against him."

"I am pleased to see that you have finally succumbed to your conscience."

Veera remained silent.

"What did the Nayaks pay you for your loyalty?"

"The Nayaks can't buy me!" Veera exclaimed, trying to haul himself up from the depths of his heavily cushioned chair.

"And that fool of a man, Samar Chandar, has quit his job so he can revive the anti-dam movement. Does he think people will listen to *him*, someone with no social clout?"

"You may be surprised. He was very close with Raj Nayak and remains close to the family. People are almost certain to trust him, follow him. The scandal and death haven't caused as much damage as you—as we—would have liked. People are understanding, almost sympathetic. Raj was their beloved leader, and they want to hold on to that during these uncertain times. And, let's not forget those horrible deaths in the flood...."

THE HANUMAN TEMPLE had survived mostly intact, only a few loose roof tiles had washed away. A pillar outside had crumbled, causing a portion of the veranda to collapse, but Lord Hanuman still stood tall and regal. He continued flying through the skies with a mace in one hand and the Dronagiri mountain, with its lifesaving Sanjeevani herb, in the other.

The people of Nilgi were too busy restoring their homes and had not the time to clean and restore the temple. That had to wait. So, unlike countless dusks when the villagers gathered at the temple to talk, gossip, and socialize, today was silent and still, like a mad person who can be tipped over at the slightest provocation.

The water in the Krishna ran black and murky, taking with it all the things it had collected from villages and towns: bits of mud houses, wooden beams, cooking pots, clothes, and children's toys. The trees were bent from the onslaught of the floods but the birds and monkeys that had survived were returning. A mad, ravaged beauty settled over Nilgi like a shroud over a living person.

A few people had braved the silence and stillness and come to the temple. Raj's death had drawn them closer, but not like old times. They were now acutely aware of the unpredictability of the future, the fleetingness of life, the futility of pride, the danger of judgment and unforgiveness.

"How can you be so forgiving, Ma?" Rohan asked Daya. "He betrayed us and then didn't give us a chance to talk it over, understand and forgive him. There are moments when I hate him. Loathe him."

"Nothing is black and white, son," Daya answered, her heart shattered into a million pieces, every shard with so many sharp edges that when it dug in, she wanted to scream from physical agony. But she knew she did not have the luxury of nursing her own pain because her children needed her. Jai, Rohan and, now, Reshma.

"How can you say that?" Rohan said. "It is a question of being moral or immoral and he was immoral. Hardest part is I still love him."

Daya hugged her distraught son.

"We are complicated, us humans. It is true he cheated on me, but it is also true that he loved me and loved her. His feelings for Reshma's mother did not diminish what he had for me. I never knew this about him, that he could love two women with the same intensity but in different ways. Love isn't something you give or take, demand or deny. It is something you feel, and you can't help feeling it because it becomes a part of you. Love is supposed to bring you happiness, but your dad's love ultimately devastated him."

"How can you be so understanding?" Jai asked.

"I can carry my anger and pain for the rest of my life but what will that achieve? It will eat at my insides, poison me, make me bitter. And you will suffer the most. Not just you and Rohan, but also Reshma. Look at her. She is your sister. What did she do to deserve all this? Born in a brothel, her mother murdered, someone out there still wanting to kill her for unknown reasons, and a father who drowned. My only purpose in life from now on is to protect my three children."

"I can learn to love Reshma," Jai said. "And I will always love Daddy, but I can't forgive him. Ever."

"What is the point of that, Jai? Daddy has more than paid for his deceit and there is nothing to gain from not forgiving him. If people know we haven't forgiven him, they will only add fuel to fire, make sure we hate him for the rest of our lives. If they know we have made our peace and moved on no one can touch us and we can hold our heads high. He did a lot for people in this district all his life without expecting anything in return. People loved him, they still do, and I will make sure they continue to."

"She *is* sweet," Jai said looking towards the temple where Reshma was crouched over something on the ground with Samar. "You are right, Ma. She has been through enough. She doesn't deserve our resentment. Remember how Daddy had Rohan and me convinced that we would be a perfect family if only we had a little sister and how you said you were done having children? Ironic, how he provided us with a sister."

"Yes," Daya said, choking on the word. "Have you noticed how Reshma looks at you, begging to be accepted? Her parents are both dead, but she isn't grieving because she has found a whole new family and friends who love her."

They looked towards the riverbank behind the temple, where a group of people had gathered, silhouetted against the setting sun.

"WHAT CAN WE do with this brass pot?" Reshma asked Samar. "There are holes in it but it is so pretty."

"Where did you find it?"

"There," Reshma said, pointing to a spot upstream. "The flood brought it. Should we try and find the owners? We can't keep it if it

233

belongs to someone and they are missing it."

Samar felt a pang. That was exactly the reason he and Usha could not adopt Reshma. She had been lost, so Usha and he had believed they could keep her. But now she had been found by her real family and they could not keep her.

But that was a little girl, and this was a brass vessel.

"We can keep it," Samar said. "Even if it is being missed, it will be impossible to find the owners."

"Are you sure it will be alright?"

"Tell you what, let's build a stone house for your dolls in the vada's kitchen courtyard and use this as a pond. You can fill it with water, and it will slowly seep out just like a real pond and you can use a watering can to make it rain over the pond and fill it again."

"Really? Will Daya awwa let me do that? She is very proud of her kitchen garden and may not like a doll house in it."

"I am certain she won't mind," Samar said. "You are the daughter of the house now."

Reshma nodded her head and ran to Guru and Bharati, picking interesting things the floods had brought to the muddy riverbank. It would take a while for Reshma to get used to her new status and, deep down, Samar did not want her to. He wanted her to be miserable at the vada, never feel comfortable there so Usha and he could have her back. But Samar knew that even if she hated being Reshma Nayak and Usha and he managed to adopt her, Reshma would never truly be *their* daughter because the world knew she was not.

"Is this how it will always be?" Usha asked. She had gone inside the temple to pray.

"I suppose," Samar said. "We will have to watch her being someone else's daughter. Maybe we should move away?"

"No, Samar. I want to live here. I want to watch Reshma grow up. I want to be part of her life."

"Are you still asking Lord Hanuman for a child? After he gave us one and then took her away?"

"So what if I still ask? At least I am not sitting around feeling sorry for myself. At least I have started hoping we may still get our *own* child."

"I am sorry. I am sorry, my love."

Samar embraced her and she cried into his neck. Not loud sobs but quiet sniffs as if she were saving her sobs for something far worse. Their lives had been full of tragedies and losses, but their love had brought them dreams and hope that they might come true. Now, suddenly, their love was not enough to carry them forward. They needed something bigger, a grand purpose, so they could minimize their heartbreak and get on with their lives.

"We can't let Reshma see us like this," Samar said, inhaling the familiar scent of Usha's hair. It still tantalized him, even after almost a decade of marriage. "She still looks to us for comfort and we have to give her that. It will be a long time before she lets down her guard completely and accepts Daya as her mother."

"She may never, Samar. She had a mother who was killed. And what happens when her memories return? Or if they never return?"

"We don't know the future, Usha. The best we can do is take it a day at a time and pray Reshma will be alright. She is resilient. We cannot decide what we mean to Reshma or what she means to us. Or what Daya means to her. The truth is Daya will do everything she can to make Reshma happy. She will care for her as if she were her own child. It is just the way she is."

"How can you be so logical?"

"I have to be. We have to be because far worse things are about to happen in our district."

People were focusing their energies on rebuilding their lives destroyed by the floods. The fury and pain caused by the lives lost was being ignored for now, but once some order had been restored, it would erupt like a volcano. Already, a recklessness was seeping in, a self-destructive fearlessness that terrified Samar. Santosh's repeated, relentless attempts at discrediting Raj and the anti-dam movement were backfiring. Instead of instigating people against Raj, it was bringing them together.

CHAPTER TWENTY-TWO

In the run-down stone house of his mother's ancestors, Veera felt at ease after months of living in dread, at the edge of insanity. He had left Nilgi at the end of monsoon, when the district was still recovering from floods.. His past was less likely to catch up with him here in his mother's childhood home and, for the first time in his life, he prayed for obscurity. The only people who knew him in this tiny village were his two estranged uncles and their families—it was their house he was living in. Veera, encouraged by his mother who despised her humble roots, had made it a point to never associate with her brothers, both simple, uneducated farmers. Then, a cruel twist of fate and Veera was begging to be accepted. They welcomed him because they were uncomplicated people who did not hold grudges. They believed their dead sister had willed their unmarried nephew, Veera, to come to their village so he could be taken care of.

For his part, Veera, had relinquished his biggest dream: a new, modern house in Shantur's outskirts, and a car. For the first time in his life, no one rejected him. His uncles and their families embraced him, accepted his considerable flaws and he was content in their tiny house, filled with people. He felt safe and loved—something he had not experienced since his mother died. When he lay down on his thin mattress at night, he thought about what he had found and was moved to tears.

As the village's only police officer, Veera had more power than when he was in Shantur. His duties were simple: squabbles between farmers, squabbles between housewives, squabbles between husbands and wives and parents and children. All he had to do was threaten to take the case to higher authorities and things sorted themselves out.

It was September and he was far away from the world of floods, sordid affairs, illegitimate children and drownings. He could not believe he had been in the midst of it just weeks ago. Now, he watched as a bystander, uncaring what happened to the players in the drama. He was free at last, beholden to no one.

This time last year, Veera had returned to his home town, to the house his mother had left him, after many years. He would have preferred to never return but Santosh was pressuring him to find him a suitable mistress and there were no women left in Shantur for the job. Desperate, Veera decided to try the brothel in his home town.

Those few days he had spent trying to convince a prostitute to become Santosh's mistress still haunted Veera. He was terrified of looking back but his mind never cooperated. When images of that time clouded his mind, he closed his eyes and drifted out of his body. Suspended from above, Veera watched a pathetic man who could not even control a prostitute. He had let anger and pride get the better of him and he would have to pay the price for it for the rest of his life, even if he was never caught. His nightmares were more than enough punishment.

That first night he was back in his home town, Veera lay down on the single aluminum bed of his childhood home, a one-room concrete structure in which his widowed mother had showered him with expensive presents and a devotion that did not waver in the face of all his failures. He had taken love for granted until she died, and he realized, with great shock, that no one else loved him. The house was his only inheritance and he had not sold it, even if he would never admit to this, because of sentimental reasons. The happiest days of his life had been spent here. Suddenly, Veera missed his mother so much, he curled into himself and sobbed into his chest in self-pity.

"No one loves me except you," he whispered, sure his mother could hear him.

THE NEXT DAY he went to the brothel that had once been his second home. The building was more dismal than he remembered, and Veera wondered how he had found happiness within its walls. He felt proud at having broken the shackles, leaving behind a pathetic life where he was the subject of ridicule and derision. He had built a life for himself in the district's capital and risen to the rank of police inspector. He knew people envied him. What he did not know was they were in awe of his blatant corruption and dishonesty, unhindered by conscience.

He was unprepared for the emotions that assailed him when he stepped inside, into a front room he knew too well. The air still smelled of Dettol and cheap incense and the tattered sofa had been patched up in an attempt to make it more presentable. There was no one in the room and Veera called out, "Namaskar!"

A man ambled in, his cheeks filled with paan juice, as if he were blowing a balloon. He saw Veera in his policeman's uniform and a guarded look entered his eyes.

"Is something wrong?" he asked, pulling up his lower lip to prevent the red paan juice from dribbling down his chin.

"Don't you remember me?" Veera said, taking off his hat.

Recognition dawned and the man laughed, "Yaar, it is you! I had heard that you had become a big man and I see it is true. After all these years."

"Things don't seem to have changed much," Veera responded looking at the stained walls, the peeling paint. He had ignored it when he was frequenting this place, but it now repelled him. The brothels he went to these days were well-run businesses and offered women of much higher quality.

"It is a hard business," the man responded. "Our main source of income was wealthy men who chose one of our girls to be their long-term mistresses. Now, women, especially the wealthy ones, have become bold and demanding. They threaten to expose their husbands who value their reputations above all else. It is becoming hard to support my family. I can't even afford to take my kids to the movies once a week like I did before."

"I think I can help you," Veera said. "I have a proposition."

"I don't want to take any risks with the law. It is just luck that I haven't been closed down yet. I know what I am doing is not entirely legal, but people will never understand I am helping these girls, keeping them safe under my roof."

"No, you won't be risking anything. Quite the opposite. You see, I am looking for a long-term mistress for MLA Santosh. Someone young, beautiful, intelligent, who will appreciate the privilege of being his mistress. Santosh is very different. He doesn't hide his women. He respects them too much and likes to be seen with them in public."

"How much will he pay?"

"He will be very generous. You will be able to keep your family in style. The thing is his wife ran away with another man and he is devastated. He needs someone who can ease his grief."

"I may have the right woman. She was just abandoned by her client, a rich businessman who manufactures burlap bags for farmers, called Ravi Thakur. His wife found out a few weeks ago and threatened to kill him and Champa."

"That's her name? Can I meet her?"

"Yes. And the more I think about it, she will be a great match for the MLA."

The man went in and returned with a young woman with thick waist-length hair and the most beautiful eyes Veera had seen. His heart missed a beat and he wished *he* could have her. He examined her from head to toe and she stood, unflinching, looking down at the floor.

"Go now, Champa," the owner said and turned to Veera.

"She is trained in the arts, in politics, and can talk intelligently. Champa was a city courtesan for some of the most influential men in the country. But there is a little child, a daughter, she has to care for."

"She won't have to worry about that. Santosh will pay for the girl's school and upkeep. This is very good for her. Being associated with such a prominent, respected man will help her. She can hope for a better life for herself and her child. Can you arrange it?"

"I will speak with her and get back to you."

"Call me as soon as you can," Veera said. "Here is my cell number."

VEERA'S DINNER AT the small restaurant down the street had been surprisingly delicious: a rich mutton curry with hot, fluffy rotis and an onion-green chilli salad. Veera was pleasantly surprised at all the restaurants that had opened in his home town after he had left for Shantur. It would have been perfect to finish the day with a visit to the brothel, but Veera had risen in life and could not be seen going to the cheap and dowdy place he had once frequented. The brothel owner had still not called, and he was becoming restless. Of course, Champa would not pass up this opportunity, but he needed verbal confirmation before speaking with Santosh and working out the details of payment and expectations. Some of the past mistresses had to be groomed for the role, but Champa would be ready immediately.

The cell phone rang as Veera was drifting off. He recognized the number, but let it ring a few times before answering.

"Hello, who is this?"

"Is this Inspector Veera?"

"Yes, this is him."

A pause and then, "I am calling about Champa."

"Oh, yes!"

"I am sorry, but she has refused. She doesn't want to be seen in public, even as the mistress of a powerful man. I tried everything. Cajoling, pleading, even threatening to throw her out. She did not budge."

"Did you explain to her the financial benefits?"

"I did. But nothing made a difference."

"This is preposterous. I would like to speak with her."

"She is very firm, and I can't force her, but you can try."

"It will be good for you and your daughter," Veera said, sitting on the tattered, badly patched-up sofa in the brothel's front room.

"I can't do it," Champa replied, staring down at the floor. "I don't want to be seen in public with the MLA. Or any other man for that matter."

"Think about it tangi," the brothel owner pressed.

"My family is from this area and they will be heartbroken if they see me. I ran away from home years ago and they don't know I work in a brothel. My younger siblings won't be able to marry because of the disrepute I will bring on them, being publicly displayed as a politician's mistress."

"You don't have to worry about that," Veera cajoled. "Everyone knows how rich and influential Santosh is and all will be forgiven."

Champa continued staring down.

"How about you think this through?" the brothel owner said, gently. "We can discuss in a day or two."

"I don't have all the time in the world," Veera said. "But I can wait a day or two. Hell, I wish someone paid *me* to do nothing except grace the bed of a rich man."

"I AM SORRY, Sir," Veera said holding the phone between his cheek and shoulder. "I am traveling, trying to find you a worthy mistress. There is no one in Shantur."

"Better make it quick, Veera," Santosh said. "I have several social engagements and don't want to go alone. It will remind people that my wife ran away. It is a slur on my manhood."

"I have someone in mind, Sir. She is perfect for you, but she is wary, having never been in the limelight. I will convince her, I promise."

"Do whatever it takes." And the line went dead.

Veera was furious. How had it happened? He was at the mercy of a corrupt, ruthless politician who lacked ideals and a stubborn prostitute with high ideals. He called the brothel owner.

"I can't wait for Champa to change her mind. I am getting a lot of pressure from the top. I have to see her tomorrow and try convincing her again."

"There is yet another complication. Her previous client,

Ravi Thakur, wants her back, despite his wife's outrage. She is threatening to have him and Champa killed but Ravi Thakur is taking no notice. He says he is in love with Champa."

"Don't worry about that. I can buy him out. What time shall I come tomorrow?"

"I have to visit my sister, but you can come around anytime," the brothel owner said. "The girls are all going to the town fair but Champa never goes to those things. Her room is the last one down the corridor, to the right."

THE NEXT MORNING Veera, dressed in his ironed uniform, doused in Brut aftershave, walked to the brothel. It was warm and humid, the end of monsoon and the beginning of winter. Auto-rickshaws, cycles, cars and bullock carts jostled for space on the narrow main street. Fruit and vegetable sellers, squatting by the roadside behind piles of apples, oranges, brinjal, and cucumbers, shouted out prices. People stopped to haggle, uncaring they were holding up traffic, oblivious to the frustrated honking of cars.

The side street on which the brothel stood was mostly deserted and Veera looked around furtively to make sure no one was watching him. He had come here without qualms, sometimes in broad daylight, when he lived here. But it was different now, he had a reputation to keep.

A little girl was sitting on the front steps leading to the door, playing with a doll, and Veera guessed she was Champa's daughter. A beautiful child who looked up and then quickly down, without acknowledging him as he climbed the steps. He wondered if she was deaf and dumb. Or, perhaps, she was slow in the head, which was very likely, as she undoubtedly owed her existence to the depravity of her mother and brazen lust of her father.

The corridor upstairs was dimly lit, lined with rooms from

which the usual cries of copulation did not come as the girls were all out. He knocked on the last door to the right and it opened.

"I am not working, sir," Champa said, seeing Veera.

"I am here to talk to you," he said, walking past her into the room. "You have no idea what you are throwing away, refusing MLA Santosh."

"I realize, but as I explained, I can't put my family through the scandal."

"How many times do I have to tell you that it won't matter once you are with Santosh. People excuse you anything when you have money."

"I will not change my mind."

"You are being insolent," Veera shouted. "I can destroy you if you don't come with me."

"Please be quiet, sir," Champa said, soothingly, closing the door. "My daughter can hear you."

"Do you think I care? If you don't come willingly, I will make you curse the day you denied me."

"Do what you will. I, too, can destroy you if I wish. All I have to do is go out and tell people you are a regular customer here."

"How dare you threaten me," Veera grasped Champa by her braid and dragged her to the bed. "I will teach you a lesson."

Champa bit him as he began tearing off her clothes and he howled with pain, letting her go. A blind fury blurred his vision as he was taken back to the rejections of the past, where the women he propositioned tore him down with their words. He had not faced that degradation since moving to Shantur and had not expected it, especially in a brothel as low as this one.

He got hold of Champa just before she reached the door and, grabbing her, hurled her towards the bed. Champa hit her head against the corner and fell to the ground, still.

"I will be back," Veera said, kicking her as he left the room.

The little girl looked up as he walked out the front door, stared at him, then looked back down and continued playing with her doll.

It was only after he reached home that the foreboding set in. He wondered how hurt Champa was. Perhaps, he should have waited to make sure she was all right, but it was too late for regrets. He decided it was best to lie low and returned to Shantur. He would call the brothel owner tomorrow to make sure everything was fine.

His cell phone rang that evening.

"Sir, there is some bad news," the brothel owner said. "Champa was found dead late this afternoon."

Veera broke into a sweat and sat down hard on his sofa.

"How? What happened?"

"There appears to have been a fight, and her head hit the corner of the bed in the struggle. It is surely a brain injury."

"I am sorry to hear it. Who found her?"

"Her daughter, Reshma. When did you see Champa today?"

Veera made a quick calculation.

"I didn't go after all. Some urgent business brought me back to Shantur and I decided it wasn't worth my time to try convincing her."

"We are trying to find out who may have done this. The child is too distraught and won't tell us anything. She never spoke much to begin with, but she has gone completely quiet now. My feeling is that this must have something to do with Ravi Thakur's wife. If she did, indeed, follow on her threat to have Champa murdered, she will never be indicted. Her husband is too powerful."

Now, LIVING WITH his mother's family, Veera told himself to forget the past. It seemed so far away, as if it had happened to someone else. He could hear laughter and shrieks outside. It was a clear night and the village children had gathered after dinner to play. Veera's nephews and nieces where out there, he knew. He did not, yet, know all their names and when he addressed them wrongly, they just laughed. To his own surprise, he realized he wanted to know all of them—their names, their grades, their dreams. Entrenching himself in the lives of his new family was the only way to leave behind all that he did not want to remember. He pulled the cotton blanket over his head and fell asleep.

CHAPTER TWENTY-THREE

The three villages, two kilometers apart, were the poorest in the district. They were also the first to flood as they were at a low level, built on the banks of the Krishna by people from centuries ago when the river behaved as it naturally did, never overflowing its banks. Decades ago, when National Mining had mined the area aggressively, stripping vegetation, rainwater began flowing down slopes unhindered, causing floods. Those floods, however, were not severe enough that the villages needed to be evacuated. But since the dam wall had been raised, the villages were flooded two or three weeks a year, so the inhabitants abandoned their homes and stayed in makeshift shacks on higher ground until the waters receded.

The villages had not been prepared for the swiftness of the floods when torrential rains broke the severe drought this year. They did not have the means or the know-how for a safe evacuation and as the water rose rapidly, the elders lay prostrate and prayed to be spared while the younger population despaired. When the prayers went unanswered, they began fleeing, piling their children and elders and meager possessions in bullock carts. Two carts toppled while crossing a bridge across a stream that was now gushing like a river, disgorging the passengers who were carried away by the strong currents. Most perished, their bodies washing up in far-off banks and two bodies were never found: a pregnant woman and a two-year-old boy.

The death toll was twenty-seven.

A deep silence had descended in the three villages of the dead, an indefinite mourning period for the people who had died in the floods. Instead of succumbing to their tragedies, the families of the dead rose in toxic smoke, permeating every town and village affected by the floods, further fueling the madness that had already taken root in the district.

Samar's initial attempts at reviving and reorganizing the anti-dam movement through some of the key players and activists had not worked. He had once feared the repercussions of the government if he, as a government employee, incited the people against authority. But after what had happened, Samar did not care. But people were beyond listening to reason and it became apparent they were unwilling to wait and wanted what they deserved right now. He sensed an underlying recklessness that worried him. After much soul-searching, Samar resigned from his job so he was no longer a government employee and there was no conflict of interest. He could now represent the people, channel their emotions into something constructive. He could openly speak out against the government, criticize it.

THE MOVEMENT COULD not be revived from where Raj Nayak had left it because the circumstances had changed. Before, people's demands were monetary—compensation for property loss. But there was no compensation for the unbearable grief of those who had lost someone they loved.

"We need to continue petitioning the government, perhaps try the central government, even," Samar told the crowd gathered outside the Hanuman temple. "I have a few contacts in Delhi who might help us."

"Are you serious, sir?" a young farmer asked. "You want us to write and plead to the government after having lost our friends and families to the flood? My aged mother drowned. She was in one of the bullock carts that toppled."

"This isn't a time to sit around, politely requesting crumbs," an old woman said.

"What do you propose we do?" Mahesh, Samar's activist friend asked. "Nothing will be achieved by hasty decisions."

"And we will get somewhere, writing to the government?" the young farmer scoffed.

In the end, Samar consulted with the leaders of the 86 villages and planned a strike outside Santosh's house.

IT WAS DUSK when the riots began and no one knew, exactly, why they began. A group of anti-dam activists, led by Samar, had gathered the previous morning to picket on the street in front of Santosh's mansion. An effigy of Santosh bounced like an escaped balloon over the heads of the crowd. There were banners and cries:

"Our rights are our rights, and we will take them by force if you don't give them to us,"

"We want market-rate compensation for our property,"

"We will not be bullied." "Santosh has a potbelly and no guts!"

Santosh, of course, did not come out and the front gates of his mansion remained closed, manned by two frightened sentries no more than twenty-five years old. They did not feel safe despite the twenty-foot-high compound wall with sharp shards of glass embedded at the top to discourage and injure thieves and interlopers.

"When will the MLA come out?" Samar shouted into his bullhorn.

Finally, as the sun was setting, the front gates opened a crack and the secretary squeezed out, sideways.

"Sir was busy all day talking to the dam authorities. He is on your side. He wants you to be fairly compensated for all your losses."

"Things have changed, then," a man in the front shouted. "Just a few days ago Santosh said the government was not responsible for flood damages because they were caused by heavy rains and not the dam."

"That is not true," the secretary said, wiping his brow with his handkerchief.

"When will he come out?" Samar asked.

"Tomorrow morning," the secretary said, hoping to convince Santosh to appear before the protestors.

"Tell him we are going on hunger strike until he shows up," Samar said.

The secretary disappeared through the crack in the gates knowing he had not appeased the crowds and had, in fact, made matters worse.

"You don't all have to stay," Samar said to the crowd. "I feel the only way to be really heard is to go on a hunger strike. But, we hadn't discussed that so if you cannot do it, leave. There will be other things you can help with, later. This is going to take a while."

Inside his mansion, Santosh despaired. He was regretting brushing off public demand, refusing outright to pay compensation, blaming the floods on farming practices and rains. He could have been diplomatic and dragged things on until the next election when he would be retiring from political life. Because of his lack of foresight, a mostly peaceful resistance had turned violent.

THAT NIGHT, HOWEVER, a temporary unthreatening silence pervaded the protestors.

They all slept outside Santosh's mansion.

Mallayya. Ummappa. Shekawwa. Bagawwa. Somappa. Kalmesh. Preeti, Ganesh and Sankalp Sagar.

And they all slept.

More people gathered the next morning, eager to be part of the unfolding drama. They declared their solidarity by planting themselves with the protestors, further fueling their anger. The day dragged on and Santosh had still not shown up. Some protestors who had not eaten or drank since the previous morning sat down, too feeble to do anything else. Some began shouting slogans through the closed gates and others started pummeling it with sticks.

The police arrived and tried to disperse the crowd with their lathis but the protestors refused to be bullied and became violent. Santosh's effigy was burned, and someone tossed a burning stick over the compound into the garden. The police began beating people but it only made the mob more intractable.

Inside his house, Santosh cowered knowing the barely restrained madness of the strikers had just burst forth. He knew he had to leave. His staff and servants planted a tall ladder against his back compound wall and another one down on the other side. Santosh, his secretary, and two servants climbed out and were whisked away in a waiting car.

Outside, the fighting was getting worse. The mob that day was of a different caliber than the one that had rioted before. These rioters were younger, harder, more focused and better equipped and Samar did not know where they had come from. They knew where to find the empty buses to burn, which houses belonged to government officials so they could set them on fire, who to hurt and how much. They had swords, knives, rifles.

A new contingent of armed policemen were deployed. It was hard to say who fired the first shot, but it rang out above the commotion. The crowd panicked. There were screams, beastly cries and guns going off in every direction. At a certain point, when madness sets in, the mind stops differentiating between friend and foe. The true, peaceful protestors like Samar fled, leaving behind those whose hate had turned into vehemence.

SEVERAL DOZEN PEOPLE were injured, five were in critical condition, including one policeman, and two were dead.

When the newspapers reported it, when the anchors discussed it, when the international media salivated over it, they all called it a planned riot. Planned for dusk, when the rioters could flee more easily. However, they all agreed that the government deserved the violence even if those killed and injured were mostly the protestors.

Samar was called in the next morning to help identify a body. He looked at the young man, no more than a boy, in a mint-green shirt with a big red stain, like a giant hibiscus, and his heart sank. He was the son of Nilgi's tailor, a student in Shantur's college. The two investigators questioned Samar as a formality, and released the body for the family to cremate.

CHAPTER TWENTY-FOUR

The silence that had sunk into Nilgi like a stone in still water now rose and drifted into every crevice, every space, every moment, every thought. It was a deafening quiet filled with the cacophony of sounds from the past. Marriage music, a newborn calf's mooing, the red-wattled lapwing's call, children's shouts, jowar heads bursting with grain, whispering. Bees humming, jackals howling, a radio blasting Bollywood music.

Now, a quiet funeral procession, punctuated by the occasional sob.

The boy's body, covered with flowers, was being carried on a wooden plank with four handles. Samar, the boy's father and two brothers gripped a handle each. A father should not have to carry his child's body to a funeral pyre, pour ghee over it and set it on fire. When the woodpile burst into flames, the tailor keeled over and wailed like a child. His wife, held back by a group of women, pushed them aside and went to her husband, collapsing by him so their combined grief became a black cloud that hung over an entire village, devastated further by the loss of a son.

In the light of the flames, Samar's face glowed orange and he turned his gaze on Usha standing by him. A disbelieving, grieving, humbled village stood around the pyre. Everyone was there—the old, the young, the ones who knew the boy and the ones who did not. They were there not because of how the boy had lived but because of how he had died, way before his time. The village poured its grief into the boy, lamenting that he would never finish college, marry, have children.

AT THE BACK of the crowd, Daya stood holding Reshma's small hand. She did not want to draw too much attention to herself. Raj's death was still too raw and Daya was not ready for questions and commiserations.

"Death always shocks," Daya thought, philosophically. "Even though that is the only reality we are moving towards since the day we arrive on the planet. Birth is only the beginning of death."

She felt Reshma's body shaking and looked down to see her sobbing.

"You don't need to see more tragedy, my little darling," Daya whispered to Reshma, tucking her head into the folds of her sari.

"He has gone," Reshma said. "My father. Where is he now?"

"In a safe, beautiful place," Daya replied. "He is watching over you, over us."

"I want him," Reshma sobbed.

"Yes, he is not here but I am," Daya said picking up Reshma. "Let's go home. We have paid our respects."

Behind Daya, Sharada's body heaved with sniffles and Guru sat down, his head between his knees.

For the millionth time, Daya wondered how long Reshma

would remain silent about her mother, choose to not remember her. Daya tried protecting Reshma but there was always the occasional, insensitive person who mentioned Priya's murder. Even then, Reshma showed no reaction.

Before the funeral, the village flocked to the tailor's house, covering the son's body with wilted flowers bought from markets selling shriveled cucumbers, eggplants and papayas that still smelled of dank floodwaters. Raj was buried discretely by the police and Nilgi was not going to be cheated of another funeral.

People's anger against the government turned into an even wilder fury that could not be contained and Samar feared more riots, more violence, and more deaths. A threshold had been crossed and Nilgi was no longer afraid—it knew it could bear big losses. Boundaries, limits, prejudices, grudges melted away as Nilgi grieved another death. It regretted its faith in itself realizing that its tragedies and the nature of them had ejected it into the modern world. It was no longer the village it thought it was and now had its own brand of corruption, devastation, and depravation.

RAJ HAD WORRIED about his reputation, whether Nilgi would accept him after his affair became known. The village, in the past, had been unforgiving of infidelity. He had also worried about Reshma, if the nature of her mother's profession would forever taint her so she was denied a place in Nilgi.

But Nilgi had experienced so much sorrow that its sensibilities had changed. The government's corruption and neglect had lowered its patience with authority while simultaneously raising its tolerance for personal immorality.

"She is his child," Sharada said. "She is Raj dhani's child. He always wanted a daughter."

"Yes, she is," Basu responded. "And we can never let anyone

forget it. She is the daughter of this house."

"And we cannot allow people to reject her."

"No, we will make sure they don't."

"How?" Sharada responded.

"By never allowing anyone to forget all that he did for us, for Nilgi, for the victims of the dam."

"COME HERE CHILD," an old woman, sitting cross-legged outside the Hanuman temple, said to Reshma. "Has no one combed your hair today?"

"It was combed but she keeps undoing her braids," Bharati said.

"Oh, so naughty," the woman said. "Let's tie it up."

"Don't do it that way," another women said. "There will be so many knots tomorrow morning."

"You should not be talking. Look at your hair."

Beyond the temple, the Krishna glimmered, and gurgled like a gentle brook. Hard to imagine that it had uprooted everything in its way just a few weeks ago. It seemed oddly content because it had got what it wanted.

So much had changed.

No man ever steps in the same river twice for it's not the same river and he is not the same man. – Heraclitus.

EPILOGUE

Five Years Later

Nilgi has escaped yet another monsoon flood. It has been five years since the village was swallowed whole by the Krishna and it has not happened again. The river is behaving and Nilgi's faith in Lord Hanuman's ability to protect it from the river has been revived though, this time, the village's trust in the monkey god is not absolute and it prepares itself for floods before the onset of every monsoon.

Even god makes mistakes, the village now knows.

Under the largest banyan tree, Usha bounces a baby on her knee. A little girl named Tara with Samar's eyes and Usha's mouth. Lord Hanuman finally heard Usha's prayers and gave her a child. The day Usha became pregnant, Samar put his reservations about religion and god aside and began praying in the temple every day.

Usha distractedly passes the squealing baby to Guru who tosses her in the air, catches her and takes her to a group of old women squatting in a circle. They fuss over the baby, snap their knuckles against the sides of their heads in gestures of adoration. They discuss whom she resembles.

Samar is sitting with a group of men outside the temple. He is now a member of the state legislative assembly. He won the elections with a promise that he would fight for adequate dam compensation and that is what consumes him now. Samar has made many enemies among politicians and government officials, who are finding it increasingly hard to become rich misappropriating allocated compensation funds, but he does not care. He owes it to Raj Nayak's memory to see this battle through.

Reshma and Bharati are giggling over the scantily-dressed women in the latest issue of Femina. Bharati swears she will never dress that way even though she will soon be getting married and moving to the city which is more permissible. Daya, after finally accepting that Bharati is not at all interested in school, has found her the perfect bridegroom. The boy is the grocer's nephew and lives in the city where he has a Dalda oil wholesale business. Losing his parents when he was a teenager has made him responsible and independent and it is the perfect situation because Bharati does not have to deal with in-laws and dowry.

Reshma is taller, less skinny and grows more beautiful each day. She, now, has no inhibitions calling Daya "Ma," and Jai and Rohan "Anna." Jai and Rohan have not yet completely forgiven their father but their love for Reshma is unconditional and indulgent. Reshma is a happy girl but deep, dark secrets enter her eyes sometimes and when she is like that everyone leaves her alone. People have stopped pressing her for information. In fact, they do not want to know.

Daya knows she will never love another man or marry again and is throwing all her energy into raising her three children. Her pain has eased, and she is grateful for Reshma who does little things for her like leaving "I love you," notes by her bed. It is something Jai and Rohan would never do.

As for the rest of the village.

Some, like Sharada the toothless roti-maker, have grown too old to leave the house. They spend their days in prayer and giving people around them irrelevant, useless advice. Some have passed away. Some young people have left for better jobs and opportunities. Some have remained in the village to fight for their rights and find ways to farm their doomed fields.

So, life goes on, finds reasons to go on since the dead will remain dead and misdeeds are never forgotten.

It was a good summer and monsoon, and it looks like the winter harvest will be abundant. Yellow maize heads whisper secrets to each other, sugarcane sways like green dancers on stage, every movement synchronized. Sunflowers open their faces to the sun, smiling. Guavas ripen in the trees and jasmine, hibiscus and bougainvillea bloom.

The village glimmers.

In a field, a farmer is weeding a patch underneath a hibiscus creeper. It was where Reshma was attacked, and he has been avoiding clearing it all these years. Now, Reshma has recovered, and the farmer wants to plant there again. He digs the sharp edge of his sickle deep into the ground to get to a stubborn root, triumphantly wrenching out a huge lump of soil and root. That is when he notices a shining object in the soil. He thinks it is a piece of glass but when he picks it out he sees that it is a silver amulet on a black thread, the kind mothers put around the necks of their children to protect them from evil. He wipes the dirt off the silver and sees an inscription. The farmer is illiterate and pockets it with the intention of asking someone to read it for him. Someone must have dropped it and, the farmer is sure, will be happy to find it.

It is days before the farmer remembers to show the amulet to a friend. The friend reads the name out, shrugs and hands it back to the farmer. There is no one by that name in Nilgi.

Veera.

Glossary

- Appa – father
- Apsara – supernatural female beings, beautiful dancers in Hindu mythology
- Ashram – a place of retreat, often religious
- Attar – a fragrant oil usually from flowers
- Avaaru – respect form for addressing people, equivalent to "they"
- Awwa - mother
- Barfi – a milk-based sweet
- Bazar – a marketplace
- Bhel poori – a snack made with puffed rice, potatoes, onions, tomatoes and tamarind sauce
- Bhidis – thin, hand-rolled cigarettes
- Brinjal - eggplant
- Chamcha – a person who tries really hard to please someone
- Chutney – a condiment-like side dish, integral to Indian cuisine and made with a variety of ingredients like peanuts, tomatoes, mint, cilantro, spices
- Dal – a staple in Indian cuisine, lentils cooked and spiced in different ways
- Dhani – a formal way of addressing a man of importance
- Dhoklas – steamed lentil cakes
- Dodda Awwa – older mother: Awwa is mother and Dodda is older, bigger.
- Ghee – clarified butter

- Hafta – one week
- Harmonium – an Indian keyboard instrument that works like an organ
- Henna – a natural, plant-based dye used since ancient Egypt
- Jaggery – a cane sugar used on the Indian subcontinent, dark brown in color because it is made without separating the crystals and molasses
- Jowar – a staple grain native to India
- Kikar – a small, thorny tree found in India
- Koel – a song bird found on the Indian subcontinent
- Kohl – an ancient eye cosmetic prepared by grinding a charcoal-like mineral
- Kurta – a loose, collar-less shirt worn on the Indian subcontinent by both women and men
- Laddu – a spherical-shaped sweet made with flour, sugar, nuts, and raisins
- Lakhs – a unit in the Indian numbering system which is equal to 100,000
- Lathis – bamboo batons British in India used to regulate crowds and which Indian police continue to use
- Lehenga – an ankle length skirt
- Maami – aunt
- Maidan – town square or a place for public gathering
- Namaskar – a traditional Indian greeting of respect, made by bringing both palms together
- Paan – betel leaf stuffed with areca nut and cloves and used as a stimulant
- Pakoras – Indian version of vegetable fritters made by dipping vegetables in spicy gram-flour mixture and then deep fried.
- Pav bhaji – a fast food, a thick vegetable curry served with soft bread rolls
- Payasam – a dessert made with milk, rice, coconut, jaggery,

and cardamom

- Peda – a sweet made by reducing milk and sugar until it is of thick enough consistency so it can be molded into different shapes
- Pipal – a variety of the fig tree considered sacred, it is believed that Buddha attained enlightenment under this tree
- Pooja – a Hindu worship ritual that uses all five elements: earth, fire, water, air and ether
- Police Chowki – a police station
- Pujari – a Hindu priest
- Pyjamas – loose trousers worn on the Indian sub-continent by men and women
- Rickshaw Wallahs – someone driving a rickshaw, an open three-wheeled vehicle used in south and southeast Asia
- Rishis – a Sanskrit term for an enlightened person
- Roti – a traditional Indian flatbread made with stoneground wheat or millet flour
- Salwar-Kameez – loose pants (salwar) worn with a tunic (kameez)
- San Awwa – younger mother: San means smaller, younger and Awwa is mother
- Sari – a drape of fabric worn by Indian women that goes around the waist with one end falling over the shoulder
- Shamiyana – a ceremonial tent
- Shikakai – an Ayurvedic herb used as a shampoo
- Tabla – a pair of hand drums
- Tangi – younger sister
- Tiffin carrier – lunchboxes with two to four steel containers that fit one above the other
- Vada – traditional, residential mansion in southwest India that also serves as an administrative center for a particular area
- Yaar – slang that means "friend"

About the Author

Sena Desai Gopal is a journalist specializing in science and medicine, food, and travel. She was born and raised in India and now lives in Boston with her husband and two children. Her work has been published in The Boston Globe, The Atlantic, Modern Farmer, and The Times of India, among others. She holds master's degrees in Environmental Science from India, Tropical Agricultural and Environmental Science from England, and Science and Medical Journalism from the United States. Sena herself is from a small village in southern India, doomed to submerge in the backwaters of one of India's biggest dam projects—The Upper Krishna Project. Her family has lived in the village for 18 generations and she grew up on stories of its residents and a fair dose of dam politics. Her father was one of the people who fought for and forced the government to fairly compensate the people who will lose their livelihoods and property because of the dam. Sena can be found at www.senadesaigopal.com and on Twitter at @senadesaigopal.

Acknowledgements

Thank you Chantelle Aimée Osman, my indefatigable editor at Polis/Agora, who got to know my book better than me and suggested changes I never questioned because I knew she was right.

To my dear photographer friends—Ronny Sequeira in India and Teresa Curtin in Newton, MA—who shot my author photos.

To Sheryl Julian, the former food editor at the Boston Globe, my friend, mentor and tireless auntie to my children, who gave her frank opinion on every aspect of the book and its publicity.

For you, too, Ellen Ruppel Shell and Doug Starr, my science journalism professors who taught me how to analyze scientific data and translate it into something that people would understand. It is because of you that I could write with so much confidence the effects of mining and dam projects.

Drs. Amita and Sanjiv Chopra whose positivity and unerring belief in all that is good, helped me rise above all my disappointments and put them in the perspective of a larger universe we have no control over.

I cannot thank enough all the women in my life, the sisters of my heart, who stood steadfast by me, ever-confident of my book's success. And, especially, you, Gauri Nargolkar, my childhood friend and soul sister who never for one second doubted my success.

I owe so much gratitude to my parents, Rekha and Kumar Desai, who supported this project of my vanity and never asked me when I would finish writing it. They gave me the space to create.

And all my aunts, uncles, cousins, and friends spread across continents, who watched with pride as I waved my book off into the world. My beloved aunt and uncle, Chinna and Rajat Sarnaik, whose house I grew up in and my dear cousin, Nivedita Sarnaik, whose presence took away the loneliness of being an only child.

Jaya and Raj Desai, more my friends than aunt and uncle, who kept me grounded as I oscillated between hopelessness and optimism every time the book was rejected.

The people of Yadahalli inspired me to write this as they struggled with a dam that was causing their village to flood. Their trials and tribulations, their optimism and faith became the soul of this book.

For my beloved mother-in-law, Indira Gopal, mother of my heart, who connected me to Priya Doraswamy, my agent. Priya's faith in me was absolute and never wavered and she continues to be involved in my book every step of the way.

For my darling children, Surya and Anya, who showed so much confidence in me and my work that I couldn't let them down.

And, finally, to Harsha Gopal, my love, my life, my anchor. Sweetheart, you have always believed in me. Come share my limelight even if you hate being the center of attention.

CPSIA information can be obtained
at www.ICGtesting.com
Printed in the USA
JSHW022303180322
24049JS00006B/6